To Each Her Own

By Molly Mirren

To Each Her Own

For my husband, who would have been disappointed if my idea for a story had been normal. I love you.

Chapter 1

Funny how words could be sharp as daggers, how they could pierce deep enough to wound the soul. Erin could feel Blond Guy's words ripping into hers, and, God, did it hurt, like her stomach was being yanked out by a jagged hook.

If Luis had looked away, he would have seen her, but he was too absorbed in what his friend—the blond guy with his back to her—was saying. Luis and Blond Guy were in the kitchen, along with Erin's purse, which she had remembered just as she'd reached the front door of Luis's apartment. She was on her way through the living room to retrieve it when Blond Guy began his tirade.

"Devs are bottom-feeders," he was saying. His blond hair was long enough to barely touch his broad shoulders and was sticking out from a backward black baseball cap with an Oakland A's emblem. Obviously, he was the friend from California Luis had vaguely mentioned last night.

"Devs are even more perverted than those weirdos

who wish they were paralyzed," Blond Guy went on, "those people who pretend." His tone got darker. "Don't tell me you fucked the freak."

"Yes, we fucked," Luis answered in his lyrical voice. He had the hint of a Hispanic accent, even though he'd been born and raised in the U.S. It was a common thing for San Antonio, which had a lot of Latinos. "I'm exhausted," he said. "After the sex, we had to have the standard 'deep' dev convo—blah, blah, blah—where I got to hear how hard it's been for her to come to terms with what she is."

Erin cringed at her own gullibility. She was officially the worst judge of character on the planet. And to think she'd bared all to him, mind and body.

"It was a long time coming," said Luis. "We've been talking for weeks."

"How was it?" Blond Guy asked.

"I rocked her world, of course," he said with a leer, dimples flashing in his cheeks.

Erin drew in a sharp, silent breath. Just ten minutes ago, when she'd kissed him good-bye, she'd thought those dimples and his glossy, wavy black hair were adorable. Now they mocked her.

For the record, Luis hadn't rocked her world, and she knew she hadn't rocked his either. Still, she'd thought there'd been some kind of connection, some kind of bond between them. Apparently she was a freaking idiot.

Blond Guy let out a wry snort. "Right. You rocked her world. But what are you doing messing around with devs? You can do better."

Luis shrugged and lifted his hands, calling attention to his oddly curved, thin fingers as if to make a point. "Hey, man. Quadriplegic here. Not exactly a great catch—at least not to most AB women. They can't see beyond the fact that I'm a cripple. They don't know what they're missing, but devs do. With devs, at least I already have my foot in the door."

"They're all nutcases."

Luis shook his head. "I'm telling you, some devs are okay. Erin seemed normal enough, and she didn't bat an eye when I told her I needed help with a few personal things—no awkwardness about my catheter or helping me get undressed or any of that stuff."

"That's because she was probably getting off on it."

Erin clenched her jaw, hot anger coursing through her.

"Probably," said Luis. "But you have to admit, she's got nice chichis and a tight ass."

Oh, my God, thought Erin. What a compliment. Chivalry wasn't dead after all.

Blond Guy's deep voice was filled with disgust. "I don't care how hot she is or how nice her tits and ass are. There's something wrong with anyone who's attracted to floppy, paralyzed body parts. Is it some kind of power trip or something? Is it a low self-esteem thing, like devs think us cripples will stick with them because we can't get anyone better, because we can't run away? That's bullshit."

He gripped his wheels, squeezing the handrims and tires together in his large hands, and the blades of his shoulders went back, drawing attention to the TiLite logo on the backrest of his sleek, compact, all-black wheelchair. Judging by the sureness of his grip and the arm muscles bulging beneath the sleeves of his long-sleeved T-shirt, he was a para, not a quad like Luis. "I've heard some of those freaks are attracted to actual wheelchairs," he said, "and they don't care whether there's a dude sitting in the chair or not. They get off on humping an empty wheelchair. Devs are just gross, dude. They're fuckin' weird. Subhuman."

Erin felt the usual shame and denial twist her insides. It wasn't like that. She wasn't like that. Granted, she had just noticed the brand of his wheelchair, which no normal person would probably do, but she didn't want to fuck the damn thing! It was the same as noticing a cool sports car or admiring a badass guitar.

"Christ. Name something disturbing in the world," Blond Guy continued, "and there's always someone who gets off on it. I saw a thing once on TV where a woman got horny every time she saw saw someone throw up."

"Damn," Luis said, his face screwed up in revulsion.

"Yeah, I know. She'd try to get guys to throw up for her because she got off on it. But you know what? Devs are even sicker. People who get off on all the shit we have to deal with because of our paralysis are pervs and sadists. It's as simple as that, and there's no way in hell that'll ever be normal, no matter how some people try to sugarcoat it. A lot of child molesters seem like normal, upstanding citizens, too. Just ask the Catholic Church."

Erin felt like she'd just been punched in the gut. She wasn't even Catholic, but that insult dug a little deeper and was a little more humiliating than all the others. She started shaking with a terrible and sudden cold, filled with fury, embarrassment, and—although she tried hard to keep it at bay—self-hate.

She'd had enough. Fighting not to show the turmoil inside her, she dug her nails into her palms, then stalked into the kitchen. Luis saw her first and went pale beneath his caramel-brown skin, his face registering shock and then guilt.

Blond Guy, whose back was still to Erin, swiveled his chair around. His eyes widened a little when he saw her, but that was it. There was no guilt or remorse in his demeanor, no awkwardness, no sign he cared that he'd just annihilated her character. What was it he'd said? Subhuman. In his eyes, she was less than human.

Erin's nose and eyes started stinging, a signal of oncoming tears, but she'd be damned if she'd let these two assholes see her cry. She swallowed hard and cleared her throat. "I forgot my bag," she said in a flat tone that sliced through the tense silence.

Luis and his friend stared. She stared back long and hard, telling them each without words that she'd heard everything they'd said. When she finally moved, the thick soles of her black leather boots—the biker boots she never left home without—thunked as she walked across the wide ceramic tiles of the kitchen floor to grab her bag from the counter. She didn't look back as she strode out of the kitchen with as much dignity as she could muster, feeling their eyes on her back.

She was almost out of the apartment when she heard Luis call her name. He'd apparently found his tongue, but it was too late. Erin never broke stride. She quietly shut the door behind her, too proud to allow herself the satisfaction of slamming it. She held herself together until she made it to her car, and then the dam burst. As she sat in the driver's seat, hot tears poured down her cheeks, and her throat felt thick and tight.

"Don't tell me you fucked the freak." The sentence reverberated through Erin's skull.

Yes. She (said freak) had spent the night with Luis. The evening was a culmination of weeks of talking with him online and meeting him a couple of times in person for coffee. Last night had been their first real date because she'd wanted to do things right this time by getting to know a guy before she got drunk and screwed him. She hadn't exactly been a nun for the last five years—since the day her fiancé, Trynt, had dumped her and kicked her ass to the curb—but she'd been trying to change that.

In her sluttiness, she hadn't discriminated. She'd liked able-bodied guys (also known as ABs in the world of disability) and wheelers (wheelchair users) alike, but the wheelers were the ones who really got her attention— the cute ones, anyway.

Wheelers came in all shapes and sizes, just like AB

guys. Some wheelers were assholes (Blond Guy being a perfect example), and some were nice. Some were incredibly hot and sexy, and some were not. Some were nerdy. Some were cool. And, yes, some were pervs. Some just wanted a fuck and would say anything to get into a girl's panties. After all, boys will be boys, wheelchair or no.

It wasn't like disabled guys were on every corner and easy to find, but there were a few websites for people like Erin—people called "devotees" or "devs"—where wheelers who supposedly appreciated devs could chat with them. For some reason, it seemed a lot of dev women were primarily attracted to spinal cord injuries (SCI), while dev men were attracted to amputees, but that wasn't written in stone. There were also some who were attracted to other disabilities, like blindness or deafness. Name the disability, pretty much, and there was someone attracted to it.

The site Erin frequented focused mainly on SCI and was originally meant to be a support group for the devotees who were attracted to that type of disability. It was a place where devs could meet other devs, where they could find others who understood what it was like to be a devotee and help each other deal with the stigma and guilt of it. Eventually the objects of their affection—the wheelers themselves—showed an interest in the site, and it evolved into an unofficial way for devs and wheelers to "meet" each other.

When Erin was a newbie, she'd been played by a

few guys before she developed an instinct for figuring out which wheelers were stringing her along and which were for real. Once she'd driven all the way to Seattle only to be blown off by a guy with paraplegia she'd been chatting with online for eight weeks and really liked. When she'd called him from her motel room, the guy had chickened out at the prospect of actually meeting her in person, saying he didn't think devs were his thing after all. Too bad he couldn't have decided that before she'd wasted two long days of her life on the road, racking up unpaid days off from her job and maxing out her Valero gas card.

Apparently her instincts were still for shit. Luis was proof of that. She hadn't planned on spending the night with him. She'd wanted to take things slowly with him, show him she was a regular person, a person he could respect. Unfortunately, beer and several shots had gotten in the way of her good intentions, not for the first time in her life. She'd gone home with him and, yes, fucked him. Last night, however, she would have termed it making love.

She'd trusted Luis, thought they had something special developing between them. He'd said he was okay with the dev thing, said he understood. So how could he let his friend say such disturbing things about her?

Rummaging in her glove compartment, Erin found a McDonald's napkin that still smelled like french fries. She wiped her wet face and blew her nose. Maybe Blond Guy was right. Maybe devs—maybe *she*—didn't deserve the status of human being. Maybe devs *were* on a par with child molesters, rapists, and serial killers, people with sick urges they couldn't conquer. It was a thought she'd grappled with and tried to deny many, many times, but there were dark moments like this when she was afraid it was true.

When her tears subsided enough for her to see where she was going, she started her piece-of-crap car and pulled away from the curb. Luis's apartment was in a new complex close to The Quarry shopping area, near Lincoln Heights. It wasn't that far from her house in Olmos Park.

As she turned onto Basse Road, she tried to stop replaying Blond Guy's words in her head, tried to think of other things, but her mind kept going over and over what he'd said. She was a bottom-feeder. A perv. A freak.

It hurt with a pain that was physical, that contorted her insides into a gnarled tangle. She slammed her hands against the steering wheel as rage flooded through her. Why was she like this? Why couldn't she make her bizarre desires go away? Why couldn't she just be normal?

She hooked a left onto Jones Maltsberger, entering Olmos Basin Park, and felt the car veer off the road, as if it had a mind of its own. The park was small, but it had lots of trees.

Erin knew she should steer the car back onto the road, that heading for a tree was a bad thing, that pressing the pedal to the metal was even worse. Her heart pounded in her ears and her hands shook. She told herself to take her foot off the gas, to slow down, but something dark and utterly desolate inside her wouldn't let her foot obey. It was stealing her reason and her will to live.

Strange how many thoughts flashed through her head in the next few seconds. Would it hurt? Would it kill her? Did she want to die? As she got closer to the trees, her fear lessened and morphed into a numb resolve. She was detached from her body and unable to feel.

No, she didn't want to kill herself, but she did want the bad, perverse part of herself to die. She was tired of feeling tainted, of being scorned, of being alone. She couldn't see an end in sight, just a continual string of failed relationships and a constant, exhausting fight to find self-respect and acceptance.

She thought of her twin brother, and guilt slashed through her numbness. Zac would be devastated and so angry at her for doing this, for giving up, for killing herself the same awful way their parents had died.

What the hell was she doing? She needed to turn the wheel and stomp on the brake. She needed to choose life for Zac's sake, if not her own.

But by the time she made that decision, it was already too late.

Chapter 2

It was the painkiller. It was causing hallucinations. That was the only explanation Erin could think of for why, when she forced her heavy eyelids up, a fuzzy version of Blond Guy was sitting before her in his wheelchair, hands gripping his wheels, broad shoulders back and squared toward her.

"Erin?" said Zac, distracting her from the disturbing vision. He was shaking her shoulder. She blinked and squinted at her twin, who was younger than she was by five minutes. Mentally, it was more like five years. It couldn't be said that either of them had their shit together, but still, she was by far the more mature of the two.

Zac's wavy, mop-looking black hair came into better focus. Black wasn't its natural color. It was brown, like hers. He dyed it, and Erin thought it looked hideous. The hair dye shade had been called "black plague." Where does a person even find hair dye with a name like that? It was a color that would never be found in nature.

Well, that might not be quite true. Erin had seen sad, pathetic photos of animals covered in black, inky oil—victims of the BP oil spill in the Gulf of Mexico—and those pictures brought the color of Zac's hair to mind. Still, for reasons she didn't understand, the state of his hair never seemed to stunt his love life. It must be the musician thing. There were always girls willing to be band groupies.

"Erin," Zac repeated, sounding a bit exasperated, "did you hear what I said?" He was looming over her, his face close to hers, his brown eyes expectant.

She blinked again and tried to see around his big head at her surroundings, tried to slog her way through the potato soup in her brain and figure out where she was. Oh, yeah. Now she remembered. She'd been released from the hospital earlier that morning and had been blissfully lost in dreamland until Zac woke her up. She was lying on the sofa in the living room—what her grandmother had always called the parlor—in the small, shabby-but-not-so-chic 1930s Olmos Park house Erin had inherited, along with Zac, when Nana passed.

There were soft, down-filled pillows underneath Erin, one supporting her head and the other under the bulky splint of her shattered right ankle. She felt a little disconnected from her body, like she was floating, but at least she was feeling no pain, thanks to the outstanding painkiller she was on. It was making everything seem surreal, and she'd obviously been imagining things, like, for instance, Blond Guy.

She raised her hand and stared at it, opening and closing her fingers. It seemed normal and real enough, so she peeked around Zac again to see if she was still hallucinating Blond Guy. Yep. Still there. Of all things for her brain to conjure up, why him?

She felt like giggling at the absurdity of it because there was no way he could possibly be in her living room, but her mirth died quickly when she remembered what he'd said about her. She shoved the memory away. Bad thoughts didn't belong in her world right now.

If the Blond Guy illusion was any indication, Percocet was some powerful stuff. She'd never taken the drug before, but now she understood why it was a controlled substance. She hadn't been this fucked up in at least a couple of months. She was high as a kite.

No, not a kite, she thought as her mind began to wander. That was too common. High as a hot-air balloon? No. High as a jet? No. High as a cloud? No. Lame.

She scoffed at herself. It was one of her greatest frustrations as a writer, this thing of trying to find descriptions and phrases that hadn't been used a million times before.

Her talent was mediocre, despite all the practice and the college degree she'd earned in writing. She'd finished several novels but never submitted a single one for publication because she knew they sucked. Some might call her a perfectionist or an underachiever or a coward. She called herself a realist.

"Earth to Erin," said Zac, snapping his fingers in front of her face. He gave her a lazy, affectionate smile and drawled, "You're fuckin' blazed, little sister." He always talked like that, like a stoner. Well, okay. He was a stoner. He was a walking cliché, the standard druggie musician.

Zac said getting high freed his mind to be creative. Erin argued he didn't need the pot (or sometimes the stronger stuff), that he was just as talented and creative without it. Not that she could talk. She felt more creative when she was drunk, less inhibited, and God knew she was no saint when it came to drugs. She didn't smoke nearly as often as Zac, but she'd been known to smoke a bowl or two. The high got rid of her demons, at least for a little while.

Zac was watching her, still amused. Erin decided it was time to speak. "'M not"—she paused and licked her bottom lip, trying to get her tongue and mouth to perk up and form coherent words—"your li'l sister." It was her standard, pat response whenever he called her that, although usually delivered more lucidly. It was juvenile, just a way for her brother to rib her, and she knew it, but neither of them would let it die.

Zac voiced his usual response in return. "Size matters more than a measly five minutes in the delivery room. I'm tall; you're a freakin' pygmy." He tweaked her nose. "That makes you my *little* sister."

She was about to protest but was distracted when Zac turned and swept a hand toward the specter of Blond Guy. Erin was more awake now and starting to get worried. Shouldn't Blond Guy have poofed away or morphed into something tangible by now, like a potted plant or a TV? Why was she still seeing him?

To her dismay, he was sharpening into focus instead of shimmering away like an apparition should. Blond stubble that matched his longish blond hair covered a well-shaped, firm jaw. His lips, pressed together in a neutral line, were part of a face that was symmetrical and masculine. He was good-looking, no doubt about it, but Erin didn't care. She wasn't into blond guys, especially ones who equated her with pond scum.

Zac suddenly put his hands on her cheeks and turned her face so that she was forced to pay attention to him. "That dude over there is Jay—" Zac stopped and looked over his shoulder at Blond Guy. "How do you say your last name again?"

"Bon-tray-grrr," Blond Guy answered.

"What's the origin of that?"

Erin snickered. Sometimes Zac asked the dorkiest questions.

Blond Guy's brows went up and the corners of his mouth went down. His expression said he really had no idea. "Um, German, maybe?"

Zac nodded. "Thought so."

Erin rolled her eyes, and the room spun in a slow, fascinating circle.

Zac turned back to her and resumed his introduction. "That dude is Jay Bontrager, your new roommate."

Fighting to hold on to the loopy, soothing remnants of the Percocet, Erin let out a sloppy, skeptical snort. Her new roommate? That wasn't possible. "I have a roomie." She pressed the tip of Zac's nose with her finger. "You.

You're my wombmate."

Zac groaned and Blond Guy's lips curved upward, like he might be slightly amused.

"Okay," said Zac, sitting down on the old mahogany coffee table a few inches across from the couch. "Erin, I need you to, like, try to focus on what I'm saying."

She didn't want to focus. She didn't want to be in this conversation. Blond Guy as a roommate was too horrible to contemplate.

"You were in a car wreck, remember?" Zac was frowning and kind of serious, for once. "You have a bad concussion and a really fucked-up ankle, which you had to have surgery on. No way you're going on tour with the band. Remember what we talked about at the hospital? I'm leaving in a couple of days, and you need someone to help pay the bills, especially since you won't be able to work at Lars Bar for a while. Doctor said crutches for twelve weeks and then at least four weeks of therapy after that. Jay has signed a six-month lease. You'll be roommates while I'm on the tour, and then we'll reevaluate once you're back to normal."

Erin stared at her brother for a moment, then let her gaze flick over to Blond Guy. Her heart sank. She couldn't deny it anymore. He wasn't going to poof away. He wasn't a hallucination. He was real.

His mouth quirked to one side, and he raised his eyebrows, giving her a look that was part curiosity and part insolent challenge. He was clearly waiting to see what she would say, but he didn't seem too worried. Erin found that unbelievable, considering he had to have an inkling of how she despised him.

"No fucking way he's moving in here." Her voice was suddenly stronger and more deliberate, and she tried to make it clear there was no room for argument. "He's an asshole."

Zac blinked in surprise and shot Blond Guy a sheepish look. "Sorry, dude. She's *so* out of it. She doesn't know what she's saying. She's on a pretty strong painkiller."

"It's okay," said Blond Guy, now the picture of compassion as his eyes settled on Erin. "I understand."

The rumbling timbre of his voice was confident and masculine, and Erin remembered the sound of it all too well. During his rant against devs at Luis's apartment, that voice had bulldozed through any self-esteem she might have salvaged over the years. Narrowing her eyes, she said caustically, "How noble of you."

He met her gaze, almost daring her to expose him, which pissed Erin off even more.

Zac's brow furrowed, and he looked from Erin to Blond Guy and then back to Erin. "So, do you know this dude or something?"

"No, but—" She clamped her mouth shut. She wanted so badly to tell Zac who Blond Guy really was and how he'd made her loathe herself, how she'd almost— stupidly—killed herself because of him.

But Zac knew nothing about the whole dev thing, and she wanted to keep it that way. She didn't want anyone in her family or any of her friends to know. She'd learned her lesson with her ex, and she didn't want a repeat. She couldn't stand the thought of her brother thinking she was a perv, looking at her with disgust.

"I don't know him," she said, answering Zac's question. "He just seems . . . arrogant. I think he'd be hard to live with and—" she eyed Blond Guy's wheelchair pointedly "—and high maintenance. I'm not gonna be some crippled guy's nurse."

Blond Guy's shoulders went rigid, his hands tightened on his wheels, and a muscle twitched in his jaw, but he let the barb go.

Erin felt a pang of remorse for using the word "crippled" (totally not politically correct) but dismissed it. Whatever his game was, she wasn't going to make things easy for him. Besides, what she'd just said was downright sweet compared to what he'd said about her.

Zac's eyes widened as if Erin had suddenly sprouted an extra head. He turned to Blond Guy. "Whoa. I swear she's not usually like this. She's usually so nice. She likes everybody she meets. Would you—could you just give us a sec?"

"Sure. No problem," Blond Guy answered magnanimously, erasing any trace that Erin's comment had hit its mark.

Erin snorted, which earned her another sharp look from her brother. She ignored him and watched as Blond Guy deftly skirted his chair around the sofa and coffee table.

His chair was sporty and fit him like a glove. It

looked like the type of wheelchair made with a rigid frame, where the wheels popped off for stowage, instead of the type of chair that folded up and tended to be bulkier. Erin figured it had probably been custom made for his needs—a common solution for those wheelers who could afford it. He propelled his wheels with long, fluid pushes, and he seemed to have a symmetry with his chair that was second nature, like it was a part of him.

He was wearing a blue plaid flannel shirt and loose jeans, and his thin legs were tucked neatly in, close to his chair. His feet, shod in white Nikes, were placed evenly on the solid piece of metal that made up the footplate. Normally Erin would have thought white Nikes were a little too *Seinfeld*, but she had to grudgingly admit that, somehow, Blond Guy made the look work.

She hated herself for noticing so many details about him, and her anger spiked all over again. What was he trying to pull here? Why would he want to be her roommate, especially in light of the excruciatingly low opinion he had of her? The guy hated devs. Why would he want to live with one?

"Erin," Zac hissed after Blond Guy had disappeared down the hallway that led to the bedrooms. "What the hell? The dude is *handicapped*, and you just totally, like, mowed him down for no reason!"

Not for no reason, but it wasn't like she could tell Zac that. "Don't say 'handicapped.'"

"Huh?"

"'Handicapped' is offensive to some. Just say he has

a disability."

Zac gave her another look that said he thought she'd lost her mind. "Oh, like calling him a cripple is better?" He didn't wait for a reply. "Listen to me. This guy is willing to pay double what we were asking for rent."

Erin frowned. "Why would he do that?"

"Because I thought it would be better for you to have a girl roommate, and I already had one lined up when Jay came to see the house. When I told him we already had a renter, he offered to pay double what she was, and he was willing to do a six-month lease instead of three, like the girl wanted."

Erin ground her teeth, which didn't help her sore head any. The drugs must be wearing off, because it was starting to hurt. "What if he's a serial killer, Zac? You're just gonna leave me alone with a strange guy you don't know?"

Eye roll. "The dude's a computer nerd. He does software support."

She was skeptical, although it made sense, since he was a friend of Luis's, and Luis owned an IT company. But Blond Guy didn't look anything like an IT guy, and there wasn't a nerdy bone in his body. Maybe the whole computer nerd thing was just a cover. "Ted Bundy was an innocuous, well-liked law student," she pointed out.

"Erin," said Zac, tilting his head to the side, "you know I wouldn't leave you with someone I thought might hurt you. I get a good vibe from Jay."

"A good vibe?" she asked, incredulous. "You're

leaving me with a totally strange man, when I'm all injured and vulnerable, because you get a 'good vibe' from him?"

Zac nodded like that was completely reasonable and added, "I talked to his boss on the phone, and he gave him a stellar rec, too. The guy couldn't say enough good things about him."

His boss who was probably Luis. So now Luis was in on the deception, and he'd actually spoken with her brother. Erin felt like there was a lead ball in her stomach, and then panic flashed through her.

Calm down, she told herself. Luis couldn't have outed her as a dev to Zac. Zac definitely would have said something if he knew.

She frowned, which seemed to make her head throb more, and then her ankle decided to join the fray. She rubbed her forehead with her hand. "Please, Zac. I've just got a bad feeling about this guy. I don't want him here."

"Erin, the dude's handi—has a disability, for fuck's sake. What's he gonna do? Run over you with his wheelchair?"

She felt an illogical spark of indignation on Blond Guy's behalf and on behalf of wheelers everywhere who constantly had to put up with the assumption they were weak and ineffectual. "He can't walk, Zac. That doesn't mean he's helpless. I'm sure he's far from it." Then she remembered her purpose and that she hated the guy. "He could—he could strangle me in my sleep or smother me or hack me to bits with a machete. He has incredible upper body strength."

"How would you know that?"

She knew because she knew way more than she should about paraplegics. *Freak* echoed in her head, but she said, "Just a guess. He probably has to use his arms a lot. Stands to reason he'd be strong."

"Oh. Yeah." Zac sounded uncertain, but, never one to mull things over too closely, he switched gears. "He's got a dog."

That piqued Erin's interest, despite her desperation to convince her brother not to let Blond Guy move in. "What kind of dog?"

Zac's mouth curved into a knowing smirk. Erin was a sucker for animals, especially dogs, and it was no secret she'd always wanted one. "Some kind of Rottweiler mix."

She grumbled, "So what. Serial killers can have dogs, too."

Zac flashed her the goofy rock-star grin he used to dazzle his groupies. "Yeah, but I think the difference is that, like, the serial killers eat their dogs or something, not play fetch with them."

"Ew."

Zac grew serious again. "The tour lasts four months. You only have to live with him for that long without me, and then I'll be back."

"No. Absolutely not," said Erin with an emphatic shake of her head. "I don't want him here. And four months is a long time!"

"Why are you so against him? Just because he's handicapped or disabled or whatever?"

Ah, the irony.

"That's not like you, Erin," Zac said reproachfully. "I've never known you to be prejudiced like that. And it's not like the dude can help it."

She shrugged.

"Besides, the house is already equipped with handicapped—um, I mean, disabled stuff. Nana's room is perfect for him."

Erin stiffened. "No!" They'd both been close to Nana, but Erin and Nana had had a special bond. Nana had used a wheelchair for the last few years of her life, and her room had been left untouched since her death.

"I know you and Nana were close, Erin," Zac went on. "I loved her, too, but her room's not a shrine. There's no reason Jay shouldn't use it. I mean, seriously. It's time we face reality. Nana doesn't need it anymore."

That was harsh, even if it was true, and it made Erin feel weepy. She swallowed the huge lump in her throat and said, "Find someone else, Zac. Call that girl you were talking about, the one who almost rented. See if she's still interested."

"Jay's paying double, Erin, and you need the money. It'll be at least twelve weeks before you're on your feet again and probably longer before you can work at Lars full time on that ankle. I can send you a little money from the road, but you need Jay's rent."

She didn't say anything. She knew Zac was right about the money, but she didn't want to give in.

His eyes were pleading. "Just give him a chance. I can't understand why you're so against him. I think you're just overly emotional and whacked-out because of, like, the concussion or the meds. You're not thinking straight."

"He's a *stranger*," she argued again.

"So is that girl," Zac countered. "What if she's psycho like that girl in *Single White Female*?"

Erin searched for another argument, but she was getting tired and her brain hurt. She let out a sigh and her head sank deeper into her pillow.

Zac took it as acquiescence. He dropped a brotherly kiss on her forehead. "Thanks. It'll work out great. You'll see."

She responded with an inelegant sniff that meant "I highly doubt it."

"I'll go tell Jay he doesn't have to move out," he said with a grin.

She raised her brows in a combination of dismay and disbelief. "He's already moved in?" Her brother was thoughtless sometimes, but she couldn't believe he would be so high-handed.

"Oh. Uh, yeah." Zac was already getting up and heading toward the hall, and he shrugged off her disapproval. "I really didn't think you'd care. I thought you'd just be glad I found someone."

"Wow," she said. "Thanks for asking me first. Loved

the 'Hey, Erin. I've got someone I'd like you to meet. I think he'd make a good roommate for you, and I want to see what you think.'"

Zac mimed choking her. "I did! You just don't remember. This is the first, like, really coherent conversation I've had with you. You've been really fucked up." He shrugged again as if to say, *What was I supposed to do?* "Jay was anxious to get out of his friend's apartment, so I said he could move in. You were still in la-la land at the hospital and weren't up to conversations of more than five words. I seriously had no idea you would have any objection to the dude."

Erin took in a massively annoyed breath.

"Just relax, little sister. It's all good," Zac drawled in his stoner's voice, and then he disappeared down the hallway.

Erin slung her arm across her forehead and muttered, "I'm not your little sister." A second later, she could hear him knocking on Nana's—Blond Guy's—*Jay's* door.

Slowly closing her eyes, Erin wondered how the hell she was supposed to live with a guy who thought she was the lowest of pervs—or how she was supposed to live with herself. She hated being a dev, and her recent, if somewhat pitiful, suicide attempt (thank God no one knew about *that*) was a glaring testament to how detrimental the whole devotee thing was for her. She needed to be normal.

From now on, she was going to be a freakin' paragon of the conventional and boring. Nothing but missionary style with perfectly able-bodied guys for her. No kinky wheelchair sex (with the guy in it, of course) ever again. And she did *not* just feel a stab of regret in her girlie bits at that declaration.

She decided she'd been going about it all wrong for the past five years. She'd been trying to find herself and all that existential crap, trying to come to terms with the deviant part of her, trying to understand it instead of denying it. It was time to stop perpetuating it by dallying with disabled guys like Luis. Out of sight, out of mind, right?

But how was she supposed to do that if she was living with a wheeler?

Chapter 3

Jay was eavesdropping, ear straining at his bedroom door while he gripped the wheels of his chair for balance. Unfortunately, he only caught snippets of the conversation—mostly Erin's side of it, since Zac was keeping his voice down. Jay heard lots of adamant *no*s and something about a serial killer, which he assumed referred to himself. Obviously, things were not going in his favor.

He pulled his ear away from the door and pressed his palms into the seat cushion of his chair, lifting his butt up for a moment. It was something he did often to help prevent pressure sores on his ass, and it also gave him something to do with his hands when he felt antsy. He glanced at the boxes he hadn't unpacked yet. Maybe he should repack the stuff he'd already gotten out instead of unpacking more. It was looking like he would probably be homeless and back on Luis's doorstep soon.

That was a serious downer. Luis was a good friend, but they got on each other's nerves as roommates. However, the real deal breaker was Chopper, Jay's overgrown mutt. Luis was allergic to him—or so he said.

Jay figured the real truth was that Chopper, who was what some would call butt-ugly and what Jay himself called ferocious-looking, scared Luis. No matter how much Jay assured Luis that Chopper was harmless, Luis had the same reaction everyone else had: fear and trepidation.

There was a knock, and Jay twisted the knob with one hand and used his other to wheel his chair away as he opened the door.

Zac was standing in the hall. "You're in, dude," he said with a lopsided smile. "Sorry about the 'asshole' comment and Erin's not-so-stellar reception. Like I said, she's still kind of out of it."

Jay felt a twinge of remorse. He knew damn well why Erin had been so angry, and she had every right to be. What the hell was he doing? Why was he taking advantage of the situation? He used to have some morals.

Unfortunately, those morals had all gone out the window when he'd seen the appealing, if slightly rundown, old house where Erin lived. He'd been surprised to see there was a wheelchair ramp leading to the front door, although given the whole devotee thing, it made sense in a way that creeped him out. It stood to reason her house would be welcoming to wheelers.

The house sat on a street that was a mixture of modest houses like Erin's and the huge old mansions Olmos Park was known for. The house was already made accessible for his disability with widened doorways, hardwood floors, handrails in the master bathroom, and ramps. Even better, the large detached garage in the back was the perfect place to store and rebuild his Harley in his spare time, something not many apartment complexes could offer. And the decent-sized backyard where Chopper could have some stretching room was gravy.

So, three days ago, when a tall, lanky guy in a black concert T-shirt and jeans too skinny for a dude to be wearing had opened the front door and assumed Jay was there to inquire about the roommate ad on Craig's list, Jay, acting on impulse, hadn't corrected him—and that was before Jay had even seen the inside of the house. Once he'd taken the tour, he was sold.

The house had great bones, although it had seen better days and could use some repair work. He could probably help out some in that regard and looked forward to it, if his landlords were willing to let him. He liked working with his hands, and he knew a thing or two about replacing rotted wood and painting.

Olmos Park was a historic, mostly affluent little city with its own police force. The area had been swallowed up and surrounded by the much larger city of San Antonio but had kept its identity. Jay hadn't lived in San Antonio long, but even he knew paying double the low rent Zac had asked for was still a good deal in Olmos Park. Hell, since the house was accessible, a feature that was hard to find, Jay would have paid triple what Zac asked. The only drawback was his new roommate probably wanted him to die a slow, painful death.

Jay followed Zac back into the living room and approached Erin. It was time to face the music. She obviously hadn't told Zac she knew Jay from somewhere else, which was surprising but a relief. He still hadn't come up with a plausible explanation for why he'd come to apologize to her and ended up as her roommate instead.

Jay got the vibe she hadn't said anything about how they met because her brother didn't know about her weird sexual preference, and she didn't want him to know. Still, judging by her fierce resistance to Jay moving in, she was far from ready to forgive and forget.

She looked small and childlike lying there on the couch, bulky ankle splint almost up to her knee and puffy pillows dwarfing her. She was wearing a tight white pajama T-shirt that emphasized a nice rack and flat belly. Luis had been right. Freak she might be, but she definitely wasn't unattractive. Loose drawstring pajama pants with clouds and red, kissy lips on them rode low on her hips, exposing a small strip of pale skin between the bottom of the tank and the top of the pants. Her skin looked like it would be soft.

Her long brown hair was tangled wildly and spilled out over her pillow, giving her a serious case of bed-head. There was a cowlick in her bangs that exposed her forehead along with a large, nasty-looking bruise on it. Jay couldn't help but wince a little at the sight of it. She'd taken quite a knock in that wreck.

He inched his chair as close to her as the coffee table would allow. Her eyes were closed, but the pained grimace on her face and the stiffness of her shoulders told him she wasn't asleep. He cleared his throat, trying to get her attention.

Slowly, she turned her head toward him, and then her gaze burned into him, suspicious and unwavering.

Her brother shifted his weight from foot to foot, watching their interaction warily. Only the whine of a distant leaf blower broke through the thick, awkward silence in the living room. It was interrupted by the sudden, tinny beats of a song Jay didn't recognize coming from the cell phone in Zac's jeans pocket.

"Um, I'll be right back," Zac said with a hint of relief on his face. He loped into the kitchen to take the call, leaving Jay and Erin alone.

Erin's eyes were locked on Jay, relentless and penetrating. They were an uncommon hazel color that reminded him of that famous picture of the Afghan girl on the cover of *National Geographic:* pale sea green mixed with gold, then ringed on the outer edge with a dark forest green. Ignoring the unease he felt from her scrutiny, he said, "So, you didn't rat me out."

Her features hardened. "I don't know what your deal is, but you need to tell Zac you changed your mind. Think of an excuse. I want you out of my house."

"You need my rent money."

"I'd rather starve."

At that moment, Zac walked back into the room and approached Erin from the other end of the couch, and she looked away from Jay.

Zac held out a glass of water and a couple of pills. "Time for your next dose of antibiotic and your happy pill."

Erin accepted the glass and the pills, but she only swallowed one of them. "I'll take the antibiotic but not the pain pill. It makes me too loopy." Her eyes slid to Jay, making it clear she didn't trust him. "I'm not taking anything that might hinder my faculties. I want to be alert."

Zac rolled his eyes. "Just take it. I can tell you're hurting. You look like you just swallowed a buttload of hominy. Why suffer if you don't have to?"

"Will you be here?" she asked. There was a hint of pleading and vulnerability in her tone. "You won't leave me alone . . . ?" She left the question open-ended, and everyone knew she meant alone with Jay, the serial killer.

"No," answered Zac. "I won't leave you alone. I'm not leaving for three more days. Hopefully, your 'faculties' will be functioning better by then," he added wryly.

She cast one more distrustful glance in Jay's direction and then, with a little sigh, took the other pill. "I'm serious, Zac." She grabbed his wrist. "Don't . . . leave . . . me."

Zac crouched down so they could talk at eye level. Gently taking the glass of water from her hand, he helped her adjust the pillow behind her head. "Erin," he said in a quieter voice, "I wouldn't leave you with someone if I thought they would hurt you. You know that. Jay's a good dude."

Erin shook her head, her chin wobbling like she was

on the verge of tears. Jay suddenly felt kind of shitty knowing he was the cause of her distress, finagling his way into her home like he was.

Zac drew her into a comforting hug and let her cry on his shoulder. "Shhh," he soothed. He held her for a long time and then carefully lowered her back onto the pillow. He might be a flake and a burner, but it was clear he loved his sister.

Jay grabbed a Kleenex from the box on the coffee table and handed it to Zac. The whole dev thing was fucking weird, and Jay despised them with an intensity even he couldn't quite explain, but he wasn't a completely heartless bastard. He didn't like to see a woman cry, even if it was some crazy dev.

Still, there was something about Erin he couldn't put his finger on. She made him feel almost . . . protective. That wasn't the right word exactly, but he didn't know what else to call it. He might have even been attracted to her if he'd met her out someplace, like a bar, and didn't know her secret. It wasn't like she had "I'm a devotee" tattooed on her forehead. She looked perfectly normal on the outside.

Her brother took the tissue and tenderly wiped her face, then held it to her nose. She blew into it, making a faint little honking noise that made her seem even more vulnerable and kind of cute.

Jay felt a strange tug on his heart that made him oddly restless. He pressed his palms into his seat cushion and did a quick pressure lift.

Brushing Erin's hair back from her face, Zac said, "You'll feel better once you get some more rest."

Her lips tightened and her eyes slanted in Jay's direction. "I doubt it."

Just then, Jay heard Chopper scratching at the back door that led outside from the kitchen, and he was glad for the reprieve. He wheeled over and let the dog in. Chopper, a black, sleek-haired, hugely muscular dog that was at least part Rottweiler and part anyone's guess (maybe horse), bounded over to his water bowl, sloppily lapped up a few gulps of water, and licked his huge jowls. Then he sniffed a trail into the living room, where he noticed Zac and Erin. His floppy Rottie-style ears pricked up as much as they could, and his out-of-place, shaggy, undocked tail, which looked like it should be attached to another dog, stood at attention.

"Chopper, sit!" Jay commanded when he realized Chopper was about a second away from leaping onto the couch and giving Erin a slobbery bath she probably didn't want. Plus, Jay was afraid the 150-pound mutant giant might accidentally hurt her in his exuberance.

Chopper immediately sat, knowing not to ignore a command from his master, but his whimper, his fidgets, and the way his stumpy tan eyebrows furrowed together in a woeful canine look said he was barely containing himself.

The painkiller Erin had taken seemed to be already kicking in, if her droopy eyelids were any indication, but when she saw Chopper, they went wide.

Although Erin's brother had had a few days to get used to Chopper, it was clear the jury was still out about what he thought of the dog, judging by the way he abruptly stood and shielded his sister behind him. Yes, Chopper looked like some kind of hound from hell, but looks could be deceiving. He was about as vicious as the Easter Bunny, and he was a terrible guard dog. The only danger Chopper posed to a burglar was possibly drowning him with doggy kisses. He was loyal, however, and his goofy antics as a puppy had brought Jay through some dark days in those first few years after his accident.

Erin shifted on the couch, trying to see around her brother. "Zac, move," she said, but he continued to stand guard.

Jay pushed his chair closer to Chopper and affectionately scratched between the dog's ears. His fur was still cool from the nippy February air outside. "He's harmless. I swear."

Zac still didn't appear to be convinced. "He's—he's not hungry, is he?"

Jay grinned. "He's always hungry, but he prefers chunks of Velveeta cheese to human flesh."

Erin pushed weakly at Zac's leg. "Move, Zac," she repeated.

Zac stepped back so he was standing near the end of the couch where Erin's head rested, still close enough to protect her. Erin looked at Jay, her expression unreadable. "His name is Chopper?"

"Yeah," Jay said, expecting her to react with fear like

everyone else.

Instead she held out her fist, offering it to the dog, and said, "Chopper, come."

"Erin . . . ," Zac started in warning, but he trailed off when Chopper, well-trained and eager to meet Erin, padded over to her and sniffed her fist, then licked it.

She smiled faintly and rubbed his chest, then scratched between his ears like Jay had done. "You're a handsome boy, Chopper. Nice to meet you."

Jay couldn't believe it. Maybe the painkiller she was on clouded her judgment, but she was absolutely unafraid, even though she was small enough for Chopper to swallow in one gulp.

Chopper breathed a wet, noisy sigh of contentment and rested his chin and mammoth black front paws on the edge of the couch by Erin's side, making it clear he was in heaven and wasn't planning on leaving anytime soon. Erin's small smile widened into something that was . . . well . . . stunning. With her long brown hair, delicate features, and small pert nose, she was already pretty, but when her smile was uninhibited like that, showing dainty white teeth that were slightly uneven and just a promise of dimples that didn't quite materialize, she went from pretty to radiant.

Jay's pulse picked up and his mouth suddenly went dry. He swallowed and glanced down at his lap to make sure his numb dick hadn't risen to attention. It hadn't, of course. He couldn't get wood from emotions or simple attraction anymore; he could only get it from direct touch. Still, he hadn't reacted like this to a girl in a very long time.

He stared at Erin, a little dumbstruck and a lot horny, and wanted nothing more than to feel her small hands rub the parts of his body that still had sensation. He felt envious of Chopper as he watched her gently pet the dog. He had to give her a few brownie points for that. Anyone who could see through Chopper's grisly beast of an exterior to the gentle teddy bear within couldn't be all bad, even if her penchant for gimps was wacko.

As if sensing Jay's eyes on her, Erin glanced up. The light of amusement and fondness for Chopper instantly faded from her strikingly colored eyes, and, to Jay's immense disappointment, the heart-stopping smile fell from her face.

Chapter 4

Erin woke to a shrill noise coming from the kitchen. She opened her eyes groggily and squinted at the digital clock on her nightstand. 11:16 a.m. So early. She hadn't gone to sleep until sometime around six that morning and was supremely annoyed to be woken at such an ungodly hour. She took a deep breath and tried not to think about how much the incision on her ankle itched and hurt.

When she'd finally fallen asleep, she hadn't slept well. Zac had left yesterday to go on tour with his band, Silver, and Erin had vowed that once the safety net of her brother was gone she wouldn't take any more painkillers. She wanted to be alert and on guard against her new roommate. So last night she'd swallowed a couple of Motrin instead of one of her happy pills.

The Motrin had only helped a little, and the itching and constant ache in her ankle had caused her to sleep fitfully. She would be a zombie if she had many more nights like last night—or many more mornings getting woken up by what sounded like a maniacal dentist in the kitchen.

She wondered where Chopper was. She and the dog

had fallen into an unlikely routine of sorts in the three days since she'd come home from the hospital. He'd made a huge commotion outside her bedroom door that first morning after the big reveal that Jay was there to stay. Chopper whined and scratched until Jay gave in and let him into her room before going to work. Not up to interacting with Jay, Erin had played possum and pretended to be asleep (as if anyone could sleep through Chopper leaping onto their bed and licking them).

As a result, a precedent had been set. Now, every day before Jay left for work, Chopper would end up in Erin's bed, sleeping next to her until she woke up for good. This morning, however, his enormous warm body, which was almost as big as a man's, wasn't snuggled next to her, and she kind of missed him.

It had been beyond presumptuous and rude of Jay to let his gargantuan pet into her room while she slept without asking her, and she should have complained— but she hadn't. Apparently Jay had taken her silence as permission.

The truth was, Erin really liked Chopper. She'd made her dislike of Jay clear, but she hadn't hidden the fact that his dog was exempt from that dislike. Besides, it wasn't like the poor animal could help who his master was.

She sighed as the shrill *zzzzzzzzzzzzzz* noise went off again, making her teeth hurt. It was clear she wasn't going to get any more sleep, which meant she needed caffeine pronto. She hoped who or whatever was making the noise in the kitchen wasn't a crazed lunatic. Maybe she should be more worried. She was supposed to be alone.

It was a Tuesday, so Jay should be at work, but maybe he'd stayed home for some reason. If he hadn't and she was about to die a horrible death at the hands of Jack the Driller, she hoped she would at least have some caffeine in her body first to make it more bearable. She sat up, reached for the crutches lying on the floor next to her bed, and hobble-thumped her way into the kitchen.

She found Jay sitting on the colorful Spanish-tiled floor, in front of the cabinet under the sink. His wheelchair sat empty, within his easy reach. Erin had only once seen a wheeler do a chair-to-floor transfer, and the strength it took to do such a feat had amazed her. Judging by the broadness of Jay's shoulders and the hint of well-developed biceps that showed through the sleeves of his dark gray hoodie, he had the strength to do it. He was holding a drill, about to screw in one of the old hinges on the cabinet door. That explained the noise, but what was he doing here? He was supposed to be at work.

He was sitting sideways in relation to the cabinet and seemed to be able to sit up okay without support, which meant he must have at least some abdominal control. She wondered what level his injury was. Probably around the T7 vertebra or lower.

His thin legs, covered by loose jeans, were positioned together in front of him. One of them jiggled a little. To someone who didn't know, it looked like he was moving it on purpose, but Erin knew it wasn't voluntary. A lot of people with paraplegia had to deal with spasticity—the random, uncontrollable expanding and contracting or, in some cases, stiffening of paralyzed muscles—but it was the first time she'd seen any evidence Jay had it.

And she didn't care! Why would she care? That wasn't what a normal, non-icky person would think about. A normal person wouldn't know about spasticity, and they sure as hell wouldn't know about levels of spinal cord injury and what they meant, unless maybe they knew someone with one.

Freak.

Angry with herself and irritable, she yelled above the noise of the drill, "What the hell are you doing?"—even though it was obvious.

The drill stopped spinning, and he looked up at her. Sunlight streaming in through the window over the sink illuminated his eyes, making them a bottomless grayish blue. It was the first time she'd really noticed them. They were . . . nice.

Nice! What the fuck? She didn't care what color his eyes were.

"Morning," he said pleasantly in his deep, whiskey-tinged voice. "How you feeling?"

"What are you doing?" she repeated.

One corner of his mouth curved upward, and he seemed unfazed by her surliness. "Some of the cabinet doors keep falling off because the hinges are shot, especially this one." He waved the drill toward the door he was working on under the sink, bracing his other hand on the floor. "The hinges are really old and hard to find, but I found some that matched the originals from a specialty salvage store on the Internet. They came in yesterday, so I thought I'd do some repairs this morning."

She made a noncommittal grunt, trying her best not to be impressed. That cabinet door had bugged her for years, but she didn't feel like acknowledging he was doing a good thing. This was the calm before the storm. They had a lot to discuss, and she wasn't about to let his Bob Vila act disarm her.

His lips curved a little more. It seemed like he was always on the verge of a smirk. He had little laugh lines at the corners of his eyes, around his mouth, and a few wrinkles on his brow that made her think he was older than her twenty-six, probably closer to thirty. She tried not to notice the other details of his face, like his strong chin and the ever-present blond five-o'clock shadow on his jaw.

The sun highlighted white-blond streaks in his shoulder-length hair that most sorority girls would pay big bucks for, but Erin seriously doubted Jay paid a hairdresser to add highlights to his hair. They had to be natural, because the vision she got of him sitting at a hairdresser's workstation with highlight foils in his hair was absurd.

She didn't know much about Jay Bontrager, but he was the type of guy that oozed masculinity. It came off him in waves. Erin figured there were probably plenty of normal, able-bodied girls who would be attracted to him, with or without the wheelchair, and she found it ironic that she wasn't one of them, since she had a thing— correction—*used* to have a thing for disabled men. But she wasn't into blonds, and she wasn't into guys who thought she was on a par with a child molester. Her belly tightened uncomfortably at the reminder.

"Hope you don't mind that I took the initiative," he said.

"What?"

"The hinges," he said, bringing her back to their conversation. "I hope you don't mind that I'm replacing them. Zac told me I could repair whatever I thought needed fixing around the house."

Oh, of course Zac would say that. What was next? Signing the deed over to Jay? And how did Mr. Fixit expect to be compensated? It wasn't like they had a lot of money lying around for house repairs. If they did, they would have gotten stuff fixed a long time ago.

More annoyed than ever, Erin headed for the coffeepot on the far counter, carefully maneuvering on her crutches. The last thing she wanted was to fall on her ass in front of him. "Whatever," she responded tersely, swinging her legs through the crutches. "It's not like you care what I think, right?"

"That's not true, darlin'."

She shot him a look. "We both know I'm not your darlin', so don't call me that."

"It's just something I say. It's automatic."

Somehow that made it worse, knowing he called every girl that. It was sexist, too, but she wasn't a bra-burning feminist. No. It was more that the endearment, delivered in his buttery voice, was a caress she didn't want.

"How much did those special hinges cost?"

"Don't worry about it. You didn't ask me to fix them. I don't expect you guys to pay me back."

She clamped her lips together to quash the urge to thank him.

"How you feeling?" he asked again.

Clenching her armpits to hold her crutches in place, she used her hands to pour coffee into the filter. Ignoring his question, she asked one of her own. "You're blowing off work just to fix a cabinet?"

"Erin," he said, his tone a bit stern, "my question first. How are you feeling? You look . . . haggard."

"Wow, thanks. You really know how to charm a girl."

He let out an exasperated breath. "I didn't mean it like that. I'm just concerned."

"Oh, cut the crap," she retorted. "I mean, I'm a bottom-feeder, right? I disgust you. You don't care how I feel."

He shifted his shoulders and pressed his palms into the floor, as if adjusting his body for a better seat. "I'm sorry you heard that."

She scoffed. "You're sorry I heard you say it, but you're not sorry you said it."

He studied her for a moment. "Maybe I was talking

about something I didn't fully understand."

She pressed the Brew button. "But now you do understand? Are you suddenly an expert on devotees? You ready to embrace us—them—with open arms?"

"Uh . . . no, not exactly." And then his mouth curved into that smirk that had threatened earlier. "But I'm willing to live with one, right?"

She shot him a dark look. "You think that redeems you?"

"Hey, I just meant I'm making progress."

"You are such an asshole." She turned away and reached up, stretching to open a cabinet door above the coffeemaker. When she reached for a mug, she nearly lost her balance for a second. She almost lost one of her crutches, too, but caught it just in time.

Jay set down the drill and quickly transferred from the floor to his wheelchair. He looked like a gymnast, like one of those guys that did the rings, the way he gripped the frame of his chair with one hand and had his other hand fisted on the floor, then dipped his head and lifted his hips enough to swing his butt into the seat of his chair. The whole process took less than a second.

Once he was settled with his feet on the footplate, he wheeled closer to her. "You're going to need help with that," he said, looking up at her and eyeing the mug in her hand.

"Not from you," she said, even though she knew he was right. She wouldn't be able to hobble to the table on her crutches and carry a mug of coffee, too. She didn't care. She'd just stay at the counter and drink there. It was petty, but she didn't want any help from him.

His brow wrinkled into an earnest expression. "Look, you have every right to hate me. I don't blame you, but I'm not moving out. I need a place to live, and you need my rent money, so let's find a way to live with each other."

She didn't respond. All she could think of to say was "Fuck you," and that seemed juvenile. She needed to gather her thoughts and regroup. When the coffee was ready, she poured some into her mug, then set it on the counter so she could turn, using her crutches, to face Jay fully. Once she felt like she was balanced, she tensed the muscles under her arms again to keep the crutches in place and grabbed the mug, taking a sip of the hot, bitter brew. Its pungent aroma and the warm steam wafting up to her nose were paradise.

Now fortified with caffeine, Erin could feel her thoughts coming together. "How did you even know we were looking for a renter? Did Luis send you?" She couldn't remember if she'd mentioned the renter thing to Luis, but maybe she had. They'd talked about everything. God, what a dumbass she'd been to trust him.

Jay sat back in his chair, hands on his wheels. "I came because of Luis, but he didn't know you were looking for a renter. That was a fluke. I swear. I came to apologize to you, and the next thing I knew, Zac was giving me the tour. One thing led to another, and I was moving in.

"I feel bad that I ruined things between you and Luis.

He really likes you. Just because I was a bastard, don't take it out on him. He's got nothing against devs."

"I didn't hear him taking up for me."

"Okay. Maybe that's true, but nobody's perfect. He was mostly just letting me rant—blow smoke—but that doesn't mean he agreed with me."

"Yes, he did," said Erin. "He practically admitted he was only going out with me for a fuck." Which, slut that she was, she'd given him.

Jay's brow wrinkled again. It made him appear so soulful, so apologetic, so genuinely concerned for his friend. "Give Luis a second chance, Erin. He's a good guy, and he felt shitty about what happened. He tried to get in touch with you, to say he was sorry. He didn't know about the car accident and didn't know you were out of commission, so he kept trying and trying to call and text you."

She knew that. She'd seen the messages on her cell phone. At first she'd been too out of it to respond to any of them, and when she emerged from the hazy fog of painkillers, she hadn't wanted to respond.

"When you didn't answer any of his messages," Jay went on, "I felt bad for him. I knew all that was my fault, so I came to apologize. I swear I only came to ask you to give him another chance. I didn't know you and your brother were looking for a roommate."

"We weren't. We needed someone to rent the house while we were on tour."

Jay frowned a bit, looking bemused.

"We weren't looking for a roommate," Erin clarified. "I was supposed to go on the road, too."

She hadn't even begun to deal with that yet. It was a big deal, the tour for the band. It was maybe their big break, their chance to gain national status, and now, because of one colossal moment of insanity, she was stuck in San Antonio with a broken ankle and her worst nightmare for a roommate. She had her reasons for not being as excited about the tour as she should have been, but she would have taken traveling in a cramped RV with three other people for months over her current situation any day.

"I'm sorry," Jay said.

She took a sip of her coffee and shrugged. "Whatever. You were explaining how you ended up as my roommate. I mean, first of all, why would you even want to share a place with me, knowing . . . " She'd started to say "what I am," but she didn't want to cop to the dev thing anymore. Deny, deny, deny. If she told herself she wasn't a dev long enough, maybe it would be true.

"Like I said, it just happened."

Erin raised her brows. She had a better guess. "Or, you liked the house and its location, and you were sick of staying with Luis."

Jay nodded. "That, too. There's not too many choice houses in old, historic neighborhoods already equipped for someone with a disability."

"What did you tell my brother? He hasn't said anything about Luis. I'm assuming you didn't tell him about"—

she paused, feeling her ears grow warm, and glanced down at her coffee mug to hide her embarrassment—"how we met?"

Jay shook his head. "Your brother did all the work for me. When he opened the front door, he automatically assumed I was a random guy here to inquire about his ad."

She couldn't believe Jay's gall, and when she spoke, she could hear the accusation in her tone. "And you didn't bother to correct him. Instead, you took advantage of the situation."

The corners of Jay's mouth dipped downward nonchalantly, but he glanced away for a second before meeting her eyes and rephrasing her words: "I seized an opportunity."

"And you thought I'd just roll out the welcome mat?" She huffed mirthlessly. "You're the freak, not me. Or else you're delusional."

His features hardened. "In case you haven't noticed"—he made a show of looking down at his legs—"my number of options for just about everything has dwindled now that I get to spend my life in this chair, so I take what I can get when it's offered."

She thunked her mug down on the counter. Some of the coffee sloshed out and burned her thumb, but she was too mad to care about the pain. "Oh, spare me the sob story! That chair doesn't give you the right to be an asshole. It doesn't give you a license to screw people over, to—to blackmail them!"

His jaw turned to cement, and his eyes burned like blue coals. "You don't know what it's like to be in this chair, so don't fucking tell me how to live in it!"

She scoffed. "Is that supposed to make me feel sorry for you? Now you're playing the cripple card?"

"No." He scrubbed both hands over his face and then pressed them together, index fingers touching his lips, as if trying to rein in his anger. "Look, I know what I did was shitty."

"Which time?" she asked caustically.

He dropped his hands down to his tires, gripping them, and drew his broad shoulders back. "Both times," he answered. "I'm sorry for all of it—for what I said about . . . devotees . . . and for being less than completely honest about the situation so your brother would rent the room to me."

Erin hadn't missed the distaste he tried to hide when he'd said "devotees," even though the word was framed in an apology. "I want you gone," she said. "I'll tell my brother who you really are, what you said, that you totally scammed him. He might seem like a flake, but when it comes to me, he doesn't put up with any shit. He'll make you leave."

Jay's mouth curved cynically. "Now, do you really wanna go there, darlin'? Because I'm thinking you don't. I'm thinking your threat is a bunch of hot air. Your brother has no clue about your little fetish, and I don't think you want him to know, or you would have already told him everything."

She hated him for guessing the truth. "I'm not a dev," she said through clenched teeth.

"Right," Jay said. "That's why your house is all tricked out for wheelers. I'm curious. How did you explain it all to Zac? Was it for an old boyfriend or something? It must have been expensive to have all that work done."

That made Erin stop short. "What are you talking about?"

He made a sweeping motion with his hand. "The ramps, the way everything in your house is accessible. It's like fucking *Field of Dreams,* the devotee version." He leaned forward and imitated the whispering voice in the movie, his expression sardonic and mocking. "If you build it, wheelers will come."

At first, Erin couldn't believe what she was hearing. The magnitude of the insult punched her in the gut. Then overwhelming fury began to rage through her veins, and she started to tremble. If she'd had a gun, she would have gladly blown his head off. "You dumb shit," she said. "My grandmother used a wheelchair the last few years of her life. The house was modified for her."

Red stained Jay's face as he stared at her, clearly stunned. After a moment of heavy silence, he wiped his fingers over his mouth and shook his head, his manner contrite. "You're right. I am a dumb shit. I was distracted by a phone call from one of my customers when Zac was giving me the tour, and I must have missed the part about it all being for your grandmother." His gaze homed in on her, intense and filled with regret. "Because I knew you were a dev, I jumped to conclusions."

Erin didn't trust herself to speak. She closed her eyes for a moment and took a deep breath, trying to regain her composure. When she did, she felt dead inside, numb. "Like I said, I'm not a dev. I'll never date another wheeler."

He glanced down, clearing his throat. "Is it . . . " He looked up at her. "Is it that easy to turn off?"

No, it wasn't, but she wasn't about to admit that. "It was just something I experimented with. It's in the past."

His look said he didn't believe her, but he didn't argue. After completely humiliating her, at least he had that much tact.

"You implied you'd tell my brother," said Erin. "Would you really stoop that low?"

His forehead creased and he looked remorseful, but he didn't deny it. Instead, he said quietly, "This isn't at all how I wanted this conversation to play out."

"But you won't go?" Her hands squeezed the padded grips of her crutches. "You'd force me to tell my brother about the dev thing?"

Jay looked her in the eye for a long moment, jaw squared. "Yes." To his credit, it sounded like it pained him to admit it.

"Nice." Erin gave a short, bleak laugh, but she suddenly felt like crying.

"Look," he said with a sigh, "I know I haven't given you any reason to believe it, but I'm not as bad as you think. Give me a second chance to prove it to you.

Things will go a lot smoother if we're not at each other's throats."

She was appalled. "A second chance? Are you serious? You're blackmailing me!"

"Erin—"

"Fuck you, Jay." So much for not being juvenile.

Steadying her crutches, she found her balance and hobbled around him. When she was almost to the living room, she stopped and, not quite looking at him over her shoulder, said, "I don't give second chances."

Chapter 5

Christ. Could that have gone any worse?

Jay watched Erin crutch out of the kitchen and gritted his teeth. What was wrong with him? He couldn't say anything right to her. He'd wanted to at least establish a truce between them, but instead he'd threatened her with blackmail, not to mention the asinine assumption he'd made that she'd modified her house for wheelers. Of course it was for her grandmother. He'd stuck a gigantic foot in his mouth and was still choking on it.

And where had that burst of self-pity come from? He'd broken his back eight years ago. He had his bad days, but he'd long since moved past the grief and anger stages of dealing with his SCI. He'd accepted it, or so he'd thought, and he was embarrassed to have played the cripple card with her, even it had been in the heat of the moment.

Erin, on the other hand, obviously felt no pity for him. She hated him as much as she would any AB guy who was putting the screws to her. Jay wasn't used to that. Most people gave him a free pass whenever he was a dick, the same way they would treat a small child who didn't know any better, chalking it up to what they figured must be a dismal existence in a wheelchair.

"Of course he's a jerk sometimes. Wouldn't you be if you were like him?"

Erin had given him the gift of equality and held him accountable, and he realized, as a small smile played across his face, that he respected her for that.

A few hours later, Jay found himself outside Erin's door. She hadn't responded to his knock, and he wondered if she was asleep or if she was just not answering. Given their stormy relationship, it probably wasn't smart to go in without her permission. He didn't want to make things worse with her than they already were, but she hated him anyway. What was one more transgression in a list of many?

She hadn't had a decent meal since Zac left. Jay knew because he'd been keeping track. Other than to take a bath or get coffee, Erin hardly left her room, at least from what Jay had seen when he wasn't at work. He was feeling guilty about everything that had gone down, and he didn't want her to starve to death on top of everything else. So he'd brought a peace offering.

He knocked one more time. No answer.

"Fuck it," he muttered, and let himself quietly into her room. He stopped just inside the doorway and watched her for a moment, trying to see whether she was truly sleeping. She was lying on her side, her back to him, legs bent at the knees and bulky ankle splint propped on a pillow.

The wooden tray on Jay's lap held a turkey sandwich, a glass of iced water, and a napkin, and as he wheeled around to her side of the bed, he was careful not to spill any of it. Now face-to-face with her, he saw that she was asleep for real and not playing possum like she did whenever he let Chopper into her room in the mornings. Her dark brown hair was still a mess, but at least her bangs were straight and hid the giant green-gold bruise on her forehead. That thing seemed to get uglier and scarier by the day as it healed.

She looked almost childlike when she slept, innocent and vulnerable, with long dark lashes fanning over her cheeks and the lips of her expressive mouth parted into a tiny O. Actually, in a quirky sort of way, she was really beautiful.

She was wearing the same tight pink pajama tank and black cotton drawstring pants she'd had on since yesterday evening, the fabric of one leg bunched up where it met her splint. He could see a small section of her taut stomach just above the top of the pants. It was soft-looking and pale, and it never seemed to be covered, no matter what pajamas she wore. It tantalized him, and for a second he forgot to breathe.

Her breath was slow and steady, in the rhythm of a deep sleep. He could see her ribs expand and contract with each easy inhale and exhale. The thin cotton of the tank top did nothing to hide the peaks of her nipples; it was clear that she wasn't wearing a bra.

He was breathing again, but his breath was stilted,

kind of like a phone stalker's, and he felt too warm. He had the urge to do a pressure lift, but the laden tray on his lap kept him from it. What he really wanted was to put a hand on her small rib cage just for the simple pleasure of feeling her breathe. A nice squeeze of one of her round, perky tits would be nice, too. He had to grip his wheels until the tires dug into his palms to keep from doing either one.

Jesus. He needed to find a woman. It had obviously been too long since he'd had a date, but things hadn't gotten so desperate yet that he was ready to cop a feel from a sleeping dev.

He cleared his throat, then said gently, "Erin?"

She wrinkled her nose for a second but didn't wake up.

"Erin," he said a little louder, "I need you to wake up."

Lashes fluttered, and then her eyelids rose, revealing the startling light hazel of her eyes. With a surly groan, she squinted and said, "Oh, God. It's you. Go away," and then her eyelids slid down again.

"You gotta wake up, darlin'."

"Go . . . away." This time, she said it slowly and succinctly, like he was a knuckle-dragger.

In an exaggerated monotone, he said, "I brought you a delicious sandwich." It was a play on a line from *Napoleon Dynamite,* but he didn't really expect her to get the reference. He didn't even know why he'd said it.

He was surprised when her eyes popped open and

made contact with his. Her mouth twitched, and a flash of recognition, a fleeting moment of shared humor, passed between the two of them before her face reverted to the usual expression of dislike she reserved for him.

Still, it was cool she'd gotten the movie reference, and he almost smiled.

"I'm not hungry," she said, eyeing the sandwich with disdain.

Jay liked her voice. It was a mixture of baby doll and smokiness that was enhanced by her sleepiness, and it was sexy as hell.

She yawned and snuggled into her pillow, closing her eyes again. "I'm going back to sleep."

"Sorry, darlin'. You need to eat, and you've got a doctor's appointment soon."

Her eyes flipped open. "Don't call me darlin', and how do you know that?"

"Your brother told me. He asked me to look out for you."

She rose up on one elbow. "What?"

"He asked me to look out for you, and I promised him I would. That's the main reason I decided to work from home today."

"I thought you wanted to fix the hinges."

"That too."

She looked skeptical. "Why would you want to do my brother a favor?"

"I'm not as heartless as you think, darlin'. Your brother seems like a decent guy. I don't mind helping him out."

She searched his face, appearing to mull that over, and added absently, "Stop calling me darlin'."

Jay smiled. "Zac made sure I knew you had a follow-up doctor's appointment today at four. I'm your ride."

"Uh, no, you're not."

"Hate to point it out, dar—Erin, but you don't have a car."

She grimaced. Her car had been totaled in the wreck.

"Face it," said Jay. "You need me."

She snorted. "Hardly. I have friends I can call."

"It's kind of short notice," he countered.

"If no one can take me, I'll call a taxi."

"I'm already here and willing, and I'm free."

"I don't care. I'm not riding anywhere with you."

Stubborn. No other word for it. Jay rolled his head on his shoulders, trying to get the tension out of his neck. "Do you think we could find something not to argue about?"

She sat up fully, scooting herself back against the headboard, and gave him a level stare, a challenge. "Doesn't look like it."

He sighed and ran his hands through his hair. "I'm sorry. I'm sorry for everything I said. I'm sorry for . . . " He searched for the right words.

Her brows went up, disappearing beneath her bangs, and she picked up where he left off. "Worming, conning, manipulating, lying, inveigling, *blackmailing* your way into my home?"

"That's not how I'd put it," he said, not wanting to admit those words were pretty close to true.

"Just trying to be helpful."

"I needed a place to live," he said with growing irritation. "Your brother needed a renter. Problem solved. It's basic economics."

"He had a renter! You didn't fight fair, and you know it!"

Jay wanted to strangle her. "I offered double the rent! Most people would think that's a good thing!"

Erin's cheeks were flushed with the heat of anger, her chest heaving. "Yeah. But *most people* wouldn't be called pervs and bottom-feeders by their prospective roomies, now, would they? How many of those people do you think would want to live with someone who is repulsed by them?"

Jay was breathing hard too, frustrated because she was right. Their gazes caught and held, and the animosity coming from Erin pierced him. Forcing his voice to sound calmer than he felt, he said, "Help me to understand it, then, the devoteeism. I want to understand it."

She stared at him for another moment. "I don't need to justify who or what I am to you. I'm not some zoo animal here for you to study and stare at."

"Oh, come on, Erin! I don't think of you as a fucking zoo animal. But how do you expect me to accept what you are if you won't explain it?"

She glared at him, those amazing eyes of hers bright and intense. "I don't expect you to accept anything. What part of 'Get the fuck out of my house and my life' do you not understand? I don't care if I ever earn your respect, and I don't owe you any explanations. I just want you gone."

Jay wasn't sure what was wrong with him, but he couldn't stop. He was consumed with a relentless, driving need to know what made her tick. "Is it a dominant/ submissive thing?" he asked.

She steepled her hands over her mouth and shook her head. "Oh, my God. You are *such* an asshole."

"I think that's been established."

"I'm not having this discussion with you."

"Are you attracted to me?" Jay looked down at himself. "Are you attracted to my chair? To my paralyzed legs?"

Tears were gathering in her eyes, and her chin was starting to tremble. He felt like a bastard for pushing her, but he didn't stop. "Do you like it when you see crippled guys like Luis and me struggling with things that able-bodied guys don't think twice about? Do you get pleasure from our pain? Do you get off on our humiliation?"

"Get out," she hissed.

Jay was gripping his wheels, his shoulders tense, his voice deliberate and maybe too harsh, but he didn't hold back. "Goddammit. If I'm wrong, Erin, tell me."

She swallowed hard. "Get out," she repeated.

"I just want to know . . . ," he began, almost pleading. "I just want to know what makes you attracted to someone like me."

"What, are you afraid of me? You afraid of getting my taint? You want to know how to ward me off, how to protect yourself?"

Of course that wasn't what he'd meant, but before he could deny it, the full force of her gaze zeroed in on him, and the stark loneliness and despair in it stunned him speechless.

"Well, rest assured, Jay," she said darkly, "you're safe from me."

He closed his eyes, knowing he'd fully fucked up this time. "Erin, I didn't mean—"

"I'm not attracted to you," she went on vehemently, talking over him. "And I won't ever be. Ever."

Her declaration felt like a blow to the stomach, bothering Jay more than he would've thought. He drew in a deep breath and exhaled. It was time to quit before he made things worse.

Grabbing a wheel with one hand for leverage to maintain his balance, he reached over with his other hand and set the tray of food next to Erin on the bed, even though he knew there was a good chance she would dump it all on his head. Then he looked her in the eye. "For what it's worth, I'm sorry. And I'm not afraid of you. That wasn't what I meant."

"Get out." She didn't acknowledge the tray, just stared at him stonily.

He nodded and started to wheel toward the door, but halfway there he stopped. "My offer of a ride still stands."

She scoffed. "Really? I think you can guess my answer to that."

Yes, he could. It was a resounding "Fuck off."

Chapter 6

Pride goeth before a fall, and Erin was about to fall hard. It rankled, but she really had no choice. She was in desperate need of a trip to the grocery store, and it was either get Jay to take her or starve. She hobbled on her crutches to the large kitchen window next to the back door, trying to ignore the incessant itching of her broken right ankle, which was now encased in a hard, waterproof, dark blue fiberglass cast.

She could see Jay in the driveway in front of the old-fashioned detached garage working on his motorcycle, which he'd been doing more often lately since the weather was getting warmer. Winter only lasted about two months in San Antonio, usually January through February, and spring usually came early. It was March now, and some days—like today—got up into the seventies and were gorgeous.

For four weeks, Erin had been bumming rides or calling taxis when she needed to go somewhere, and it was getting old, not to mention expensive. Angie, the girl she worked with as a waitress at Lars Bar, was willing to help her out, but Angie worked a lot and wasn't always available. Plus, Angie and Erin weren't really that close—not close enough that Erin felt comfortable hitching rides for who knew how long.

Insurance was covering her totaled car, but the deductible was huge. It would be a while before she could afford to replace it, even after her right ankle healed enough for her to drive.

So, despite what she'd told Jay, Erin was short on people she could call. With Zac and her other two close friends from the band, Michelle and Norf, all gone on the band's road trip, it looked like Jay was her last resort.

As he'd made clear every time he'd seen her waiting at the front door, watching for a ride, he was willing to take her wherever she needed to go. She'd always refused him on principle—and because he was a constant reminder she was defective. He made her feel base and dirty in her own skin, which wasn't conducive to achieving the self-respect Erin so desperately craved.

She tried to avoid him as much as possible, but Jay was kind of hard to ignore. He'd started working at the house more, usually at the kitchen table on his laptop, which Erin figured he did just to annoy her.

He exuded a charisma and physical arrogance that was distracting, that made any room he was in seem smaller. When he talked to customers on the phone, his rich voice permeated the room and wrapped itself around Erin like a hypnotic male vapor. If he was around, it was impossible to concentrate on whatever she was doing— which, okay, was pretty much just watching TV, but that wasn't the point. He was an intruder.

An intruder with a car.

Taking a deep, fortifying breath, Erin steeled herself and crutched out the door. When she made it to Jay, his back was to her, and he was intent on installing some shiny new chrome thing on his Harley. He'd somehow gotten the motorcycle mounted and secured up on an old worktable that rolled so he could reach the bike better and move it back into the garage when he was done.

Why he was restoring a motorcycle, she had no idea. How would he be able to ride it? She was curious, but she'd never wanted to have an actual conversation with him enough to ask.

He didn't seem to notice she was standing behind him. He was sitting in his wheelchair, shirtless. His broad shoulders had already soaked in some sun and were turning brown. He had the coloring of someone with Scandinavian ancestry—blue eyes, blond hair, and a natural bronze skin tone that tanned easily—and Erin decided there must be some Viking mixed in with his German blood. Erin, with her fair skin, was the antithesis of that. Thirty minutes in the sun without protection, and she was a boiled lobster.

He was wearing the faded black baseball cap with the gold Oakland A's emblem on it Erin had first seen that fateful morning at Luis's apartment. Jay wore it a lot, and, as usual, it was on backward. His long hair brushed his shoulders as he leaned toward his bike, and the ends of it flipped up slightly—but not in a girlie way.

His appearance and the easy, confident way he moved, especially considering he had paraplegia, didn't fit his nerdy profession. He had a working-class vibe, seemed more blue collar, more rugged. She had visions of IT guys wearing polos, khakis, and loafers, but she rarely saw Jay dressed like that. Then again, most of his work was done over the phone, so he didn't need to dress professionally very often.

On the nicely defined deltoid muscle of his right shoulder, he had a badass tattoo of an archaic-style compass in black ink. There were no letters designating directions, just the spikes of the compass making what sort of resembled a star.

Another tattoo on his left shoulder was also done in black ink. It was a word or a name, but the scrolled lettering was so elaborate Erin couldn't make out what it was. The tats seemed to come alive as Jay moved, the sinew of his arm and back muscles rippling under his golden skin.

Because he was leaning forward a bit, Erin also had a good view of the long, vertical surgical scar that ran about ten inches along his spine. The scar looked silvery and well-healed, and Erin wondered how long ago he'd been injured.

A pang of empathy tightened her belly. She didn't want to feel compassion for him, but the scar was a reminder of all the pain and heartache he must have been through at some point. No one deserved a spinal cord injury, no matter how much of a scrote they were.

Erin was pulled out of her musings by Chopper, who'd been lying on his side in the sun but heaved his great body up as soon as he saw her. She leaned down to pet his large, gargoyle-like head, trying not to lose her balance on her crutches. Chopper soaked in her affection like a sponge, and she couldn't help but smile at the dog's sweet, gentle nature, which was so contrary to his ferocious appearance.

Jay dropped the ratchet he was working with onto his lap and swiveled his chair around to face Erin, and if she'd thought his back muscles were impressive, his pectoral muscles were stunning. In fact, his muscles were ripped down to his waist, where his muscle tone abruptly morphed into a slight paunch that didn't show so much when he was wearing a shirt. Obviously, the area of his navel was where his paralysis began.

He was wearing the same loose, worn jeans he wore often, but Erin quickly bounced her eyes away from his atrophied legs. She didn't want him to think she was perving on them.

His disability didn't detract from his fluid grace, and the fact that he used a wheelchair didn't make him appear weak. The well-engineered chair fit him perfectly, like a second skin, and insinuated strength.

Erin's pulse picked up, and she got an urgent zing down in her nether bits, a longing. She hated her body for its betrayal and fought not to clench her eyes shut to block out the sight of him.

He's not hot, he's not hot, he's not hot, she chanted

to herself. He was a blond, for God's sake. She'd never been into blonds. Ever. She liked darkly handsome guys like Luis. Yeah, Luis had been a massive mistake, but that didn't mean he wasn't nice to look at. She wasn't about to start lusting after blonds now, especially not Jay Bontrager.

He looked up at her, squinting into the sun, two little creases between his brows, and his sunlit blue-gray eyes were so gorgeous that her heart did a flippy thing against her will. She bit her lip, almost drawing blood, hoping the pain would bring her back to her senses.

"What's up?" he said in his relaxed, rumbling voice. He picked up an old, grease-stained rag from his lap and wiped his hands.

"I just . . . " She cleared her throat, not liking how shaky her voice sounded. "Nothing, really."

When she didn't go on, he asked, "Did you need something?" His brows were raised a little, and he had that curve to his mouth that threatened a cocky smirk. She thought it was an unconscious thing he did, like it was ingrained in him to be flirty—like he knew the effect he had on women and what she'd been thinking about him. "You just out here smelling the roses?"

Erin glanced at the barren backyard, which had been neglected for years, and laughed wryly. "No. I was, um, wondering if you were planning on going to HEB anytime soon?"

He glanced down at his hands and then back up to her, just one eye squinting this time. It was almost a wink. "Just went yesterday, but that doesn't matter. I'll take you if you need to go."

She wasn't surprised he'd just gone because he went often. He liked that fancy HEB, the Central Market grocery store on Broadway, the expensive one with all the gourmet stuff. She'd noticed he bought a lot of healthy things like fresh produce. It was weird because he was so unpretentious. She wouldn't have pegged him as being someone who was particular about the groceries he bought, but she had to admit, whatever he cooked usually smelled *really* good. She was more into processed, prepackaged stuff herself and preferred the regular, cheaper HEB on Olmos Drive.

Gripping her crutch handgrips tightly, Erin tried to say yes, she did need a ride, but it was killing her to ask him for help. She started to backpedal instead. "That's okay. Forget it. I don't really need to go."

A total lie. She mentally tallied what was left in her section of the pantry. She still had some Froot Loops left. Maybe. But she was for sure out of milk.

He tilted his head a bit. "Erin, if you need to go to the store, just say so. It's not a big deal for me to take you."

She looked down at her feet—one shod in a new black leather biker boot (since her old ones were trashed in the wreck) and one wearing a cast—and felt suddenly like an awkward teenager. The toenails of her right foot, painted a midnight blue that looked almost black, were sticking out of the cast. She wiggled them. "I guess I kind of do need to go," she admitted. She lifted her gaze, forcing herself to look Jay in the eye.

His mouth curved into a definite smirk this time—the Jay smirk—but it wasn't condescending or derisive. He seemed pleased that she'd finally relented. He set his ratchet and the greasy rag on the worktable and said, "Just let me go get a shirt on and wash my hands."

Erin nodded and watched him wheel himself toward the house with sure, strong pushes. If it was possible for someone to swagger in a wheelchair, Jay did it.

His car was what she would expect from him: a loud, sleek, black, muscle-looking thing. It was modified with hand controls, and he made driving it look easy. They drove to the cheap HEB in silence.

Once they got to the grocery store, Erin sat on one of the scooter carts, tucking her crutches between her cast and the seat of the scooter. She was embarrassed to have to use a scooter cart—she'd always thought they were for super-old or super-fat people—but she didn't have a choice. She couldn't push a regular cart and use her crutches at the same time.

Did that make her a hypocrite, the fact that she appreciated, had even been attracted to, guys with a disability but was snobby about it when faced with it herself? Yeah, it pretty much did, and she resolved not to be so judgmental the next time she saw someone using a scooter.

As she went up and down the aisles, Jay followed her in his chair, occasionally throwing something in the scooter's basket that he needed, but most of the stuff was hers. They garnered a lot of furtive, curious looks in their roles as Gimpy and Gimpier, but Jay didn't seem bothered by it. Erin figured he was used to it.

She tossed several cans of Pringles into the basket and said, "That should do it. That's everything on my list."

Jay arched his brows, causing his forehead to crease in a way that was somehow sort of charming—or it would be, if it weren't Jay. "Glad to see you finally put some vegetables in the cart, darlin'," he drawled.

"Don't call me darlin'," she responded. It was rote now, something she said automatically without any real heat. She perused the less-than-healthy contents of her cart as she and Jay made their way to the checkout lanes and shrugged. "Pringles are made out of potatoes. Potatoes are vegetables."

Jay just shook his head.

The store was crowded, so they had to wait in line behind two other people at the checkout stand. A lanky, nerdy-looking white guy was browsing the magazine rack next to Erin, and he bumped into the bulky leather purse hanging from her shoulder. "Excuse me," he said with a polite smile.

She gave him a short nod and small smile back. "That's okay."

Wheeling up beside Erin's scooter cart, Jay continued to mock her grocery-buying habits. "Do you ever buy anything that isn't encased in some kind of man-made packaging? Do you ever, you know, actually cook anything?"

"Yeah. Of course." It was a lie, but she didn't want him to know she was a terrible cook.

He looked skeptical. "Kraft mac 'n' cheese doesn't count as cooking."

"I like mac 'n' cheese," she defended. "And, by the way, what I eat is none of your business."

He considered her, his eyes thoughtful. "How about I make you dinner tonight, darlin'? Show you what a real meal is."

"Uh, no," she retorted. "And I'm not your darlin'."

He glanced toward the ceiling as if he might get some help from above. "You know, most women would like it if a guy wanted to cook them dinner."

She looked around and lowered her voice, trying not to keep their argument from calling more attention to them than they were already getting, but her tone was still hard. "You know damn well why I don't want you to cook me dinner."

"Actually, I don't, Erin." Jay punctuated his words like he was fed up with her. "I just want to do something nice. Why is that such a bad thing?"

Fury simmered in her blood. How could he not know why? He had to know, and it pissed her off that he was pretending to be Mr. Magnanimous and making her out to be the bad guy.

Did he think just because they hadn't had a knock-down-drag-out in the last three weeks that all was good between them, that she could ever forget what he'd said?

The uneasy truce of the last few weeks was only because she'd gone out of her way to avoid him. Every time she remembered his scathing tirade against devs, not to mention that he was also blackmailing her, it gutted her. And now he wanted to cook her dinner?

She leaned toward him and hissed, "I don't want anything from you. And why would you even want to sit at the same table with someone like me, let alone cook me dinner?"

His nostrils flared. "Jesus Christ. I—" He stopped abruptly and focused on a point beyond her shoulder, then reached with lightning-quick speed across her body.

Startled, she turned her head to see Lanky Guy standing on the other side of her scooter with his hand inside her purse. She'd forgotten to zip the bag when she put her grocery list back in it. One of Jay's hands was gripping the wheel of his chair for leverage, and one was clamped down on Lanky Guy's wrist. Jay was scowling, those expressive brows drawn together, his eyes boring into the pickpocket. "What the hell do you think you're doing?" he growled.

Lanky Guy reared back with his free hand and brutally punched Jay in the face, then took off running. The blow was completely unexpected and shocking in its intensity.

Jay's head snapped back, his back slamming against the backrest of his chair, and the force caused the chair to tip over. With a hard thud, his skull hit the white floor tiles. He grunted and then stared at the ceiling with dazed eyes.

Time stopped for a split second, then chaos erupted. The customers around Erin and Jay gasped and said lots of "Oh, my Gods," while Erin's heart lurched into her throat. Two HEB employees, men who had been stocking a bin of sale items near the exit, saw Lanky Guy running for the automatic doors and tackled him.

Another couple of guys, off-duty soldiers dressed in sand-colored camouflage uniforms, helped Jay right his chair and get back in his seat. He was breathing hard and dabbing at the corner of his eye. When his fingers came away, there was blood on them. "Son of a bitch," he muttered, wincing.

One of the soldiers kept holding on to Jay's arm, even after he was settled in his chair. "I'm fine," Jay told him. Erin wasn't so sure, but at least his breathing was starting to return to normal.

When the soldier didn't look convinced, Jay clenched his jaw like he was annoyed that the soldier was coddling him. As he spoke, however, his tone was firm but polite. "Really. I'm fine. Thanks."

The soldier nodded and let go.

Alarmed that Jay was bleeding, Erin turned toward the stunned lady behind the checkout stand. "We need something to wipe his eye."

A few seconds later, someone shoved a wad of brown paper towels into Erin's hand. She stood up on her good leg, then leaned toward Jay and braced herself with one hand on his leg for balance so she wouldn't fall. It felt weird to be touching him, to feel the knobby bone of his knee under the denim of his jeans, but she reminded herself that he couldn't feel it. He probably had no idea she was touching him. Still, being so close to him, she could sense his warmth. Her heartbeat picked up at the disconcerting intimacy of it. "Let me see," she said to him softly.

He let his hand drop and turned the injured side of his face a little toward her. He had a cut near the corner of his eye, and the area around the eye was red and starting to swell. "You're gonna have a nice shiner," she observed, gently dabbing at the bleeding cut with the wad of paper towels.

"Shithead must have had a ring on," Jay grumbled.

Erin was close enough to feel the soft stirring of his breath on her face when he spoke, and she ignored the little shiver down her spine it caused. His breath smelled nice, sort of minty. If she weren't so grateful to him, she might have been annoyed by that. Did he always have to be so perfect?

She lifted the paper towels away from his face and inspected the cut. "I think it'll be okay. It's already almost stopped bleeding. I don't think you need stitches."

He nodded and swallowed hard, still looking pissed off.

It started to really sink in what he'd done for her, and Erin started to feel shaky now that the adrenaline rush was fading. She'd had nearly three hundred dollars worth of tip money she'd saved up for a rainy day in her wallet—money she desperately needed now that she couldn't work. If Lanky Guy had stolen it, she either would have been stuck with dry Froot Loops to eat until Zac could send her some money or would have maxed out her credit card, which was already precariously close to that point.

Jay's gaze wandered from her face down to her hand, the one still on his knee. His focus lingered there, and a frown flickered across his face. God, it must repulse him, the fact that she was touching him—on his paralyzed leg, no less. He probably thought she was turned on or something.

Embarrassed, Erin hastily pushed off—causing Jay's chair to roll away from her a bit—and plopped back down on the seat of her scooter. She wouldn't meet his eyes, but she could feel him staring. The weight of it made her feel flustered, so she inspected the contents of her purse to give her hands something to do. When she gathered her dignity and found the courage to look up, she was startled to see a warm glow in Jay's grayish blue eyes instead of revulsion or disdain. It wasn't what she'd expected to see, and she was captivated.

A woman put a hand on Jay's shoulder, distracting him, and whatever had passed between him and Erin was broken by the concerned HEB employees. Someone put a Band-Aid on his cut and gave him one cold pack for his battered eye and another for the back of his head.

The next hour was filled with answering questions from the police for an arrest report and Jay being fawned over by the HEB staff, including an awkward moment where an employee thought Jay was a veteran and thanked him for his "sacrifice," assuming he'd gotten his spinal cord injury as a soldier. Jay seemed embarrassed, almost apologetic. He corrected the guy politely and told him he wasn't a veteran, but he didn't elaborate on what had caused his injury.

Erin could see how someone might mistake him for a veteran: San Antonio was home to four different military bases, two major military hospitals, and a lot of young soldiers with disabilities. Still, cause of injury was a very personal thing for a lot of wheelers—most of whom didn't like to relive that traumatic moment of their lives by talking about it—and it must be irritating for Jay to have to explain himself.

When it was all over and their groceries were loaded in Jay's car, they started back to Erin's house, neither of them speaking. From his profile, she could see his bruised, damaged eye and the Band-Aid just above it. She tried not to wince. It looked painful and marred his movie-star-handsome good looks, but only a little. She hated that he'd been hurt because of her.

Breaking the lull, Erin said, "So, I guess I owe you a big thanks for stopping that guy from stealing my wallet."

"Don't strain yourself, darlin'." Jay's voice was wry. "I know it must be killing you to say that."

She glanced down at her lap, her lips forming a small, involuntary smile. "Yeah, it is." Looking at him more soberly, she said, "But I mean it. Thanks."

"You're welcome." He grinned at her, flashing his pearly teeth and completely disarming her.

That was bad. She didn't want him breaching the carefully constructed wall she'd built around her heart. She looked out her window so he couldn't see her face, afraid of what it might reveal.

Chapter 7

In the end, Erin was the one who made dinner—sort of. They picked up burgers and fries from Whataburger. While Jay would have avoided getting socked in the eye if given the choice, and was still feeling the ache from it, Erin's animosity toward him seemed to have eased somewhat as a result of his unintentional act of chivalry. She was less aloof and had even bought his burger. He'd offered to pay, of course, but she'd insisted on buying.

They were sitting at the kitchen table now, sipping Shiner Blonde longnecks with their burgers. He sank his teeth into his and, once he was done chewing, said, "This is really good."

Erin took a pull of her beer. "That's why they're called 'what-a-burgers.'" She spoke in her laid-back, smoky little-girl voice, and there was almost a smile on her lips. He knew one was playing across his own.

"Is it a Texas thing? I've never seen one in Cali."

"Yeah. The chain started in Corpus Christi in, like, the fifties or something."

He nodded and took a sip from his longneck.

"What part of California are you from?" She dipped

a fry in ketchup and popped it in her mouth.

"Stockton originally and then Oakland after my injury."

"Why did you come to San Antonio?"

"Better job. Luis made me an offer I couldn't refuse. I had a pretty crappy help-desk job in Oakland that was going nowhere. The cost of living there is high, too. I'm making more money with Luis, and it goes a lot further here."

She took a bite and regarded Jay while she chewed. "You met Luis online, right?"

Jay laughed. "You make it sound like we met on eHarmony or something."

A real smile spread across her features then, almost-dimples showing, and it intrigued him. He could stare at that smile all day.

"You know what I mean," she said. "You took a big risk, moving to a completely new place where the only person you knew, you'd never met in person."

He nodded. "Yeah, I guess. But, like I said, I didn't have much to lose. And I'd been talking to Luis on the SCI forum for a long time." He lifted his shoulder in a half-shrug. "I don't know. I just felt like I knew him, like I could trust him."

She pressed her pretty lips together and stared at her longneck, tracing the rim with a delicate finger. "Yeah. Luis is good at that." There was an edge to her tone.

Jay guessed she was thinking of her own online relationship with Luis before Jay had ruined everything between them, and he felt guilty. "He's a good guy, Erin. You should give him another chance."

She glanced down and idly tore off a piece of bun. "What do you think'll happen to that guy who tried to steal my wallet?"

Jay exhaled, frustrated she wouldn't talk about Luis, but he followed her lead and let it go. "I hope he gets a ticket straight to the clink."

"Mmm," she said with a perfunctory nod.

"What? You don't think that's what he deserves?"

Her pale green-gold eyes, framed by dark lashes and soft black eyeliner, met his, and he felt a stir of attraction. Jesus, her eyes were incredible. She didn't wear much makeup that he could tell, aside from the eye makeup, and she didn't need it. Even if she was a freak, she was a beautiful one, and he was a red-blooded American male. A crippled one, yeah, but sure as hell not blind.

Luckily, she didn't seem aware of the effect she was having on him. She grimaced in a rueful sort of way. "I actually kind of feel sorry for the guy."

Jay raised his brows. "Erin, he was trying to steal your wallet."

"I know."

"And you feel sorry for him? I would think you'd be pissed."

"Oh, I was at first, and I hate that he hit you," she stressed, "but . . . "

"But what?"

She gave a little shrug and traced the rim of her bottle

again. "I just think—I mean, there has to be something that drives someone to do that, you know? Like, maybe his family is poor and his little sister has cancer and he needs the money to take care of her. Or maybe he lost his job, can't find another one, and is having a hard time supporting his three small kids. Or maybe both his parents are in prison, and he was in the foster care system his whole life and never had anyone to teach him right from wrong or show him love."

Jay admired her capacity for empathy and compassion, but he was more cynical. "Or maybe he's just an asshole who'd rather steal than work for a living."

"Or maybe he's just an asshole," she conceded. "Just sayin'. There's always two sides to every story."

"True." He watched her take another bite. He noticed with amusement that she was already halfway done. The girl could eat. "So, if there's always two sides to everything, why won't you tell me yours?"

Her brows knit together, partially visible beneath her dark brown bangs. "What do you mean?"

Jay was taking a risk here, possibly about to piss her off again, but the more he was around her, the more he wanted to know about her. He couldn't reconcile what he'd seen of her so far with what he'd always assumed about devotees.

He knew the instant she realized what he referred to because her mouth tightened and she put her burger down. "You never learn, do you?"

He put his hand over her small one and turned it so

he could circle his thumb over her palm. Her skin was so soft it made him ache with something he hadn't felt in a long time. He was compelled to touch her, to soothe her. It was like he didn't have a choice. "Maybe I'm wrong about devs. I don't know. You seem like a decent person, Erin. I have a tendency to make judgments and spout off shit before I know all the facts. It's a bad habit, I know."

She stared at their hands as if mesmerized, but the delicate, feminine line of her jaw was rigid.

"Talk to me, Erin," he urged. "If we're friends, if we understand each other, it'll make this whole living situation a lot better. I want to get rid of this bad blood between us."

She yanked her hand out of his and wrapped it around her beer. Her voice was harsh. "If you want us to be friends, don't *ever* bring up—" She shook her head. "I don't want to talk about it. Especially with you."

"Erin, it's okay. I won't judge you. I—"

"Don't!" She was adamant, her expression stubbornly closed off. "It's not a part of my life anymore. It never really was." Her eyes darted away and then back. "So don't bring it up again. Do you hear me?"

He nodded and knew he shouldn't push her any further, although he thought it was bullshit, what she'd said about the dev stuff. She protested too much and wanted to hide it too much for it not to matter. They ate in an awkward silence until Jay hoped it was safe enough to bring up a new topic. "So, you always lived in San Antonio?"

She took forever to answer. God, maybe he was back to square one. When she started to speak, he was relieved, even if she sounded brusque. "No," she said. "Zac and I lived in Dallas until we were sixteen. Our parents died in a car wreck, and we moved in with my grandmother and finished high school here in San Antonio."

Jay's heart contracted with an old, familiar ache. He nodded and said, "I lost my mom when I was sixteen, too. Cancer."

"That sucks. I'm sorry," Erin said, softening a little. "At least you still had your dad, though, right?"

Jay's blood went cold at the mention of his old man. "Yeah. I guess I did."

She looked guilty. "I'm sorry. I didn't mean to downplay your mom's death."

"I know. It's okay. It's not that."

"You don't get along with your dad?"

Jay let out a long breath, venting out the bad air that thoughts of his dad always caused. "No. I never really got along with him, even before my mom died. After her death, things got worse."

"Did he knock you around?"

Jay arched his brows. "Jesus. Subtle much?"

"Sorry." Her eyes flicked down. "You're right. It's none of my business."

He shrugged. "It's the same old story, same old shit, you know? Let's just say my old man wasn't into time-outs or grounding." Jay took a sip of his beer, letting the grim sarcasm of his remark sit for a moment. "My old man was a definite believer in corporal punishment. And I seemed to piss him off a lot more than my little brother, but Chad got some of it, too. We both escaped in our own way. Chad joined the army, made a career of it. He's currently vacationing in Afghanistan."

Erin's brow furrowed. "I hope he's okay."

"Trust me. He's fine. Don't feel bad for him." Jay was proud of his little bro. "He thrives on all that crap, the danger, the harsh living conditions. I don't think he could live as a civilian."

"Like that guy in *The Hurt Locker*?"

"Yeah. Great movie, by the way."

She smiled. "I love that movie."

Jay liked that they seemed to appreciate the same movies, that they had something in common. "Chad looks more like Dolph Lundgren, though, than Jeremy Renner."

"He's a big guy?"

Jay nodded. "He's taller than me. I'm six-one—or at least I used to be." It had been a long time since Jay was able to stand and let anyone measure his height. "Chad's about four inches taller." Hulking his muscles, he added, "He's burly, too, you know?"

"Wow." Erin crumpled up her bright yellow burger wrapper into a ball and sat back in her chair.

Jay's eyes widened. All her fries were gone, too, and the burger hadn't exactly been on the small side. "I can't believe you fit all that food into that little body of yours."

She scoffed like that was nothing, then eyed her

empty Shiner with a pointed look and smiled. "I'm still thirsty."

Jay shook his head, amused, and pushed away from the table, then rolled into the kitchen to get them both another beer. When he got back to the table, he grabbed one of the longnecks resting on his lap, twisted the cap off, and handed it to Erin before taking his place across from her.

"So how did you escape?" she asked.

He twisted the cap off his own longneck. "Escape what?"

"Your dad."

He took a sip. "Oh. I got married. Exchanged one ball and chain for another."

She lifted her brows so high they completely disappeared under her bangs. "You were married?"

"Yeah. High school sweetheart."

She snorted, looking doubtful. Jay was surprised. "What?"

"You don't seem like the type." she said.

"What type?"

"The marrying type or the high-school-sweetheart type."

"What? Do I seem gay or something?"

She laughed. "Uh, hardly. You seem like you'd be more of a player."

"Nope," he said with a definitive shake of his head. "I dated Jennifer all through high school and for two years after. We got married when we were twenty."

"How long were you married?"

"Two years."

"What happened?"

Jay shot her a look. "You're sure nosy all of a sudden. I think I liked you better when you were all aloof and pissy."

She smiled, unrepentant, showing her pretty, slightly uneven teeth and her almost-dimples. "You said you wanted to be friends."

"Yeah, but I didn't realize that meant a session with Dr. Phil."

"It does." Her eyes were bright with curiosity. "So what happened?"

He sighed, not exactly wanting to relive it all. It had been a shitty, painful time in his life. But he was actually having a civil conversation with Erin, and he didn't want to do anything to ruin it. "About a year into our marriage, I got hurt. Broke my back in a motorcycle accident."

"A motorcycle accident?" she repeated. Jay waited for the usual annoying expression of pity, but to his surprise, Erin sat back in her chair and said, "That's so mundane. I was hoping to hear some good war stories."

He smiled. He was glad she wasn't afraid to rib him. The veteran thing—that he must have gotten his injury in a war—was an assumption he had to correct a lot. He almost felt like he needed to apologize for not becoming paralyzed in a nobler way. Erin must have picked up on that from the HEB incident.

"Nope," he said, shaking his head. "Sorry to

disappoint you. I'm not a war hero. Just a dumbass on a Harley."

She met his gaze and smiled but looked more serious when she said, "So, your injury was the reason your marriage broke up?"

"Yeah. Jennifer and me—she divorced me six months after I got out of the hospital, almost a year to the day of my accident."

"That sucks."

"Yeah. It does." He couldn't keep the bitterness from his voice. "Apparently marriage to a paraplegic wasn't what she signed up for."

Erin had been fiddling with the label on her beer, but she stopped to look him in the eye. "She should have waited. How could she leave you so soon after you got hurt? You must have been going through hell, and she just abandoned you? She should have given it more time, especially with as much history as you guys had together."

"It was hell for her, too. And you can't blame her for not wanting to be shackled to a cripple for the rest of her life."

Erin's eyes flashed with anger. "Yeah, I can. Your wife was an idiot, Jay, and so are you for letting her off the hook. What a bitch. *I* never would have left you!"

He was taken aback by her vehemence and felt the need to explain. "My injury changed everything about our lives, Erin. *Everything*." But even as he said it, he wondered why he was defending his ex-wife. Jay understood why she'd left, but that didn't mean it hadn't hurt him beyond belief.

Erin glanced down, as if embarrassed. "Right," she murmured. Grabbing her crutches, she pulled herself into a one-legged stand, avoiding his eyes. "I, um"—she looked around, groping for an excuse—"I'm going to take a bath."

Disappointment washed through him. "Erin—"

"It's, you know, hair-washing night." She gave him a weak smile.

Jay wasn't sure why she was leaving, and before he could think of some way to convince her to stay, she crutched out of the room and was gone.

* * *

Once safely locked inside the hall bath, Erin pressed her forehead against the door. "Freak," she whispered.

"I never would have left you!" Her words echoed in her head, mocking her. Why, damn it, why had she said that?

Things had gotten way too personal with Jay tonight. She'd let herself feel comfortable with him, had let down her guard, and those embarrassing words had just slipped out. Well, not slipped out—burst out. Her reaction had been completely overboard, and she'd seen the bemusement on his face. It wasn't the response of a normal person.

His ex, Jennifer, was the normal one. The fact she left Jay after his injury was normal, if not commendable.

A lot of marriages ended in divorce after SCI. It was a sad fact.

His injury would have had a huge impact on their marriage, especially the sex. Erin knew all the implications. What sane woman would want to be shackled, as he'd put it, to a paralyzed guy?

Only someone flawed like Erin. She would never wish a spinal cord injury or any other kind of disability on anyone—ever—but if Jay had been her husband, she wouldn't have left him or loved him any less because of it.

Something had changed between them tonight. She'd seen a different side of him, and he wasn't as much of a jerk as she'd thought. It was nice to be around him without constantly feeling tense and hostile, but she needed to keep her distance. Much to her chagrin, she was starting to feel a physical attraction to him, blond hair or no. If she wasn't careful, she could end up liking him in a much deeper way, and that would be a disaster.

She couldn't be normal around Jay, and to be normal was what Erin wanted more than anything. She wanted her self-respect back. He brought out the part of her she was ashamed of, hated, wanted to destroy. She didn't want to get to know him better, and she sure as hell didn't want him to know *her* better.

Solution? Stay away from him as much as possible. It was as simple as that.

Chapter 8

"So how's Erin?" Luis asked.

Jay shrugged, feeling a surge of frustration at the mention of her name. "She's fine, I guess. Don't see much of her." The Tex-Mex place where they were having lunch had a patio that was popular with locals, and so were its margaritas. It was April Fool's Day, sunny and springlike, and Jay was tempted to have one, but it was too early. He still had a lot of work to do. Plus, he felt weird ordering a margarita. It seemed like a girlie drink, although Luis had warned him that just one from this particular hole in the wall could knock him on his ass.

Luis, who was about to scoop up a bite of cheese enchilada with a fork held in place by a utensil cuff—an adaptive device that strapped onto his hand so he could eat, since he couldn't use his fingers—arched a dark brow. "You live with the girl. How come you don't see her?"

"She stays closed up in her room or disappears in the evenings. Sometimes she doesn't get home until late." He couldn't keep the annoyance from his tone when he added, "She's got avoidance down to a science."

He didn't want to think about where she might have been or who she was with those times she came home late. She was a big girl. Jay knew that, but it didn't keep him from wondering—or from feeling something damn near jealousy.

"I would think that would be a good thing," said Luis. "I thought you weren't that eager to have a roommate, especially one who's a dev. Now it's like you don't have one. You have the house to yourself."

"Yeah." In truth, that wasn't what Jay wanted at all. The less he saw of Erin, the more he wanted to see her. It didn't help that, although she was more aloof and more guarded than ever since the one night they'd said more than three words to each other, she didn't do anything to discourage him from noticing her body.

In her defense, he didn't think she was aware of the effect she had on him, but it seemed the girl didn't own anything that wasn't tight in all the right places, especially in the neighborhood of her perfectly rounded tits. Jay would have to be a monk not to notice her on the rare occasions he and Erin were both in the same room together. Her small, slender body made his heart race, made him feel tense and restless, made him want to beg her for just a simple touch. He hadn't been this horny since he was fifteen.

He told himself it was because she ignored him that he couldn't stop thinking about her—the old grass-is-greener-on-the-other-side syndrome. Although he still wasn't sure where he stood on the whole dev thing, he wondered what sex with her would be like. He'd been scornful at the time, but now he felt a stab of envy that Luis had been with her.

Jay figured just about anything would be better than the times he and Jennifer had tried to make love after his injury. He would never forget the look of pity and revulsion on his ex-wife's face.

He'd had other sexual partners since then, but no one he cared about, and those encounters had left a lot to be desired. He knew he could please a woman, but he didn't get much out of it in return, and there was the usual awkwardness that went with it, since the women he'd been with weren't used to his disability and the effects of it. Was there some kind of secret devs knew that could make him feel sexual pleasure again? Were they more open to experimenting, less inhibited?

He told himself that would be a good thing—a really, really good thing—but he didn't see how a woman could possibly be attracted to his paralyzed body, one half strong and healthy, the other half atrophied and useless. There was something inherently wrong with getting turned on by that, and he was having a hard time getting past it. He'd always thought he would find someone who was attracted to him despite his disability, not because of it.

Still, Erin aroused his curiosity. Unfortunately, because of the troublesome talent he seemed to have developed for offending her, she had no interest in him whatsoever. When they were forced to speak to one another, she was polite but distant. He couldn't get past her defenses, couldn't get more than a brief comment from her, usually about paying bills or other household matters.

"You don't agree?" asked Luis.

Jay, still absorbed in his thoughts, was lost. "Agree on what?"

"That it's like you don't even have a roommate," Luis repeated. "I would think that's how you'd want it."

Jay shrugged and took a bite of his taco.

Luis regarded him for a moment, the sound of utensils clanking and fajitas sizzling at a table in the background, and his eyes widened. "You *like* her."

Jay chewed and swallowed before looking up. "I don't know if you could call it 'like.' I mean, she's pretty, but . . . "

"But she's a dev."

Jay didn't respond. Instead he took another bite, uncomfortable with this conversation.

"She's a good person, Jay, and like you said, she's not bad to look at. You're allowed to change your opinion of her, to admit you were wrong."

"I did admit I might be wrong."

Luis raised a censuring brow. "*Might* be?"

Jay tightened his mouth. Luis's nitpicking was annoying. "I apologized to her—more than once—but she barely gives me the time of day."

"Well, you can't blame her there. What you said about devs that day was pretty harsh. Maybe she needs more time to get over it."

"It's been two months," Jay pointed out.

Luis shook his head. "It's a painful subject for her, one she was trying to work through. I'm sure your tirade didn't help. It's not like she asked to be a dev. It's something she's really struggled with. A lot of them do."

Jay was about to take a sip of Coke, but Luis's comment made him pause. It had never occurred to him that being a dev wasn't a choice.

"You should give her a chance, Jay. Find out what devoteeism is really all about. It's not what you think."

Jay shook his head. "I don't know. It's not my thing."

"Why? How do you know it's not your thing until you get to know one of them? You've been injured a long time. I would think you would have accepted the way you are by now."

Jay stiffened. "I have. And what does that have to do with anything?"

Luis tilted his head. "Because if you were comfortable in your own skin, devs wouldn't disgust you so much. Maybe you're projecting your own hang-ups onto them."

"Cut the shrink bullshit, Garza. I've learned to live with my injury."

"Then prove it," Luis challenged. "Get to know her."

Jay was tempted, despite his misgivings. "You wouldn't care? I thought you were into her. You had sex with her."

Regret crossed Luis's features. "Yes, and I'm stupid for screwing that up, but, as you know, she won't talk to me or return my messages. She's made it clear she's no longer interested, and I can't say I don't deserve that. She heard me say some shitty things. I've definitely burned that bridge." He looked up. "Besides, I've moved on."

At Jay's cynical snort, Luis smiled. "Hey. This hunk of burnin' love is in big demand, my friend. I've got several irons in the fire. There's one I particularly like who lives in Chicago."

"That's kind of far away, don't you think?" Jay took a sip of his Coke.

"That's what planes are for."

Jay sat back in his chair and smiled. "Bro, if you can afford a long-distance relationship, I need a raise."

Luis answered with a smirk that said, *In your dreams.*

Jay steered their conversation back to the subject of his elusive roommate. "You got to know Erin pretty well, didn't you?"

Luis nodded. "Yeah. We chatted a lot on the dev website and then through e-mail."

An idea started to form in Jay's mind. "Does she still post on there?"

"She hasn't commented on anything lately, but I've noticed she's been signed in. She's still lurking, even if she doesn't actively participate."

Jay ran his index finger and thumb over the stubble on his chin. "Interesting. She told me she wasn't doing the dev thing anymore, that it was just an experiment."

Luis frowned. "I gotta say, I don't believe that. Not from the things she told me. And why would she still be lurking on the message board?"

"What's her username?"

Luis shook his head. "I'm not giving you that."

"Why not?"

"Because anonymity is what makes the site work. It's what makes the users more honest. Devoteeism is taboo. It's something some people on the site don't want anyone in their regular lives to know about. Erin only told me her real name after weeks of some pretty intense chats, after we agreed to meet in person. It's hard to build that kind of trust. I already did enough damage to her. I'm not going to sell her out on top of everything else."

Jay wiped his mouth with his napkin and dropped it on the table. "Oh, come on, Luis. It's not like you don't know me. I'm not some psycho, and I already live with the girl. I just want to know more about her. If she opened up to you on the site, maybe she would do the same with me."

Luis narrowed his eyes. "You're not going to tell her who you are? You're going to hide behind a username?"

"Well, yeah," said Jay. "How else would I do it?" He leaned toward Luis to reiterate. "Like I said, she won't give me the time of day. No matter how many times I apologize, she's never gonna let it go. She's stubborn."

Luis looked far from convinced.

"I just need a way to get close to her," said Jay.

"No."

"No?" said Jay, exasperated. "Come on, Garza!"

"It's lying. It's misleading her. Find another way to

get her to talk to you. What happens when she finds out?"

"I haven't gotten that far yet. Maybe she won't ever find out."

"Nope. It's a very bad idea."

Jay took one last sip of his Coke. Luis might be right, but Jay was out of ideas. "Look, I just want to see if we have anything in common, and you said yourself I should find out what devoteeism is really about. This way Erin and I can get to know each other without her believing I think she's a perv. Once she sees I'm not such a bad guy, I'll come clean, I'll tell her it's me—if it ever even gets that far."

Luis was silent for a long time, mulling it over. Then he spoke with less conviction. "It's still a bad idea."

"But you'll tell me?"

"She's going to think you're an asshole when she finds out," Luis warned.

"She already thinks I'm an asshole. I've got nothing to lose."

"Don't hurt her," Luis said sternly. "Some of the wheelers on the site have no respect for the devs. They're just on there to yank their chains."

Jay held up his hands in surrender. "That's the last thing I want to do," he said, and he meant it.

Luis let out a long, put-upon sigh. "It's 'emanomaly.'"

Jay grinned. "Can you spell that?"

Chapter 9

For the hundredth time, Jay's gaze drifted to Erin, who was sitting on the couch, feet propped up on the coffee table, watching TV and idly scratching Chopper between his ears. She looked hot, as usual.

She had on a charcoal gray concert T-shirt from some band he'd never heard of and jeans with a few subtle rips in them. One foot was bare, one was still in a cast, and her toes were painted a dark blue. Every sip from her mug of tea called attention to her wide, sensual mouth. The light from the lamp beside her brought out faint red highlights in her dark brown hair, which cascaded in layers that framed her face.

Jay couldn't believe she was actually sitting there in the flesh. It was like spotting some rare animal on an African safari. The TV in her room had crapped out, so he figured that was the only reason he was graced with her presence. He thought about offering to take a look at her TV, knowing she couldn't afford to have it fixed or replace it, but decided to keep his technical skills to himself for the time being. He knew he was a selfish bastard, but he liked the view of her and didn't want to give her a reason to disappear back into her room.

She turned her head a bit, like she sensed his surveillance, and he dropped his eyes back to his laptop screen. He felt her stare at him for a second and raised his eyes. She quickly looked away.

He smiled to himself. She wasn't as indifferent to him as she made out to be.

He'd been lurking on the dev website when he had time, ever since his conversation with Luis, reading over any posts he could find from Erin, or "emanomaly." None of them were recent, but he'd found a few older threads where she'd commented, and he'd used one of those as an opening to send her a private message. To his surprise, she'd replied right away.

They'd tossed a few short messages back and forth, and eventually he'd gotten her to give him an e-mail address so they could instant message each other. He'd set up an anonymous e-mail address just for that purpose. It would be faster than the private messaging provided by the dev website.

Sometimes Jay's conscience came into play, but he kept telling himself that even though technically he was deceiving her, really what he was doing was pretty harmless and probably wouldn't amount to anything. He'd chosen the username "Panhead," after his bike, a vintage 1951 Harley-Davidson Panhead. There was a small chance he was risking discovery, since Erin knew he had a bike, but she'd shown zero interest in it. He didn't think she would make the connection. She'd never said anything to indicate she was a Harley enthusiast.

The clock on his laptop said it was almost the time they'd designated for their chat. When Erin suddenly flicked the TV off and grabbed her crutches, Jay's pulse sped up. She got to her feet and crutched down the hall, leaving a forlorn Chopper in her wake.

Chopper padded over to Jay and nudged Jay's knee with his muzzle. Jay couldn't feel it, but he saw it, and he scratched the dog's large, prehistoric-looking black head. "Oh, I see how you are." He grinned. "Now that the hottie's gone, I get sloppy seconds, huh?"

Chopper wagged his tail and licked Jay's hand. Jay smiled and massaged Chopper's barrel chest with his knuckles.

Thinking Erin should have had enough time to log on to her computer, Jay entered her e-mail into the IM address box and started typing a message.

> *Panhead:* You there?
>
> *emanomaly:* Yep. Hi.
>
> *Panhead:* Hi.
>
> *emanomaly:* What's up?
>
> *Panhead:* Not much. Just working.
>
> *emanomaly:* What is your work?

Jay thought for a second. He didn't want to tell her too much because he didn't want her to figure out who she was really talking to, but he didn't want to lie if he could help it.

Panhead: I'm in the restaurant business.

He winced. It wasn't a lie, but it wasn't the whole truth either. He provided technical support for restaurants when their touchscreen computer systems went down.

emanomaly: Really? Me, too. I'm a barmaid, as sad as that is.

Panhead: Why is that sad?

emanomaly: Just that I haven't done much with my life.

Panhead: Hmm. How old are you?

emanomaly: Didn't anyone ever tell you it's not polite to ask a girl that question?

Panhead: Well, that's a relief. I wasn't sure you were a girl.

emanomaly: Ha. Yes. But let's get something straight. I am NOT interested in a hookup.

Panhead: Me either. Just trying to see what the dev thing is all about.

Jay was afraid he might have lost her when there was a long pause, but then she started typing again.

emanomaly: How long have you been injured?

Panhead: Didn't anyone ever tell you it's not polite to ask a cripple that question?

emanomaly: 26.

> *Panhead:* Huh?
> *emanomaly:* That's how old I am.

Jay's brows rose. That was already more personal information than he'd gotten from her in weeks. He hesitated to tell her how long he'd been injured, but he couldn't remember ever telling her before, so he decided it wouldn't give anything away.

> *Panhead:* I've been injured 8 years. And in case you're wondering, I'm 29.
> *emanomaly:* Then you've been injured long enough to know about devs.
> *Panhead:* True. Actually, I first heard about devs in rehab.
> *emanomaly:* And you're just now getting curious?
> *Panhead:* Let's just say I'm more open-minded than I used to be.
> *emanomaly:* Ah. You want to get laid.
> *Panhead:* No. I'm not that kind of guy.
> *emanomaly:* Ha. Right. All guys are that kind of guy.
> *Panhead:* Ouch. That's a bit cynical.
> *emanomaly:* I speak from experience.

Jay didn't like the implication of that, but he didn't want to analyze it too closely.

> *Panhead:* OK. Since we're being honest, like you said, I'm curious.

emanomaly: What do you want to know?

Panhead: Everything. I want to know what makes you tick.

emanomaly: I'm not a clock.

Panhead: How do you even know you're a dev?

Another long pause.

Panhead: You still there?

emanomaly: I'm here. I'm just trying to think of the best way to answer.

Panhead: Oh.

emanomaly: Ever since I can remember, even when I was little, I've always had a reaction whenever I saw a disabled person, a fascination and an attraction. I'm attracted to all different kinds of disability, but I find men with SCI the most attractive. Don't ask me why. I just do. I didn't realize I was a dev until I stumbled onto the dev website and saw there was a name for what I was.

Jay sat back in his chair and did a small wheelie, pondering that. This time he was the one who took a long time to respond, so she typed a question.

emanomaly: Are you freaked out now?

Panhead: No. Still just trying to understand.

emanomaly: Maybe this will make it clearer: I'm also attracted to men with dark hair, musicians (especially

> drummers), guys with a sense of humor, guys who are tall, guys who are intelligent, and guys with Australian accents. Not that I meet a lot of Australians where I live, but I wish I did. Chris Hemsworth? Yummy.

Jay smiled. It was such a normal chick thing to say.

> *emanomaly:* My interest is piqued when I meet an able-bodied guy with those traits, the same as it is when I meet a wheeler. The disability is just another physical trait to me, like eye or hair color, although, I admit, I think I feel a stronger attraction to a wheeler. Maybe just because I don't see that many around, so it's a big deal when I do. Does that make sense?

Jay still wasn't sure it did. When he again took a long time to answer, Erin added another question.

> *emanomaly:* Do you like it when people treat you differently, feel sorry for you?

Anger shot through him. That one was easy to answer. It was one of the worst things about his injury, being treated differently, being pitied. He was the same man he was before he was paralyzed, but now everyone saw the wheelchair first.

> *Panhead*: No. I hate it.
> *emanomaly:* Well, then why is it disturbing that I would

see you as a man and not as an object of pity? It's a shitty fact that a lot of able-bodied people—ABs— see you as weak because of your disability. They may even see you as someone who is like a child, someone who needs to be protected and coddled, someone who is no longer a sexual being. That is one reason, I think, why devoteeism is often seen as something sick. But a dev wouldn't view you that way. When I see a wheeler, or anyone with a disability for that matter, all I see is ability—an incredible ability to adapt and a strong will to overcome adversity. That is admirable and extremely attractive, especially in someone who has accepted his disability and moved on with his life. I know all the stuff you guys have to deal with, the pain and other things. Believe me, if I could find a cure for SCI, I would do it in a heartbeat. I don't get off on seeing you in pain—physical or mental—but I admire the class, dignity, and humor with which you deal with it. In my eyes, that is very sexy.

Panhead: But the fact still remains that my body is fucked up because of my paralysis. For one thing, my legs are abnormally thin because of atrophy. How can you find something like that attractive?

emanomaly: It's not that I'm pervin' on your legs, like I want to hump them or something. I see the whole package, the man who is shaped and made stronger by the disability. That's what I'm attracted to.

Something clicked for Jay, like a burden had been lifted. She wasn't as creepy as he'd thought. In fact, what she said made sense, and it made his attraction to her easier to accept.

There were other things he was curious about, though.

> *Panhead:* Are you attracted to all wheelers?
> *emanomaly:* God, no. A wheeler would still have to be the type of guy I would date, someone who's got a good personality, a sense of humor—someone I think is good-looking. There are plenty of wheelers I'm not attracted to.
> *Panhead:* Have you dated a lot?
> *emanomaly:* Wheelers? No. Just a few, and none of those relationships ended well. I think a lot of wheelers just want to use devs, or they say they're okay with devoteeism when deep down they're not. I'm done with wheelers. That's why I wanted to make it clear to you I'm not interested in anything other than friendship. Besides, I'm sort of dating someone.

Jay had suspected as much, but getting confirmation made him feel like he'd suddenly swallowed a stone.

> *Panhead:* Is he a wheeler?
> *emanomaly:* No. Hello? Didn't I just say I was done with wheelers?
> *Panhead:* Oh, right. So, does this AB know you're a dev?

emanomaly: Yes. We've known each other for a very long time. He just moved back to town. We went to high school together, dated through college.

Panhead: He's okay with the dev thing?

A long pause.

emanomaly: He's had a hard time dealing with it in the past, but I told him I wasn't a dev anymore. I think it's sort of a don't-ask/don't-tell thing with him right now. We had the one "talk" about it. He seemed satisfied with what I told him, and it hasn't come up since.

Panhead: Doesn't sound like a good way to start a relationship to me.

emanomaly: It's probably not, but I'm not exactly one to do things the right way. I like to see just how much I can screw things up.

Her self-deprecating humor made Jay smile.

emanomaly: I haven't even invited him to my house yet. My new roommate is a guy and a wheeler (long story, and, no, I don't have the hots for him). I dread that whole thing—you know, them meeting each other.

Panhead: Your boyfriend will be pissed?

emanomaly: I think he might be freaked, even though I'm not into my roommate at all.

Not at all? It wasn't like Erin hadn't made that clear to Jay's face, so why was it so disappointing?

> *Panhead:* Why would your boyfriend be threatened if your roommate's not even attractive?
>
> *emanomaly:* I didn't say my roommate wasn't attractive. Some people would probably think he's very good-looking.

Jay raised his brows and smiled. Maybe all was not lost.

> *emanomaly:* But, for one thing, he's a blond. I'm not into blonds.

And . . . nosedive. Jay felt like he was on a roller coaster. Nothing he could do about his hair color except dye it. For a second, he tried to picture himself with dark hair. Nope. Not gonna happen. He couldn't believe he'd considered it, even for a second. What was this girl doing to him?

> *Panhead:* What does your roommate think about your boyfriend?
>
> *emanomaly:* My roommate doesn't know about my boyfriend either, as far as I know. I don't talk to my roommate unless I have to.
>
> *Panhead:* Why?

emanomaly: Like I said, it's a long story. The short version is that my roommate hates devs. I heard him say some really shitty things about them—about me. Plus, he kind of blackmailed me into letting him live with me.

Jay gritted his teeth. Jesus Christ, the woman could hold a grudge. How many times did he have to apologize? And he'd been a model roommate, paying his share of rent and bills on time and even fixing a few things around the house (except for a certain TV). Apparently none of that counted.

Panhead: Blackmail? That sounds pretty serious. You sure you're not exaggerating?

emanomaly: I'm not exaggerating. I'm still in the closet about being a dev. None of my friends or family know. My roommate threatened to tell my brother I was a dev if I made a big stink about him moving out.

Panhead: Wow. That's pretty shitty. He never apologized?

emanomaly: Yeah. He apologized. But that doesn't mean we'll ever be BFFs. It's not like an apology can magically erase what he did and said. There's a truce between us now—we're civil to each other—but it's just better if I avoid him.

Panhead: Why?

emanomaly: Like I said, I just need to stay away from wheelers in general.

Panhead: Then why do you still log on to the dev
board?

emanomaly: Ha. Good question. I think it's kind of
like free therapy.

Panhead: Therapy?

There was no answer, but just as Jay was about to
prompt her, the IM feature indicated she was typing, so
he waited.

emanomaly: A dev is not something I choose to be.
It's sometimes hard for me to deal with. Lurking on
the boards, seeing that there are others like me and
what they have to say, sometimes helps me put it
in perspective. I wasn't going to PM with wheelers
anymore, just lurk, maybe chat with other devs.

Panhead: Then why did you answer my PM?

emanomaly: I don't know. Glutton for punishment?

Panhead: Okay. At least you're honest. Maybe you
should be honest with your boyfriend, too, and come
clean about the roomie.

emanomaly: I will eventually. We just started going
out again. I'm giving it a little time before I rock the
boat.

Panhead: Don't mean to harp, but keeping things
from him doesn't sound like a very good basis for a
relationship.

Jay winced as he typed that. He was a fucking

hypocrite, considering what he was doing. But it wasn't like he wanted a relationship with her. Did he?

Shit. What he did know was that he didn't want her dating some other guy.

> *emanomaly:* So, I gotta go.
> *Panhead:* Sorry. Was I getting too preachy?
> *emanomaly:* No. It's time for my monthly shower.

Jay chuckled.

> *Panhead:* Hmm. Monthly? Your lack of success with relationships may be because of something other than the fact you're a dev.
> *emanomaly:* Ha. Could be. But I really do have to go right now.
> *Panhead:* Hot date with the AB?
> *emanomaly:* Actually, yeah.

That stone in the pit of Jay's stomach, the one from earlier, started to expand. God. He needed to get laid—or at least the paraplegic's crappy substitute for it. He couldn't come because he couldn't feel his dick, but at this point he'd settle for being touched anywhere he could feel.

That had to be his problem. It had been too long since he'd had any sort of contact with a woman, and he was starting to obsess over his freaky but beautiful roommate—who smelled fresh and sweet like spring and definitely showered more than once a month.

> *Panhead:* Can we chat again?
> *emanomaly:* Sure. TTYL.
> *Panhead:* What does that mean?
> *emanomaly:* You don't chat much, do you?
> *Panhead:* No.
> *emanomaly:* It means 'talk to you later.'"
> *Panhead:* Oh. TTYL.
> *emanomaly:* :) (That's a smiley face.)

Jay rolled his eyes. He knew that much.

> *Panhead:* Thanks. I thought it was a colon with a parentheses.
> *emanomaly:* 'Parenthesis,' if you're talking about just one.
> *Panhead:* Anal much?
> *emanomaly:* Sorry. I'm a writer. Those kinds of things bug me.

A writer? That threw Jay for a loop. He'd had no idea. There was so much more to Erin than what she let him see. He didn't care if chatting with her like this was kind of devious. Okay, not "kind of"—it was devious. But just now he had learned more about her in fifteen minutes than he'd learned in weeks of living with her.

> *Panhead:* What do you write?

emanomaly: I HAVE TO GO. HOT DATE, REMEMBER? :)

Panhead: Next time?

emanomaly: Next time. BYE.

Panhead: Bye.

He heard the uneven thump-thump as she crutched from her room to the hall bathroom and clicked the door shut. His gut twisted at the thought of some other guy kissing and touching her, and he wanted to see who this mystery dude was.

Jay rubbed the stubble on his chin. It was time Erin's boyfriend and her roommate met each other, whether she wanted them to or not.

Chapter 10

When Trynt pulled up to the curb in his silver BMW convertible, Erin was waiting for him on her crutches. She always made sure she was outside waiting for him because she wasn't ready to reveal Jay to him. If Trynt thought it was weird she never invited him inside the house, he didn't say so, and she was glad. It really wasn't much different from when they'd been engaged. He'd rarely come in the house then either, because it was no secret that both Nana and Zac had disliked him.

Erin's relationship with Trynt began in high school and lasted through college. They'd become engaged right after they both graduated, but things ended when she'd displayed a colossal error in judgment and told him about her odd attraction.

Yes, it had been a dumb thing to do, but in her defense, the whole dev thing wasn't a big deal to her back then, just something she mentioned to Trynt one day in passing. It was just a curious thing she'd noticed about herself, this surge of attraction whenever she saw a handsome disabled guy. It was something kind of weird but harmless, sort of like Trynt's thing for the mannequins at Dillard's—which, when she thought about it, was pretty dang weird itself.

The point was, Trynt didn't go around humping mannequins, and Erin had no plans to go out and start humping disabled dudes. The thought never crossed her mind. After all, she was very much in love with her fiancé.

She explained all that to Trynt, but he freaked out anyway. God, how naive she'd been. How could she not have seen the stigma that would come with devoteeism, the creepy quotient it would have for most people?

Erin never told anyone the full story of why she and Trynt broke up, and, as far as she knew, neither did he. Nana and Zac had both said good riddance, but Erin was devastated. The demise of her engagement was a painful blow to her self-worth and self-confidence. It shattered her belief in who she was and where she was headed in life.

Despondent and lost, she did some research and learned her attraction to disabled men had a name: devoteeism. Finding this out somehow made it more real, more substantial. She got caught up in the devotee world and tried to understand it, tried to make it okay.

Now she wondered if pursuing the whole dev thing and trying to find out more about it hadn't made things worse. What started out as an occasional spark of attraction grew stronger as she acquired more knowledge and got to know actual wheelers.

Maybe if she'd ignored it all and never said anything

to Trynt, she wouldn't be so damaged and confused now. She must have wished a thousand times over the years that she could wipe the slate clean. Now, here she was, getting a second chance. She couldn't wipe Trynt's memory clean, but maybe time had mellowed the repugnance of what she'd told him, had made him more accepting.

Trynt represented everything Erin wanted to be. He was normal, the mannequin thing not withstanding. He was successful. Although he'd grown up in a wealthy Alamo Heights family, he'd made his own way in life. He'd worked his ass off in Austin as an architect, making a name for himself, and recently he'd moved back to San Antonio to start his own firm.

Why he was interested in Erin again, she wasn't sure.

San Antonio was a large city, but it had the feel of a small town in a lot of ways. So she wasn't surprised that Trynt had heard about her car wreck through the grapevine. What did surprise her was that he'd called her a couple of weeks ago and asked her out for drinks.

"I've missed you, Erin," he'd said. "I don't . . . My God. When I think of what might have happened, that you could have died—it was a wake-up call for me. So much time has passed, but I never forgot you. I couldn't stand the thought of you dying thinking I got over you. The truth is, I've hated myself for breaking the engagement. I never should have done it."

Holy Houdini. How many times had she dreamed he would say exactly that? Erin sat in stunned silence. Talk about coming from left field.

After a long pause, he said, "You still there?"

"Um, yeah."

"I should have said something a long time ago, I know. But there hasn't been a day that's gone by that I didn't think about picking up the phone and calling you."

Oh, please. How stupid did he think she was? It had been five years.

"I want to see you again, Erin. Let me take you out for a drink."

"Just one?"

"Erin." He said her name as a reprimand, like he used to when they were together.

He had no sense of humor, but there was something familiar and strangely comforting about that. It made her feel nostalgic, just like old times when she'd been in love with him and thought she was loved back. And he'd just said all the right words—namely, "take you out for a drink."

"Yeah, sure," she answered, proving she was, indeed, stupid. Or just a lush.

They'd seen each other several times since then. Deep down, Erin figured Trynt was toying with her until something better came along. He was probably just horny and thought she might be an easy lay, although, to his credit, he hadn't ditched her even after she'd made it clear she wasn't going to do the horizontal mambo with him anytime in the near future.

Whatever his motive, she was ready to get on with

her life, and she hoped Trynt would be a much-needed distraction from a certain roommate of hers who was hard to ignore, no matter how herculean her efforts were to do so. She was sick to death of being a dev and all the gut-wrenching drama that went with it—the shame, the frustration, the longing that, if her past relationships with wheelers were any indication, would never be fulfilled.

She didn't know why in the hell she'd started chatting with this new guy Panhead. It went against her resolve to ban all wheelers from her life. But he seemed nice, and it was a relief to be honest with someone. It was cathartic. Besides, no one would ever know. He wasn't real. He only existed in cyberspace, and that was where he would stay, as would emanomaly. Emanomaly was a dev; the new Erin Silver was not.

As Erin stood on the sidewalk, Trynt gave her an arrogant once-over, which she found annoying, and a short nod. Then he got out of the car, kissed her on the cheek, and helped her into the passenger seat.

Erin studied him as he slid back into the driver's seat. He wasn't bad to look at, with his teal eyes and dark hair. It kind of made up for his arrogance, at least for the time being.

Waiting for Trynt to start the car, she faced forward and suddenly saw Jay in the distance, the wheels of his chair ghosting through his hands as he coasted down the sidewalk toward her. He had on a mossy green sweatshirt that hugged his broad shoulders and muscular arms, and he wore his usual loose jeans and white tennis shoes. His legs were tucked in closely, and his feet were resting on the footplate. They bounced slightly whenever he rolled over cracks in the sidewalk. Chopper was on a leash, loping beside him.

The breath seized in Erin's lungs for a split second before she turned away, her heart racing. There was something so capable about Jay, something so vital, so strong and masculine. Simply put, he was hot, but there was much more to him than just looks. She knew that, had seen glimpses of depth and sensitivity in him, despite her best efforts to hold him at arm's length. A part of her wanted to be close to him, to bask in the golden heat of him, to uncover the intriguing guy beneath the cocky smirk.

In that moment, Erin wanted to touch every inch of him, even the paralyzed parts. She'd never admitted that to herself before, had always said it wasn't necessarily the physical aspect of a disability that attracted her but the grit and courage it took to live with it. It made the devoteeism easier to stomach.

But now, in this instant of stark clarity, she knew his thin, inert legs were a big part of what turned her on. She loved the way they contrasted with his ripped upper body. She wanted to touch them—the thought made her molten inside—because they were a part of him. Jay was the embodiment of strength over weakness, of will over adversity, of ability over disability.

But if he knew what she'd just been thinking, that she was perving on his crippled legs, he would be disgusted by it.

Deeply ashamed, Erin hid the barrage of disturbing emotions within her and leaned over to kiss Trynt on the cheek. "Ready?" she asked him, her voice sounding too high and perky. "Let's go."

The wariness on Trynt's face showed her she was acting too enthusiastic.

"Erin?" Jay called out to her, still a good distance away.

She pretended not to hear him. "Ready?" she prompted Trynt again, smiling so hard her cheeks hurt.

Trynt frowned. "That handicapped guy just yelled out your name."

She widened her eyes, trying to appear guileless, and kept her focus on Trynt. "What handicapped guy?"

"This one," answered a wry voice. The rich, deep rumble of it was unmistakably Jay. He had reached them much faster than she anticipated. "Chopper, sit," he commanded.

Erin didn't have to see it to know the mammoth dog instantly obeyed.

Schooling her features into something she hoped was neutral, she turned her head to look at Jay and tried not to notice how the evening sun lit up streaks of light gold in his longish blond hair. "Oh. Hi."

Chopper's leather leash was looped around one of Jay's wrists, and his large hands rested on his wheels. His blue-gray eyes sparked with curiosity as they took in first Erin, then Trynt, and then settled back on Erin. His face had that easy, cocky smirk that was always at the ready. "What's up, darlin'?"

She almost said, *Don't call me darlin'*, but decided it was better not to. "Nothing."

Trynt stiffened beside her, rigid as a statue. Erin laser-beamed an unmistakable go-away look at Jay, but he only raised an unrepentant brow in response. She gritted her teeth.

Chopper sat on his haunches beside Jay's chair, whimpering and wagging his tail. He obviously wanted Erin to acknowledge him but wouldn't disobey his master's command. She couldn't resist and, since Chopper's massive head was just inches from the convertible, she reached over the side and gave him a quick scratch between his shiny black ears. He licked her fingers as a thank-you.

Trying again to extricate herself from the situation, Erin sat back in her seat and said to no one in particular, "So, I guess we should be go—"

"Aren't you going to introduce us?" Jay interrupted. He was the picture of innocence, but Erin caught the subtle, sarcastic edge to his question.

She stared at him, trying to come up with an acceptable introduction without telling Trynt everything.

Apparently she delayed too long, because Jay took matters into his own hands. He raised his chin in a typical "bro" greeting toward Trynt. "How you doing? I'm Jay Bontrager, Erin's roommate."

Erin closed her eyes for a second, her stomach

sinking. Fuck. Trynt would be so pissed. She avoided looking at him, but she could sense the bitchy look on his face, the tight set to his lips.

His voice came out frosty and imperious when he said, "Trynton McCutcheon. Most people call me Trynt—spelled with a 'y.'"

Jay nodded with cordial interest, but there was a cynical curve to his mouth. Erin knew what he was thinking. She could see him judging Trynt, thinking he was a douche.

She exhaled, and when she spoke to Jay, her tone was clipped and direct, hoping he'd get the hint and go away. "Well, guess we're leaving now. See you later." Turning to Trynt, she said for the third time, "Ready?"

He gave her a terse nod. "Nice to meet you," he said to Jay, sounding about as sincere as a politician.

"You, too," Jay replied. His tone was affable enough, but his features were hard.

After they pulled away from the curb, Erin sneaked a glance in her side-view mirror. Jay hadn't moved from his spot on the sidewalk and was still looking in her direction.

Chapter 11

Trynt hadn't said a word. Not in the car, not during the meal. He answered any question Erin put to him with a caveman-like grunt.

She was starving, but her stomach was knotted so tightly she'd only eaten half of her chicken tagine, served in a reddish clay dish with a lid that reminded Erin of a volcano. The tagine was delicious, but every time she took a bite, she could feel Trynt's sullen, judgmental gaze.

So instead she kept sipping red wine. Now she was on her third glass. Or maybe it was her fourth. At this point, she didn't care. She just wanted to ease the knot.

Trynt could make her feel like an errant child. Why she let him, she wasn't sure. It was like wanting to be friends with the stuck-up, popular girls in high school in order to fit in. It didn't matter whether she liked them or not. She wanted them to like and accept her, even if she pretended not to care, and it was the same with Trynt.

Trynt had picked the new Moroccan restaurant because he always had to be on the cutting edge of things, and all his highbrow friends were into gourmet and foodie stuff. A Moroccan restaurant might not be considered that exotic in some cities, but it was a pretty brave thing to open in San Antonio, where Tex-Mex reigned.

Casablanca was a colorfully decorated establishment where belly dancers performed every Friday and Saturday night. Erin was trying not to stare in morbid fascination at the ample belly of a gray-haired dancer jiggling and tinkling near them, but it was hard, since Trynt certainly wasn't providing any distraction by way of conversation.

Once the belly dancer's song finished, she sat at a table in a far corner. A man with gray hair longer than the dancer's, woven in a braid down his back, sat waiting for her. Apparently it was break time.

Without the diversion of the belly dancer, the silence at Erin's table grew oppressive. She couldn't stand it any longer. "Are you just gonna glare at me all night, Trynt?"

He gave her his tight-lipped, bitchy look.

She set her fork down with a definitive thunk. "This is about Jay, isn't it?"

More bitch stare.

"Oh, come on, Trynt! He's just my roommate, and I don't even like him, even as a friend. I avoid him as much as possible."

Trynt gave a "yeah, sure" sniff.

She realized she was gritting her teeth and made herself stop. "I swear. I hardly ever even see him."

"He called you 'darling.'"

Erin rolled her eyes. "He calls every girl 'darlin'.' It

doesn't mean anything."

"Don't roll your eyes at me. You know I hate it when you do that."

She rolled her eyes again just to annoy him. It was petty, but she wasn't going to let him tell her what to do. She'd been a doormat the first time around with him, and it wasn't going to happen again.

When he spoke, his tone was accusatory. "You do realize your *roommate* is the very thing that broke up our engagement before."

"No, he wasn't. I didn't even know him then," she said, deliberately being obtuse.

A muscle in Trynt's jaw jumped. "Don't be cute. You know what I mean. He's *handicapped.*"

Anger started to simmer inside her. "So what if he is? Contrary to what you believe, Trynt, I don't want to fuck every guy I see who's in a wheelchair!"

His face reddened. "Keep your voice down, and don't be so crass."

"Kiss my ass." She gulped more wine, trying to control her temper.

He studied her for a moment. "What's happened to you, Erin? You weren't always so . . . coarse."

"I don't know. Maybe life happened to me." Or maybe you dumping me happened to me, she thought, but she didn't say it out loud. It sounded too pathetic.

He crossed his arms over his chest. "You're not living up to your potential. You're better than a waitress, Erin. It's making you too hard, unpolished—and so is hanging out with those musician spooks of your brother's."

"You don't know what you're talking about."

"Yes, I do. You're college educated. You grew up in Olmos Park and went to Alamo Heights High School, for God's sake." He leaned toward her for emphasis. "You should be doing more with your life."

"I didn't grow up in Olmos Park. I moved there when I was sixteen, and I never fit in with those snots at Alamo Heights."

"You know what I mean. You can do better. You're wasting your life."

She hated how disdainful he was of her life and how he'd insulted her brother. Zac's friends were her friends. "You're wrong, Trynt. For one thing, Zac's band has gained a lot of following and recognition in the last year. And there's nothing wrong with being a server in the hospitality industry. It's honest work, and it supports me while I write."

He snorted. "Oh, yeah. The elusive novel you've been working on for—how many years is it now?—that no one's ever seen."

That one stung. He was right, sort of, but she'd never admit it to him. "Maybe you're the one who's changed, Trynt. When did you become such a snobby, judgmental ass?" She pretended to ponder for a beat, index finger touching her mouth. "Oh, wait. You've always been one!"

That sparked his fury. "You didn't think so when you almost married me!"

"Maybe I did!"

He looked around, and his cheeks reddened again when he saw their argument was drawing unwanted attention.

Erin was past the point of caring. The wine was loosening her tongue and her inhibitions. She wasn't some blue-blooded socialite and never would be.

He lowered his voice. "You don't mean that. We were good together, Erin. We were close until . . . " He trailed off, looking embarrassed.

"Until I told you something I'd discovered about myself that I hadn't even begun to understand. I thought I could trust you, and you ripped my heart out of my chest and crushed it under the heel of your fucking Cole Haan."

His nostrils flared, and he looked away. "I'm sorry. You know that. And you also know what a shock the whole . . . devotee thing was to me." He waved his hand in dismissal. "We've talked about all of this. It's old news. We agreed to put it behind us." His features darkened. "You told me you weren't a dev anymore."

"I'm not!"

He shook his head. "I'm very disappointed you didn't mention your roommate is handicapped, Erin."

"It's not PC to say 'handicapped,' Trynt. I'm surprised you don't know that."

His lips thinned, but otherwise he ignored her statement. "The fact that you hid your roommate from me makes me think it's a bigger deal than you're letting on."

"I wasn't hiding him. Not really. I hardly ever see him, and I didn't say anything because I knew you'd react this way—make something out of nothing—and there is absolutely nothing between Jay and me!" She hated that Trynt had put her on the defensive. She took a deep breath to calm herself. "I was going to tell you if things worked out between you and me. I feel like things are so tentative between us. We've both changed. Things aren't like they were before. I didn't want to have this whole fight about Jay if it wasn't necessary—if you were going to dump me in a week anyway."

Trynt threw up his hands in exasperation. "That's just great, Erin. I'm glad you have so much faith in me, in us."

"In us? There is no 'us' yet. It's all new, Trynt. We're starting over, getting to know each other again."

He tilted his head, his clear, blue-green eyes piercing her, the muscle in his jaw pulsing. "Do you even want to try again? I think I'm the one who should be worried about getting dumped, especially in light of this evening's revelation. You told me a week ago you still had feelings for me. Was that a lie? Am I wasting my time here?"

She looked away before refocusing on him. "No. You're not wasting your time. I do still have feelings for you." Weak, half-assed feelings, but feelings nonetheless.

"Tell me about this Jay guy, then."

She let out an exasperated sigh. "I'm not sure I can, since I don't know him that well. What do you want to know?"

"First of all, how did he end up as your roommate?"

"My brother rented Nana's room to him while I was still in the hospital. Believe me. I was pissed when I found out I didn't get a say in the whole thing, especially since I was the one who would have to live with the guy. When I got home from the hospital, Jay was already moved in."

"Why didn't you tell him to leave?"

"I . . . " *I did.* She stopped before she said it out loud. She didn't want to go into how Jay had finagled his way into her house. It had all happened before Trynt was back in her life, and it was none of his business. Instead, she used her brother's argument. "I needed the rent money, especially since I'm stuck here and not on tour with the band."

Trynt sat back in his chair, his mouth pursed. "If it's just a money issue, I'll find you another roommate."

"He's paying double what Zac asked for."

"Why?"

She shrugged. "Great neighborhood and a decent house already made accessible for his disability. We're close to downtown. There's lots of reasons he would want to live there."

"And a girl for a roommate who's got a fetish for cripples."

That made Erin's blood boil. "That was low and uncalled for," she hissed. "Don't be a dick. And trust me, Jay's not interested in me."

Trynt scowled. "Why wouldn't he be interested? Doesn't he know what you are?"

She glared at him. "What am I, Trynt?"

He cleared his throat uncomfortably. "Does he know about your . . . inclination?"

She downed the last of her wine and poured another glass from the bottle of cabernet that sat between them, filling the stemmed glass uncouthly to the very top.

"I think you've had enough," warned Trynt, eyeing the glass with disapproval.

Erin took a defiant sip. "I think I haven't."

Bitch face number four.

"And to answer your question, yes. Jay knows I was a dev. He also knows I'm not one anymore."

Trynt sniffed. "Even if that's true, I find it hard to overlook the fact that you're living with a guy who's disabled when you had a thing for disabled guys. It's a little too much of a coincidence, don't you think?"

She was so mad she was surprised steam wasn't coming out of her ears. "You want to know what I think? I think I'm done." She threw her napkin on the table, slung her purse on messenger style, then grabbed her crutches and stood. She had to hesitate for a second because the room swayed a bit. She was buzzing hard.

When she crutched outside, the cool, brisk air of the spring night cleared her head enough that she could think. She texted Angie but wasn't surprised when Angie replied she was working and couldn't come get her.

"Dammit," she muttered to herself. She could call a

taxi. Or Jay.

She looked at the time. It was only a little after nine. Jay would be awake. And having him pick her up would be easier on her almost nonexistent bank account than calling a taxi. His number was in her contacts for practical reasons, and she tapped his name without overthinking it.

"Hello?" he answered.

"Um, hey."

"Erin?" He sounded surprised.

She cleared her throat, trying to sound more sober than she was. "I, um, just—could you . . . " God, this was embarrassing.

"Are you okay?"

"Yeah." She forced her thick tongue to work properly. "I'm okay. I'm fine." She let out a sigh. "I was just wondering if you'd mind coming to get me?"

"Sure, darlin'." He said it with no hesitation, and the warmth of his easy California drawl sent little fizzies tingling through her. Must be the wine.

"Thanks," she said. As she was giving him directions, Trynt came out of the restaurant.

When she ended her call with Jay, Trynt asked, "Who was that?"

"My ride," Erin said, refusing to look at him.

Trynt snorted. "Don't be ridiculous. I'll take you home."

"No, you won't." She gripped her crutches and shifted her weight on her booted foot, wishing she could cross her arms. The nights were still cool enough to make her glad she was wearing her favorite black leather jacket.

Trynt put his hands on her shoulders, but she still wouldn't look at him. She was pissed.

"Erin," he said, "let's be adult about this."

She glowered. "I don't like being accused of something I'm not guilty of. If you can't trust that there's nothing between Jay and me and never will be, that's your problem. I don't need this."

Trynt's mouth tightened. "Who's coming for you?"

"My roomie."

His fingers dug into her shoulders.

"Ow!" she cried. She tried to wriggle free, but he only tightened his grip. "Take . . . your hands . . . off me," she said. Her tone was deliberate and cold.

In the dim light of the parking lot, Trynt's teal eyes were darker and more sinister. He spoke with clenched teeth. "I'm the one taking you home. Do you fucking hear me?"

Erin was too livid to be afraid, and her rage and the chilly air were quickly sobering her. Looking straight into Trynt's eyes, she said, "You're hurting me. If you don't take your damn hands off me right now, I will scream bloody murder. If you thought I was making a scene inside that restaurant, you haven't seen anything yet."

Trynt scanned the surrounding parking lot nervously and then gave her an ugly, parting shake that almost unbalanced her before he loosened his grip.

The engine of Jay's black muscle car rumbled as he pulled up to Trynt and Erin, windows rolled down.

One corner of Trynt's mouth pulled back in disdain.

The ghost of Jay's familiar smirk shaped his lips, but there was no humor in it, and his gaze was flinty, almost lethal. He spoke to Erin, but his eyes stayed locked on Trynt. "Everything all right, darlin'?"

"Peachy," she muttered, feeling a little weak in the knees. She crutched around to the passenger side of Jay's car, opened the door, threw her crutches in the back alongside the wheels and frame of Jay's wheelchair, and collapsed into the seat, then leaned over Jay so she could see Trynt out of the driver-side window. Being so close to Jay made her stomach pitch, like she was weightless for a split second. He smelled nice, all clean and spicy and leathery.

Hello. Not attracted to guys who think I'm a perv, she reminded herself. Not even when they smell really good. She forced her brain to focus on her ex-fiancé, who was staring her down, and said, "Thanks for a truly shitty evening, Trynt."

Trynt pointed his finger at her, his lips pinched together. "I should have known this wouldn't work. Once a freak, always a goddamn freak."

He was good at those barbs that dug deep. It was even worse because he'd said it in front of Jay. She almost winced but stopped herself, not wanting to give Trynt the satisfaction of knowing he'd hurt her.

Jay tensed, and to her surprise, out of the corner of

her eye Erin could see his jaw harden. She put a hand on his solid arm and squeezed, partly as a thank-you and partly to stave him off.

To Trynt, she said, "Fuck off, asshole." It wasn't brilliant as comebacks went, but it got the job done.

Trynt huffed with derision. As he walked away, he tossed over his shoulder, "Have a nice life with your gimp."

Jay mashed the gas lever with his hand, revving the car's loud engine. He was glaring daggers at Trynt. As if sensing the threat, Trynt started to walk faster.

Erin settled back into her seat and let her head fall against the black leather headrest. The heavy weight of failure compressed her chest, making it hard to breathe.

"Fucking dickhead," Jay growled. "What was that all about? Did he hurt you?" His voice was hard and gravelly. Gaze still tracking Trynt, who was heading toward his BMW, he said, "If he hurt you, I swear to God, I'll run his ass over. I should anyway."

"No, I'm okay," Erin said, even as she felt bruises forming on her shoulders where Trynt had squeezed too hard. As angry as Jay was, she was half afraid he meant what he said, and Trynt sure as hell wasn't worth going to prison over.

Jay focused on her then, his brow creased in that way that made him look all soulful and earnest. His tone was gentle. "Erin, you can—"

"Don't," she said. She had the feeling he was going to say she could do better, but he didn't know. She couldn't do better.

She couldn't make it with a wheeler. She couldn't make it with an able-bodied guy. One thing was for sure: She was so damn tired of trying.

She inhaled deeply, forcing her chest to expand, and watched as her chance at normal got in his silver BMW and slammed the door.

Chapter 12

Panhead: So, how was the date last night?
emanomaly: Don't ask.
Panhead: Trouble in paradise?
emanomaly: I thought I just said don't ask.
Panhead: Oh, I thought you were just saying that.
emanomaly: I was just saying that.

She was ribbing him, and it made him smile.

Panhead: Let's start over.
emanomaly: OK. What do you want to talk about?
Panhead: Your date last night.
emanomaly: Hmm. Am I the only one getting a sense of déjà vu here?

Jay laughed.

Panhead: Come on. Talk to me. You'll feel better.
emanomaly: OK. Maybe you're right. I kinda do need to talk about it with someone.
Panhead: I'm listening. I'm like a priest you can

confess to, since it's all anonymous.

Jay looked up at the ceiling, hoping God wasn't about to smite his ass for lying.

> *emanomaly:* Hmm. Are you Catholic?
> *Panhead:* No.
> *emanomaly:* Celibate?
> *Panhead:* Fuck no. But it's been a while. Does that count?
> *emanomaly:* Ha. I guess it has to. You're as close to a priest as I'll ever get. You ready?
> *Panhead:* Bring it.
> *emanomaly:* So, my budding re-romance is over.

Jay's mouth spread into a small, grim smile. From the moment he met Trynt-with-a-Fucking-Y, he hadn't liked him. When he'd seen the pompous prick getting rough with Erin in the parking lot of the restaurant last night—Erin on crutches, no less—he'd wanted to rip the asshole's head off.

He took a deep breath and quashed his animosity. He didn't want it to bleed through to Erin and make her suspicious.

> *Panhead:* Sorry to hear it's over. What do you mean by 're-romance'?
> *emanomaly:* Remember I told you in our last chat that I'd dated this guy before?

Panhead: Yeah.

emanomaly: He was actually my fiancé at one time, right after college. Five years ago, if you want to get technical.

Jay raised his brows. *Fiancé?* Jesus. Who the hell was Erin Silver? He couldn't see the Erin he knew going out with a guy like Trynt, let alone almost marrying him. She was too cool—too good—for that metrosexual shithead.

Panhead: What happened?

emanomaly: Remember I told you he knew I was a dev and wasn't comfortable with it?

Panhead: Yes.

emanomaly: Well, that's the reason he broke off our engagement all those years ago. Like a freakin' idiot, I let it slip about my attraction to disabled guys. He didn't take it well, and duh. Who could blame him, right? But I was young and stupid, and I thought he would—I don't know—understand, I guess. Be more open-minded. I was fresh out of college and all liberal and stuff. I thought he was, too. I was wrong. Anyway, not too long ago, I was in a car wreck.

Panhead: Shit. Are you OK?

emanomaly: I'm fine. It wasn't really that big of a deal.

Not a big deal? Jay shook his head. A concussion and

a busted-up ankle weren't a big deal?

> *emanomaly:* Anyway, my ex heard about the wreck and called me out of the blue, told me he'd missed me, that he still had feelings for me after all this time. He said all the right things, so I thought I'd give him another chance. After all, I did love him once. I told him I wasn't into the dev thing anymore, and we decided to try and put all that in the past. Still, I got a bad vibe about it, you know? I knew he'd flip if he found out my roommate was a wheeler, so I kept putting off telling him.
>
> *Panhead*: Right. And?
>
> *emanomaly*: Well, when he came to pick me up last night, he met my roommate.
>
> *Panhead*: Uh-oh.

It was hard for Jay to play dumb on this. He was a dick for duping her into confiding in him, but apparently the guilt wasn't enough to make him do the right thing. He kept typing.

> *Panhead:* Does that mean you decided to tell him after all?
>
> *emanomaly:* I wish I had. It might have softened the blow. Unfortunately, my roommate took care of it for me. He was out walking his dog and saw me getting into my ex's car. He came up to talk to us and introduced himself.

Panhead: So your boyfriend was pissed?

emanomaly: Yeah. We got into a fight at dinner. The gist of his philosophy was: Once a freak, always a freak. He couldn't get past the fact that I was a dev who now has a wheeler for a roommate—even though I've sworn off wheelers forever and told him so. He said it was too much of a coincidence and implied there was more to it I wasn't telling him. It was clear he wasn't going to be able to trust me, and he acted like a complete douche about it. The whole thing is ironic, since I didn't want the wheeler guy as my roommate in the first place.

Panhead: So, are you mad at your roommate for blowing your cover?

emanomaly: No, not really. It wasn't his fault. He had no idea about my history with my ex. When he introduced himself, he couldn't have known how my boyfriend would react. I was kind of rude to my roommate, too, which I feel bad about. I mean, in a way he saved me from wasting any more time with my ex, who's a jackass—although I was pretty close to figuring that out for myself. Even worse, I had to call my roommate to come pick me up at the restaurant because my ex was being such a shit.

Guilt seeped into Jay's bones, making him uneasy. He pushed his palms down on the seat cushion of his chair and lifted his butt, then rolled his head on his shoulders to get the tension out of them.

He'd known Erin didn't want him to meet Trynt, and running into them sure as hell hadn't been a coincidence. Jay had waited with an antsy Chopper, out of sight, for at least forty-five minutes so he could "bump into" Erin at the right time.

It wasn't that Jay was sorry Trynt had shown his true colors. That asshole didn't deserve Erin. But Jay felt like a stalker. What was he gonna do, sabotage her dates every time she went out with someone?

> *emanomaly:* You still there?
>
> *Panhead:* Yeah. Sorry. So, if your ex was a jackass, why were you going out with him in the first place?
>
> *emanomaly:* I don't know. I was hoping he'd changed, that maybe we'd both grown up. He can be an arrogant ass, but he has a lot going for him, too. He's successful, smart, good-looking, and, like I said, I was in love with him once. And I was the one that screwed things up with him the first time by communicating and sharing stuff any sane person would never admit to. I guess I wanted a chance to redeem myself, to show him I wasn't flawed.
>
> *Panhead:* Do you still have feelings for him?
>
> *emanomaly:* No. Thank God. The whole engagement thing was a long time ago, and I'm definitely over him. It was worth putting up with him for a few weeks to make me see that. I think this time around I just liked the idea of him.
>
> *Panhead:* You're better off without him.

emanomaly: Yeah, yeah. Blah, blah, blah. Wish I had a dollar for every time I heard that.

Panhead: It sucks that it didn't work out, but you need to find someone who appreciates you.

emanomaly: Easier said than done. Anyway, thanks for listening.

Panhead: Anytime.

emanomaly: It's so weird, the online thing. It really is sort of like a confessional. I feel safer talking to you than I would even to a close friend. I can tell you anything because you don't know my identity and I don't know yours.

Jay's breath caught on a particularly sharp pang of guilt.

Panhead: Yeah. I know what you mean.

emanomaly: Just be careful who you chat with from the dev website, especially if you think about hooking up with someone. It's easy to get burned.

Panhead: You're probably the only one from the site I'll ever talk to.

emanomaly: Why?

Panhead: No one else has caught my interest.

emanomaly: Wow. Thanks . . . I think. You know nothing can come of our little chats, though, right? It'll never go beyond this.

Panhead: Sure. But maybe I need someone to confess to sometimes, too.

emanomaly: Anytime. :) TTYL.

Panhead: TTYL.

Jay closed his laptop and sat back in his chair, raking his hands through his hair. "I'm a bastard," he said to his empty bedroom.

Even so, he had no intention of stopping his enlightening conversations with emanomaly.

Chapter 13

It was the third night in a row Jay couldn't sleep. He was sitting in the living room, crammed into the corner of the couch because Chopper was sprawled by his side hogging the rest of it. Jay was flipping through channels, trying to ignore the annoying, uncontrollable jiggling of his legs and the pins-and-needles pain in his back.

The chronic pain, at the site where his back broke, had been a bitch lately. It was probably the reason he was having this bout of spasticity in his legs, but he refused to take medication for any of it—the pain or the spasticity. He hated how the meds made him feel, all loopy and fatigued. Plus, he knew of too many people with spinal cord injuries who got addicted to pain meds. He didn't need to add drug addiction to the list of shit he had to contend with.

Constant, unresolvable pain was common with SCI—sometimes at the site of injury, and sometimes, ironically, below the level of injury where there was no other sensation. His pain was usually manageable, though, and he'd learned to live with it. Part of that meant taking care of himself—eating right and doing a regular workout, which included passive range-of-motion exercises and stretches for his legs.

He didn't know if staying active was why he wasn't plagued with severe spasticity like some people with SCI or if he was just lucky. Either way, he figured tonight's jiggles were because his body was trying to tell him something was wrong, since spasticity could sometimes be an alarm system to warn of something haywire in the part of his body he couldn't feel (or, in the case of his back, where he *could* feel).

If that was the case, he wished his body would shut up.

There were no simple causes he could think of for why his back kept hurting so bad, and he knew anything a doctor would say couldn't be good. He was afraid he needed surgery, that something had gone haywire with the hardware pinning together his crushed vertebrae, and just the possibility of being in a hospital again, of going through weeks—maybe months—of recovery, made his gut clench and put him in a bad mood.

But those worries vanished when Erin crutched out of the darkness of the hallway into the dim living room, wearing a tight purplish blue tank top and drawstring pajama shorts with flowers all over them. At the sight of her, his heart started doing a weird, jerky mating dance.

Her petite body was perfection: nicely rounded breasts, flat stomach, tight ass, sexy thighs, and slim calves—at least the one calf he could see. She was in a removable Aircast boot now that went up to her knee.

Her ankle was slowly but surely healing. Recently, Jay had noticed her putting some weight on it, but she was still supposed to use her crutches for another couple of weeks. He'd squeezed that much out of Erin in one of his rare exchanges with her, outside of his stolen chats with emanomaly.

She paused on her way to the kitchen when she saw Jay, transferred both crutches to one hand, and reached over the back of the couch to affectionately pet Chopper's ghoulish head. He lazily wagged his tail, and Erin smiled. It never failed to amaze Jay that this woman who couldn't weigh more than a buck oh five was absolutely fearless of a dog that made even his brother, the war-hardened soldier, wary.

"What are you doing up?" she asked Jay, still scratching between Chopper's ears. "It's almost three in the morning." Her eyes traveled to Jay's jiggling legs, but she didn't comment.

Not wanting to sound like an old lady griping about her health problems, Jay steered the subject away from himself. "I could ask you the same thing, darlin'."

She hadn't corrected him lately when he called her that. He wondered if she'd just given up or if she'd grown to like it.

With a shrug, she said, "I'm usually up this late. It's hard to break years of bar hours. Lots of late nights with work and the band, you know?"

Jay nodded.

She inclined her head toward the kitchen. "I'm going

to make some chamomile tea. Want some?"

"Thanks, but I'm good."

The living room was dim except for the blue glow from the large flatscreen TV, and the hazel of her eyes looked darker than usual. She studied him for a moment. "You seem tense. The tea would help you relax."

It would also take him off his bladder routine. He was careful about when and how much liquid he drank so he could predict when to stick a catheter up his dick to make himself pee. He couldn't feel when he needed to take a piss, so being on a regular eating and drinking schedule helped avoid embarrassing accidents. Drinking tea at three in the morning wasn't part of the program.

"That's okay," he repeated. "I'm good."

She nodded, placed her crutches back under her arms with the deftness of someone who'd been using them for two and a half months, and hobbled toward the kitchen. Several minutes later, she was back with a faded ceramic Starbucks mug in one hand and only one crutch, gingerly limping on her booted ankle. "Here," she said, handing her crutch to Jay.

With a raised brow at her bossiness, he took it and reached over the arm of the couch to set it on the floor.

"Thanks," she said, one corner of her mouth curved as if she might be amused. She shoved Chopper's rump over and made a place for herself at the opposite end of the couch from Jay, curling her good leg underneath her and letting her booted foot rest on the floor. She held her tea mug with both hands, as if relishing its warmth.

Jay was surprised she was deigning to hang out with him. She usually couldn't get away from him fast enough. His surprise must have shown on his face.

"TV's broken in my room," she reminded him. "I have a crick in my neck from being on my computer, and I don't feel like reading."

He wondered if she'd been working on her novel and was curious again about what she was writing, but he couldn't ask. That was something Panhead knew, not Jay. He would have to remember to ask her about it the next time he chatted with her online.

Chopper rearranged himself so that his chin was resting on Erin's thigh. She looked down at him, giving him another scratch between the ears. He gave her a perfect puppy-dog look under lowered doggy brows, and she smiled. "You're such a flirt."

Chopper let out a contented sigh.

"What are you watching?" she asked Jay.

"Nothing, really," he said, tossing the remote onto the coffee table. "A billion channels, and there's never anything on."

"Not even *Cheaters*?"

"Now there's some titillating TV," Jay said wryly.

Her eyebrows disappeared up into her bangs. "'Titillating'?"

"Great word." He made an effort to smile, despite the foul mood he was in. "It has the word 'tit' in it."

She snickered quietly, and her almost-dimples showed before she hid her face behind her mug, taking a sip of the steaming tea. It was a shy, guileless move that was endearing and alluring.

Jay's breath caught for an instant, and he forgot about the pain in his back until it spiked again with a vengeance, radiating into his shoulders and neck. He winced and pressed his palms into the sofa, shifting his position. It didn't help. He drew in a deep breath, trying to ride out the pain.

Erin's brows lowered in concern. "You okay?"

"Yeah," he managed, trying to keep his voice normal.

"It sucks," she said, as she set her mug on the coffee table.

Jay closed his eyes and inhaled through his nose. "What sucks?"

"The pain. I know it's common for people with SCI to have chronic pain. Are you hurting?"

He hated ever admitting a weakness, so he didn't answer. Instead, he stared at the TV without really seeing it and tried hard to force himself to relax, but he couldn't. Instead, he got more tense, which caused the pain to escalate. It was a vicious cycle.

Erin was quiet, but he could feel her staring at him.

"I'm fine," he insisted. "I don't need your pity." His voice came out harsher than he intended.

"It's not pity," she said softly.

He glared at her then, suddenly furious that he had to live with this constant pain and so fucking sick of living with paraplegia in general. Why did half his body feel nothing at all and the other half hurt like hell? He didn't often feel sorry for himself, but right now he was exhausted from lack of sleep and the incessant aching. "What?" he snapped. "Is the thought that I'm hurting making you horny?"

He regretted it as soon as he said it.

She looked down, hunching her shoulders, but not before he saw the anger and hurt that flashed across her features.

Hating himself for being such a dick, he said, "I'm sorry." He'd never been more sincere, but he knew it was lame. He'd probably just undone any meager progress he'd made with her. "You didn't deserve that, Erin. I'm an ass." He scrubbed his hands over his face in frustration, feeling the rasp of three days' worth of stubble as his fingers rubbed along his jaw.

A long, heavy minute of silence ticked by, and when Erin got up from the couch, Jay figured she was pissed and was heading back to her room. Instead, she pushed on Chopper's rump, trying to get him to budge. "Scoot over, you brute," she murmured with a grunt.

Chopper complied, turning his large body in awkward circles and sniffing until he'd flattened the couch cushions to his liking. Then he curled up in the warm place Erin had vacated. There was now a small space between Chopper and Jay, and, to Jay's surprise, Erin sat down next to him and faced him.

She took one of Jay's hands in both of her small ones, sending an electric charge humming along his skin. She started massaging, kneading his palm and emphasizing certain pressure points. Jay had no idea why she was doing it, especially not after the insult he'd just dealt her, but he sure as hell wasn't about to tell her to stop.

Her touch began to soothe him. He rested his head against the back of the couch and closed his eyes, focusing on breathing and the sensation of Erin's slender fingers on his skin. His back still hurt, but the tension in his muscles was slowly releasing, relieving some of the pain.

In her dusky little-girl voice, she said, "Thanks."

He wasn't expecting that. Why the hell would she be thanking him? He opened his eyes and slid his gaze toward her. All he could see was the crown of her dark head bent over his hand. "For what?" he asked.

Not wavering on the massage, she lifted her head up and looked at him. The corners of her mouth were curved almost sheepishly. "For picking me up the other night. And for not giving me the third degree about Trynt."

Jay closed his eyes again. "I wanted to."

"Wanted to what? Pick me up or give me the third degree?"

"Both."

She paused. He looked at her, but she averted her eyes. Picking up where she left off, she pressed on a particularly sensitive spot just under his thumb.

"That feels . . . good," he said, his voice going husky. It was a little scary, how much he needed her touch. He was soaking her in like a dry sponge.

Again, she raised her eyes to his. "Is it helping?"

"Yeah." It was the most soothing thing he'd felt in a very, very long time.

"I could massage your back, if you think that would help more."

"Maybe in a minute." His pain was ebbing to a more tolerable ache, and he could finally feel himself getting drowsy. "Why are you being so nice to me after what I said to you?"

She sniffed in a self-deprecating manner. "I don't know." She didn't offer anything more, and Jay didn't push it.

Instead he closed his eyes and went back to the subject of Trynt. "That douchebag doesn't seem like your type."

He could feel Erin shrug. "He was my type at one time," she said.

"But not now?" Jay tried to sound neutral and not let anything slip out that would let her know he already knew more than he should.

"No. Not now."

"Seemed like things were getting ugly when I drove up."

She exhaled. "You saw?"

"Yeah. I saw him gripping your arms and shaking you."

She was quiet. Jay opened his eyes and tried to catch her gaze, but she was intent on massaging his hand. "Has he been rough with you before, Erin?" He tried to keep any judgment from his tone and reined in the fury he felt at the memory of seeing her manhandled.

She stopped massaging his hand for a second. "Now you're giving me the third degree."

"Sorry. Can't blame me for being curious."

She shrugged and bent over his hand again. "He never hit me or anything," she replied, "but sometimes he could be . . . intense. We have a long history. We were engaged once."

As if that explained or excused anything.

With his free hand, Jay tipped her chin up so she had no choice but to look at him. "Darlin', you can do better."

Her eyes filled with a sadness and hopelessness that made his heart ache. "I'm sure Trynt would disagree," she said dryly.

Jay leaned closer to her and slid his fingers into her silky hair, stroking her delicate jaw with his thumb. She smelled like spring and apples, and her skin was like satin. He was almost close enough to kiss her. His heartbeat kicked into overdrive, pumping endorphins into his system. Voice thick with need, he locked his gaze onto hers and said, "Trynt's a fucking idiot."

Her eyes went all sultry, and she leaned closer to him, making him think she wanted the kiss as much as he did.

Just as he closed his eyes, anticipating that her lips would be as soft and inviting as they looked, she put a finger to his mouth, stopping him. "Careful, Jay," she said in her smoky voice, then pulled back a little. When he opened his eyes, hers were trained on him, cool and direct. "Wouldn't want you to think I'm getting horny, now, would I?"

Disappointment sluiced over him like a bucket of ice water.

She got up, retrieved her crutch, and limped down the hall toward her room without even glancing back.

It was cold payback, but nothing Jay didn't deserve.

Chopper snorted, almost like he was saying, *Way to go.*

Jay suddenly felt empty. He groaned and dropped his head back against the couch in defeat.

* * *

By the time Erin made it to her room, her hands were shaking and her knees felt weak. She made it to her bed and plunked down on the edge of it, setting her crutch on the floor.

Jay had been sending out some serious pheromones, and her treacherous body had responded. Now it was like she was going through withdrawal. Being so close to him, touching his hand, feeding off his heat, had caused her blood to soar through her veins.

Holy crap. She'd almost kissed him.

She went through her mantra, telling herself over and over she wasn't attracted to him. He was blond. He was a wheeler. She was done with being a dev.

For that matter, he was a *guy*. She was done with guys—at least in any kind of capacity that required feelings. She didn't need anyone. Her main goal in life from now on was to guard her heart and regain her self-respect.

But part of her brain was calling bullshit on that.

Tonight, she'd been drawn to Jay from the moment she saw him sitting on the couch—and it wasn't because she was getting off on his pain. It was because he'd been a striking figure sitting there, with his broad shoulders and his strong, handsome face limned in the glow from the TV. And then she'd noticed how tense he was and how drawn his features were.

She'd *hated* seeing him hurting, and it had been obvious he was, no matter how hard he tried to hide it. She wanted to fix it, to ease it somehow. It was ingrained in her, a compelling need she couldn't control, not even after he'd insulted her. And that insult had fucking hurt. It had slashed through her like a knife, razor sharp and vicious.

"Is the thought that I'm hurting making you horny?"

No. The fact he was in pain didn't make her horny. It made her infinitely sad. It made her clench her fists and want to wince in pain along with him, to take some of the burden and bear it for him.

He'd apologized. She knew he hadn't really meant to hurt her. She'd been around him enough to know he wasn't quite the ogre she'd originally thought, that he wasn't the type to intentionally hurt someone. It was probably the pain and exhaustion talking. That kind of constant pain could make anyone short-tempered.

But still, he'd said it. It was an indication he still harbored an innate disgust toward devs, no matter how much he'd tried to act differently in the last few weeks. She would do well not to ever forget that, no matter the kind words he said or how seductive he could be.

And why had he tried to kiss her? She wasn't sure. Maybe he was as conflicted as she was, caught between lust and principle. Whatever the reason, Erin refused to be some experiment, some way for him to sate his curiosity about devs, or even just an easy lay. She would save that for the next AB guy that came along, someone it would be easier to protect herself from.

Jay was dangerous. He'd already hurt her—more than once—whether he'd meant to or not. What would he do to her if she opened herself up to him, let herself trust him? Closing her eyes, she pictured almost kissing him. They'd been so close—close enough to share each other's air. Her pulse surged, and she got a tight, urgent longing in the lower part of her abdomen at the mere thought.

Her body burned for him, craved him, and the more she denied herself, the more she thought about him. Maybe she should just kiss him after all. Maybe it would be awkward and slobbery and nothing like what she imagined. Maybe he would say something hurtful again that would make her come to her senses and forget about him once and for all. One thing was for sure: She needed to do something to get him out of her system.

Her body seemed to move of its own volition, her heartbeat pounding in her ears and overriding any protests from the rational part of her brain that told her this was one of the stupidest, most irrational ideas she'd ever had. As if under a spell, she crutched from her room in search of Jay and refused to let any more thoughts through, until she bumped into the back of the couch and it jolted her back to reality.

The living room was silent and almost pitch black. Only a feeble amount of moonlight glowed through the sheer curtains at the windows, and there was no Jay.

Disappointment and an aching loneliness swept through her, and Erin let out a long, deflating breath.

He must have gone to bed while she was in her room. She'd been so busy freaking out about almost kissing him that she hadn't heard his chair roll by or the click of Chopper's toenails on the hardwood in the hallway.

Gripping the padded handgrip of her crutch, she tried to smother her raging hormones, which still begged for Jay.

Good Lord. She should be happy fate had intervened and kept her from making a fool of herself. This was a sure sign she should just stay away from Jay like she'd told herself a million times before—but, obviously, that was easier said than done.

Chapter 14

Panhead: Where have you been? It's been a while.

emanomaly: Sorry. I started working again. Haven't had as much time to chat.

Jay clenched his jaw in annoyance. Three times. He'd seen her three times since the almost-kiss three weeks ago. She'd gotten the go-ahead from her orthopedist to ditch the boot and crutches a week ago, and she'd immediately gone back to waiting tables at the bar.

Jay didn't think her doctor would approve of her going back to work so soon, and he said so the one chance last week he had to talk to her. She'd insisted she could handle it, said her ankle was fine as long as she wore a brace. Judging by how badly she still limped, he wasn't convinced. She was still in physical therapy, for Christ's sake.

But what really bothered him was that when he opened her bedroom door to let in Chopper in the mornings, she wasn't there and her bed hadn't been slept in. Where the hell was she sleeping? More to the point, *who* was she sleeping *with*? Surely she hadn't gone back to the douchebag.

Jay wanted to know the answer, so he kept up the pretense and started typing.

Panhead: I didn't know you weren't working.

emanomaly: Yeah. I had to stop for a while. I broke my ankle in that car wreck I told you about. I was on crutches for twelve weeks, and I still have to wear a brace.

Panhead: I thought you said it wasn't a big deal.

emanomaly: Well, I guess the broken ankle kind of was. I had to have surgery on it to screw everything back together.

Panhead: You sure it's okay to go back to work?

emanomaly: Yeah. It's fine. And working gets me away from my roomie.

Jay's heart plunged. She went back to work—too soon—just to avoid him?

Panhead: Wow. You really must not like this guy.

emanomaly: It's not so much that I don't like him. I just need to stay away from him.

Panhead: Why?

emanomaly: He's trouble that I don't need.

Panhead: Hmm. Vague much?

emanomaly: Um, can we not talk about my roommate? Besides, he's not the only reason I went back to work. I need the money.

Panhead: Oh, like that's a good reason.

emanomaly: Yeah. Who knew? It helps pay for the little things, like food and electricity.

Panhead: Right. So, have you heard from the douchebag again?

emanomaly: No. Another relationship bites the dust.

Panhead: Sounds like a good thing, to me.

emanomaly: Yeah. I guess. I'm seeing someone else now, anyway.

Fuck. Not that it came as a shock. Empty beds didn't lie. It wasn't like she'd been at a slumber party painting her toenails and doing karaoke every night.

Jay raked his hands through his hair in frustration. She sure as hell didn't let any grass grow under her feet, did she?

Then again, why did he care? He needed to get over this obsession with Erin. He needed to get out more, find another woman. Trouble was, now that he was acutely aware of the whole dev thing, he wondered if every woman he met who showed an interest in him was secretly attracted to his disability.

He wasn't quite sure what to think of that. In fact, a part of him was angered and disturbed by it, the idea that no one but a dev would want him. But another part of him—the part that now knew and understood more about devoteeism—just shrugged it off. And if he was going to end up dating a devotee anyway, he wanted it to be Erin. Hell, even if there was a chance some girl who wasn't a dev might be interested in him, he still didn't think he'd want her.

Jesus. He swallowed hard, taken aback by the realization. He wanted Erin and no one else. Period.

> *emanomaly:* You still there?
>
> *Panhead:* Yeah. So, you work fast. You going out with another AB?
>
> *emanomaly:* Yeah. No more wheelers, remember?
>
> *Panhead:* We're not all bad.
>
> *emanomaly:* You're not all good either.
>
> *Panhead:* Who is?
>
> *emanomaly:* True. So, what have you been up to? I feel like we always talk about me. I don't really know anything about you.

You know more than you think, thought Jay. He was entering dangerous territory here and needed to be careful.

> *Panhead:* There's not much to tell.
>
> *emanomaly:* Ah, come on. At least tell me what you're thinking of the whole dev thing now.
>
> *Panhead:* I'm understanding it more. I've been lurking on the boards, reading what others say. I also have a friend who's dated a few devs.
>
> *emanomaly:* Do they still freak you out?
>
> *Panhead:* Some do, like the ones who are into S&M and want to dominate their gimpy partner and shit like

that. And the ones who want to lick the footplate of my wheelchair.

emanomaly: Ew!! No doubt, there's some crazy-assed ones, but I don't think they're the norm. I swear I'm not like that. And there's sleazy wheelers, too, you know. Did you see the guy who posted various pics of himself in his wheelchair with a boner?

Panhead: That's not desperate or anything.

emanomaly: It's okay if it was you. I won't judge.

Panhead: You're hilarious. Sorry to disappoint you, but it wasn't me.

emanomaly: Right. So what about you? You had any serious relationships?

Panhead: Yeah. Long time ago, but nothing serious since my injury. Actually, I'm kind of interested in a dev now, believe it or not.

emanomaly: Did you meet her on the dev website?

Panhead: Not really. I met her through my friend.

emanomaly: Just be careful. If your friend introduced you online, make sure the dev's not really a sixty-five-year-old man from Nigeria.

Jay smiled.

Panhead: I'm pretty sure she's not.

emanomaly: Have you seen pics of her?

Panhead: No. I've met her in person. She's beautiful.

emanomaly: Wow. So it's gone pretty far if you've met her in person. I can't believe you're just now telling me!

Panhead: It hasn't gone that far. She's made it pretty clear she's not interested.

There was a long pause before she answered.

emanomaly: Sorry. That sucks.

Panhead: You're thinking I'm roadkill, aren't you?

emanomaly: No.

Panhead: Liar.

emanomaly: Lol. I swear I'm not. Maybe you're just not her type.

Panhead: I'm not giving up. And, for the record, I'm not roadkill.

emanomaly: I wasn't thinking that! And it's good you're not giving up. Maybe she's just been burned like me. Maybe she's just gun-shy.

Panhead: Maybe. I think there's still hope. I swear she almost kissed me the other day.

Erin didn't answer, and Jay's pulse jumped. Had he said too much? Had she figured it out? Finally, to his relief, she started typing.

emanomaly: How do you know she almost kissed you?

Panhead: We had a moment.

emanomaly: A moment?

Panhead: She just had that look.

emanomaly: Was she puckered up and making kissy noises?

Panhead: No. But, you know. Sometimes you can just tell.

emanomaly: Or you're delusional.

Panhead: Or that. Thanks for the vote of confidence.

emanomaly: Haha. Just teasing you. You should keep things in perspective, though. Don't waste your energy if she's not interested.

Panhead: I won't. But she's worth a little effort before I think about giving up.

emanomaly: Good luck, then.

Panhead: Thanks.

emanomaly: So, changing the subject, can I ask you a personal question about your injury?

Panhead: Sure.

emanomaly: What level is it?

Panhead: T9 complete. Do you know what that means?

emanomaly: No muscle function or sensation below the area just above your belly button?

Panhead: Right. Why do you want to know?

emanomaly: Remember I said I'm a writer?

Panhead: Yeah.

emanomaly: Well, I'm writing a novel, a mystery, and the hero is a wheeler.

Panhead: Sort of like a gimpy Sherlock Holmes?

emanomaly: Well, yeah. Kind of. Except he's American, it's set in modern times, and he carries a Glock instead of a magnifying glass. He's pretty badass.

Panhead: Sounds interesting.

emanomaly: His injury level is similar to yours—T10 complete. I was wondering if you'd take a look at it, tell me if I got anything wrong. I'm really hesitant about showing it to anyone, but I want it to be realistic, and I need someone to tell me if he's doing something that's not possible or if there's something he's capable of that I didn't think about.

Jay was glad she was asking him to do this, but if she knew who he really was, there was no way in hell she would ask him to look at her writing. Jay Bontrager wasn't supposed to know she was writing a novel or that she was even a writer. She'd never shown him a glimpse of that part of herself in the three months they'd lived together.

Guilt settled in his gut like a brick, and he blew out a long exhale through his lips. He should say no, give her some excuse and respect her privacy, but he wasn't that honorable—and he was curious.

Panhead: Sure. I'll take a look.

emanomaly: This is a big deal, you know. No one else has seen my work before. It's really hard for me to trust someone enough to let them see it. I'm very protective of it, but I'm to the point where I need input from an outsider.

Panhead: I'm glad you trust me.

He grimaced as he typed that.

emanomaly: I don't know why, but I do.
Panhead: It's that anonymous thing.
emanomaly: Yeah. Must be. So, I'll e-mail it to you.
Panhead: OK.
emanomaly: And I need you to be honest and tell me what you really think. I won't freak out. I can take constructive criticism, even if you think it totally sucks.
Panhead: I'm sure it doesn't suck.
emanomaly: Ha. Reserve judgment until after you read it.
Panhead: OK. But I'm still sure it won't suck.
emanomaly: BTW, if I do freak out, it's not like I know where you live, right?
Panhead: Ha. Right.
emanomaly: Gotta go. I'll send you the file in a sec.
Panhead: OK.
emanomaly: TTYL.
Panhead: Later.

* * *

Erin attached her novel file to an e-mail to Panhead and hit Send. "Here goes nothing," she muttered to herself, wiping her palms on her jeans. Just the act of sending him her novel made her sweat.

She'd written other novels since she graduated from

college, but this was the first one she'd ever thought might actually be decent. Then again, she was biased. This particular story was her blood, sweat, and tears from the last five years. It was countless nights of staying up until all hours of the morning after she'd gotten home from a gig with the band or waitressing at Lars—that is, when she wasn't too wasted to write.

She cringed, thinking about the past week. She'd hardly written at all because she hadn't been home. She'd sort of taken up with the bass player for The Poonmatics, staying nights at his house so she could avoid Jay. Good for that problem, but not good for her career as a writer.

She'd been thinking since Trynt made his nasty dig about her writing. He was right, even if he was an asshole. It was way past time she stopped being so neurotic and started doing something about getting published. It was probably a pipe dream, but she was still going to give it a try. She didn't want to serve beers at Lars forever.

Letting Panhead see her work was the first step, like a Neil-Armstrong-walking-on-the-moon first step. It was that big of a deal to her. Why she was sending it to Panhead, she wasn't sure, other than she liked chatting with him and for some reason—and maybe this meant she was a complete idiot—she trusted him.

Plus, it wasn't like she would ever have to face him in person, and his injury was almost identical to her protagonist's. Panhead's insights would be invaluable.

She thought about Panhead, wondering for the millionth time what he looked like and what his real name was. He seemed intelligent and confident—not creepy or nerdy—but she was probably projecting. Maybe it was the pathetic romantic in her that imagined him to be totally hot. It wasn't completely farfetched, though. After all, she'd been right about Luis, at least in the looks department. She'd known he would be hot before she'd ever seen what he looked like. Too bad she was such a horrible judge of what he was like on the inside.

She needed to stop wondering about Panhead, though, because she had no intention of ever meeting him in person. She thought about the dev that Panhead was interested in and what he'd said, that he'd almost kissed her—just like when Jay had almost kissed Erin. The bottom fell out of her stomach for an instant. It was a weird coincidence, but it wasn't possible Jay could be Panhead. Was it?

No. That was ridiculous. There was no way Panhead could be Jay. For one thing, Panhead thought his dev was beautiful. There was no way Jay would think *she* was beautiful.

Besides, Jay was too much of a guy. He was into working on his motorcycle, fixing things around the house, his IT job, and other man stuff—except that the guy could also cook like freakin' Julia Child. Erin had been sorely tempted by the aromas that wafted from the kitchen more than once but had always resisted the temptation to join him when he offered.

Still, Jay wouldn't take the time to pose as a wheeler on the dev website just to talk to her. What would be the point? Erin couldn't picture him doing that at all. He'd made it clear what he thought about devs, and his comment about her getting horny because his back hurt was proof he was still leery of her, even if there was some physical attraction thrown into the mix.

No. There were things that were similar between Jay and Panhead, but they weren't one and the same. Even the remote possibility curdled her blood, so she quickly dismissed it. She'd already told Panhead things about herself no one else knew, and she'd just sent him her novel. She would be mortified if she found out it was really Jay.

Just stop it, she told herself. Sometimes, she had a tendency to come up with worst-case scenarios until she had herself completely freaked out over nothing. Panhead wasn't Jay. That was crazy. And it was nice to have someone she could confide in, someone she could be herself with—even if he only existed in cyberspace.

Chapter 15

"Hey, babe. Want a hit?" asked Duncan, Erin's latest bad idea, as he held out a joint. He was leaning against the beat-up eighties Mercedes station wagon he drove to haul around his instruments and stage equipment. The rest of his bandmates were inside Lars Bar getting things ready for their set while Duncan took a smoke break.

Erin had just stepped into the alley behind the bar to join him. She let the heavy steel back door shut behind her and slid down to the low doorstep, bringing her knees up and resting her elbows on them, careful not to spill the ice-cold Dos Equis longneck in her hand. Her ankle was aching, so she was taking a quick break from waiting tables before the bar got really busy. It felt good to take a load off her feet.

Her low-rise skinny jeans were tight and her underwear was probably showing above her waistband in the back. Good thing her back was to the door—not that she really cared if anyone saw her underwear, as long as she wasn't sporting a plumber's crack. She set her beer down for a second and redid her ponytail, which was getting too loose, then picked her beer up again to take a sip.

Spring had been getting steadily hotter, with temperatures up in the nineties, and the May evening was muggy. The heavy air surrounded her, making her wish for a breeze. It would be another scorching San Antonio summer, if the weather so far was any indication.

Erin studied Duncan's pale hand offering her the joint—so different from Jay's strong, masculine, bronze-skinned hands.

Oh, for the love of God! Stop thinking about Jay! she admonished herself.

Duncan was hot, too, but in a totally different way. In fact, he was more the type of guy Erin was usually attracted to, minus the wheelchair. Of average height, he dressed like her brother, which meant his attire of choice was a concert T-shirt and skinny jeans. He had a charming boyish grin, full sensuous lips, a lean, sinewy, rock-star body covered with cool tattoos, and messy, longish dark hair. However, the term "boyish" was apt. At the ripe young age of twenty-one, he was five years younger than she was.

Still, Duncan had charisma, and he could make her laugh. Plus, Erin was a sucker for musicians, and Duncan was the bass player and occasional lead singer for The Poonmatics, a band that frequently opened for her brother's band, Silver.

She wouldn't really call what she was doing with him "dating." She'd seen him hanging around the bar with his band for a couple of years, had been acquainted with him and occasionally spoken to him in passing, but last week (the night after she'd almost kissed Jay and made an ass of herself, to be exact) they'd started talking one-on-one. He asked about her ankle, one thing led to another, and she ended up going home with him. It seemed like a better idea than going home and possibly running into Jay, who was becoming an insomniac and might be awake when she got home. She'd been crashing at Duncan's house since, engaging in sessions of heavy kissing and petting, but she hadn't let things go any further.

Truth be told, Erin was using Duncan, trying to get Jay out of her system. It might seem coldhearted and selfish, but that was the advantage of messing around with a twenty-one-year-old. He wasn't looking for a serious relationship, so she didn't have to worry about hurting him.

Too bad her plan wasn't working. As bad-boy hot as Duncan was, being around him did nothing to relieve Erin's fever for Jay. Even worse, it was only a matter of time before Duncan expected more from her than she was willing to give, since the old Erin Silver hadn't exactly had a reputation for celibacy. When it got to the point where sex was an issue, they would go their separate ways, because at least for right now, there was only one guy who could scratch Erin's itch.

Until then, Duncan was an amusing diversion. And when she was at his house, she didn't have to worry about her body pulling a horny zombie and ending up in

Jay's bed.

She took a swig of her Dos Equis, savoring the tang of the lime she'd squeezed into the the bottle. Then, looking up at Duncan and eyeing the home-rolled cigarette he was still offering, she said, "What is it?" It smelled off, not like a normal joint.

One side of Duncan's mouth curled lazily upward, and his brown eyes were glassy and constricted. "It's an A-bomb."

An A-bomb was a joint with heroin mixed in. Erin shook her head. "Uh-uh. You know I don't do that shit."

"It won't hurt you. When you smoke heroin like this, in a fatty, it's not nearly as potent. Just gives the weed a little kick." He shrugged. "Hardcore users say it wastes too much boy, but it's a common method of administration in Asia and Afghanistan."

She rolled her eyes. "Oh, thank you for that enlightening information, Professor Burner. That totally makes it okay."

He chuckled.

She took another swig of beer, then pressed the cold green bottle against her neck, relishing its coolness. "I have to go back to work. I can't be fucked up." Or, well, she shouldn't be.

"It won't fuck you up," Duncan said, leaning forward off the station wagon and shoving his hand closer to her. "Come on. You'll hardly feel it. It'll just help you relax." He nodded toward the brace on her ankle, barely visible as a bulge under her skinny jeans and black Chucks. "I saw you limping. This will take some of the pain away, get you through the night."

"Or I could just take a Motrin," she said dryly.

He gave her his boyish grin, his eyes hooded and sexy. "Yeah, but where's the fun in that?"

"No, thanks."

He let it go and changed the subject. "You coming home with me tonight?"

"Maybe." She thought about Jay. If she went to her house, she ran the risk of jumping Jay's bones—or onto his lap. Her pulse surged and she got a lilt in her stomach as she visualized it, sitting on his paralyzed legs and wrapping her arms around his neck, burying her head in the curve of his shoulder and inhaling his clean, spicy male scent, feeling his arms envelop her, the peaks of her breasts rubbing against his hard chest, and all the things that could lead to.

Stop! God, it was depressing and exhausting and futile, trying to get him off her mind.

Duncan raised his brows at her vague answer. She smiled ruefully and revised it: "Probably."

"Good," he said with a grin. He held the joint between his thumb and index finger and put it to his lips. When he took a drag, the tip lit up, then he held the smoke in for a few seconds before slowly exhaling it out. Despite her earlier protests, Erin found herself tempted. Suddenly the idea of getting totally fucked up was appealing. Maybe it meant she could get rid of this constant, relentless longing for Jay.

Duncan must have sensed her wavering, because he smiled and heaved himself away from the car, then squeezed in next to her on the doorstep and put his arm around her shoulders, sticking the joint in her face. "Come on, babe," he said. His sweetly pungent breath wafted toward her, along with the smoke from the joint. "I swear it won't hurt you, and it's your first time. It'll be fucking amazing."

And it was her first time, at least for heroin. She gave him a skeptical look. "I thought you said I'd hardly feel anything."

He smiled crookedly. "Maybe you'll feel it more than someone like me, since you're not used to it."

Just say no, Erin's brain urged primly. She felt like she was in one of those antidrug commercials from the nineties and Duncan was the seedy druggie in every suburban mom's nightmare. But Erin didn't have a mother, and she was twenty-six years old. She was old enough to know better—or to do whatever the hell she wanted.

She grabbed the joint from Duncan, tired of overthinking it, and took a huge hit. The smoke she inhaled seared her throat and lungs, and the bitter taste was awful. She tried not to waste it, tried to hold it in, but she started coughing violently.

Duncan snickered. His eyes still hooded, he drawled, "Easy, Groper Girl. Don't take such a big hit next time."

Once her coughing fit was over, Erin gingerly took a few smaller, more successful puffs. She didn't feel much at first, but then, after a few minutes, it hit her. The rush was like having sunshine in her veins, slowly spreading warmth and a sense of profound well-being throughout her entire body. She leaned her head back against the door and grinned like a lunatic.

Duncan laughed. "Told ya."

Still grinning and too overwhelmed to speak, Erin met his eyes. He took it as an invitation and kissed her, probing her mouth with his tongue. His smoky, weedy taste was surprisingly pleasant, but, then, she didn't think there could be anything bad in her world ever again.

That was one of the last things she remembered until some hours later, when she woke up to someone trying to unbutton her jeans.

She opened her eyes to the harsh light of the bedside lamp in the sparsely furnished bedroom of Duncan's seventies ranch-style house. His glassy, red-rimmed, black eyes peeked down at her through several errant, dark locks of his messy long hair, a stuporous, lascivious grin on his face. He was on top of her, stark naked, his penis hard, and he was fiddling with the button and zipper of her jeans.

Heart racing and head pounding—symptoms of withdrawal from whatever the hell Erin had put into her body earlier in the evening—she reached up to push Duncan off. Her hands were shaky against his pale skin. "Get the fuck off me," she managed to slur. Her voice was scratchy, and her throat burned with the effort of speaking.

Duncan bent down and smashed his lips to her mouth. She turned her head away, only to feel him slobbering all over her neck.

"Stop. Stop it!" she rasped, fighting him harder, bucking her hips to try to throw him off. Unfortunately, that just seemed to excite him further. He was sinewy and more powerful than he looked, and she was no match for him, even if she'd been remotely coordinated in her movements. When he pinned her wrists down on either side of her head, she could barely move.

He laughed at her pathetic efforts to twist out from under him. "Come on, babe. That feels so good. You know you want it. I've been so patient. Don't you think I deserve a little reward?"

Anger, fear, and confusion pulsed through her. She was panting. How could this be happening? She'd woken up many times in guys' beds before, just like this, but this was the first time she'd failed to get one off of her. She could feel her face heating up, could feel hot tears running out of the corners of her eyes. "L't—" She stopped and started again, trying to command her mouth and tongue to work right, to form the words she wanted. "Let me go, Duncan. I'm—I'm g'na puke." It was the truth. Her stomach churned.

He let go of one of her wrists and moved his hand to her breast, twisting her nipple. It didn't really hurt, but it was humiliating. "I love it when you play hard to get," he said with a leer. This was a game to him, and he thought she was playing.

Enraged, she wrapped her free hand clumsily around his forearm, trying to wrench his hand from her breast. "Stop, Duncan!" she cried out. "I'm not kidding!"

"Stop, stop," Duncan mocked. He leaned down, getting in her face, his stale breath making her gag. "Don't worry, babe. You're gonna love every fucking minute of it."

A desperate sob escaped her, and she would have given up her very soul at that moment to be home safe with Jay instead of staring rape in the face.

Duncan started to pull her T-shirt up along her torso, trying to get it off, and Erin fought him harder, scratching his bare skin anywhere she could get in a good one-handed swipe. She kicked and writhed frantically, but the more she fought, the more he laughed and the rougher he got. He was tripping completely out of his mind.

He snaked his fingers into her tangled hair and yanked, pulling her head down so that she was forced to bare her throat to him. "I'm gonna drain you like a vamp," he grated, then began to lick her neck.

It was too much—the sour heat of his breath and his wet spit on her neck—and just as he started biting her, her stomach heaved, and bile rose and spewed from her mouth. She vomited all over him and herself. It was abundant, profuse, and disgusting, and, thank God, it had the desired effect.

"Gah! Holy shit!" Duncan jumped off her and stood, arms spread wide as he looked down at himself. Erin's fetid, lumpy, brown-and-beige barf dripped from his shoulder down onto his bare chest, and his dick began to deflate. "Goddammit!" he yelled. "What the fuck!"

Erin's heart jackhammered against her ribs, like it was buried alive and wanted to escape from this horrible situation as badly as she did. She scrambled off the bed and ran through the long hallway that led to the living room and kitchen, not caring that her Lars Bar T-shirt was now soaked in vomit.

She dodged passed-out human forms on the living room floor and crunched through fast-food wrappers, used-up joints, and other drug paraphernalia in her bare feet. She didn't know where her Chucks or her ankle brace were and didn't care. She just wanted to get the fuck out of there.

She'd never been so scared in her life, but to her relief, Duncan didn't seem to be following her. She heard no footsteps behind her, and she thought she heard the vague sound of water running somewhere in the house. As she stumbled toward the front door, she found her purse lying on the sticky brown carpet near a ratty sofa. Her wallet and lipstick and the other contents were strewn about, and she had enough presence of mind to gather them up as best she could and throw them in her bag before staggering out into the dark night.

She knew vaguely where she was—the blue-collar neighborhood behind North Star Mall—because, for God's sake, she'd been practically living there for the last week, but she was disoriented, terrified, and unable to think properly. She chose a random direction, thinking she would soon find a major street and would know where to go, but the farther she got from Duncan's, the fuzzier things got, the more her head hurt, and the more her stomach bucked and rolled. She threw up again.

When she stepped on a particularly sharp rock with her bare foot, the pain knifed through her, and she wondered why someone was trying to hurt her, maybe even kill her. She didn't know why she thought that, but she couldn't shake the terrifying feeling and started to shiver and cry, even as she kept bumbling her way along the sidewalk. Her heart wouldn't stop hammering, and she started to think maybe she'd die of a heart attack instead of being murdered. Either prospect fueled the fear that consumed her, making it harder and harder to think.

It seemed the longer she walked, the more lost she got. The neighborhood was a maze of pink-brick ranch-styles from the sixties and seventies. They all looked the same, all with the same watery porch lights and garages that had been enclosed to make extra rooms.

Where was the fucking mall? Surely she should have found it by now. She dug around in her purse like there was something in there that might help her.

She came out with her wallet. Her credit cards and any tip money she'd made that night (and she couldn't remember how much there'd been) were gone, but she wasn't about to go back to Duncan's and demand that whoever took them give them back. She couldn't find her way back to Duncan's anyway.

Then she thought maybe she was already dead and this was her version of hell, doomed forever to wander the lonely streets of this strange, dark neighborhood where she'd died. Another step on a sharp rock jolted her, and she sucked in a quick breath, telling herself she was still alive. Still alive. Still alive.

Was she talking to herself, muttering like some homeless person, somebody with schizophrenia? She thought maybe she was.

She felt something in her hand and looked down at the wallet in it. Oh, yeah. Her purse. She had her purse. She rubbed her forehead with the fingertips of her free hand, trying to soothe the achy sludge in her head enough that she could reason. She stuck the wallet back in the depths of her purse. This time, when she pulled her hand back out, she had her cell phone.

Maybe she should call a taxi? But she had no money. Maybe she could knock on the door of one of the houses and ask for help. She turned in a circle, assessing the sinister-looking homes surrounding her, but the movement made her so dizzy she had to plop down on a patch of damp, thick-bladed grass instead. The whole world was spinning now, and she felt sick again. She laid her head down on the grass and curled into a ball, then remembered the phone in her hand.

Jay. Call Jay. Jay was safety. He would help her. He would know what to do.

She held up the phone, squinting at the smooth black surface of its small screen. It reflected the glow of the porch light behind her and her own reflection: an eerie, soulless, ghostlike apparition. She closed her eyes to shut out the image and let her hand fall to the ground, thinking that maybe, if death found her, it wouldn't be such a bad thing after all.

Chapter 16

There was a giant mosquito buzzing in Jay's ear. Figured. Here was the first night in a while his back pain had been tolerable, but it wasn't in the cards for him to actually get a good night's sleep.

The buzzing was followed by a deep, throaty *woof* from Chopper, who was lying near Jay's bed on his tan papasan cushion. Jay realized the giant mosquito noise was the annoying ringtone of his cell phone—a practical joke from a coworker he hadn't fixed yet.

He was lying on his stomach, and he buried his face in his pillow. The mosquito buzzing stopped for a few blessed seconds and then started up again. "Gotta change that fucking ring," he muttered irritably.

Reaching over to his nightstand, he grabbed the phone. "'Lo?"

A pause and then, "Uh, yeah. Hey. Is this Jay Bon— Bon—Bonsomething?" It was a man's voice. It had a slightly musical cadence similar to Luis's.

"Yeah," Jay answered with a frown. "Who wants to know?" He glanced at the digital clock on the nightstand. It was 5:02 a.m.—not the middle of the night, like he'd thought. He was supposed to get up in an hour anyway.

He could hear a disturbance over the phone, someone yelling and what sounded like someone crying. "What's going on?" he said, starting to get uneasy. "Who is this?"

"Uh, my name is Hector Mendoza. Uh . . . you know a girl, kind of crazy, long brown hair, small body, green eyes?"

Jay's heart rate picked up. "You mean Erin?" It sounded like her, except for the crazy part.

Hector spoke to someone, his voice suddenly sounding distant, like he'd taken the phone away from his mouth. "Hey, he knows her. See if her name is Erin." There was shuffling and the commotion in the background seemed to die down for a minute. "It's her," Hector said back to Jay. "She your girlfriend or something?"

"No. My roommate. What's going on? Let me talk to her."

"She's freaking out, man. She's fucked up on something, all paranoid and shit. You want me to call 911, or you want to come get her?"

Jay was utterly still for a split second, hoping maybe this was a bad dream. "Is she hurt?"

"No, not that I can see. She's just flipping out. She won't let no one touch her or help her."

"Okay. Don't call 911. Give me your address." When Hector complied, Jay said, "I'll be there in twenty minutes."

His arm muscles vibrated with adrenaline as he swung his ass from the bed to his chair. Twenty minutes was pushing the envelope timewise, considering all the stuff he had to do just to get dressed. It wasn't like he could just jump out of bed and throw on a shirt and jeans.

He had to cath, for one thing, and then he had to drag on his jeans while lying on the bed—not exactly easy, since he couldn't lift his hips. It usually took him thirty-five minutes, minimum, to get dressed, and that was if he didn't take a shower or do his bowel routine. He should do it today, but fuck it. Erin needed him. He hoped he wouldn't crap his pants before he could get her home.

Breaking a personal record and several neighborhood speed limits, he made it to Hector's house in twenty-six minutes. As he pulled up in front of the house, he could see a semicircle of people surrounding a bare-footed Erin, who was sitting on the ground, hugging her knees to her chest and rocking back and forth.

The area was lit enough by streetlights and porch lights that he could see her face, tear-streaked and smudged with dirt. A few neighbors in various states of dress and undress were standing on their lawns, watching the scene. At the sight of Erin, Jay's worry ratcheted up a notch. "What the fuck, darlin'?" he muttered to himself.

He saw a stocky Hispanic man squat down next to her and place a hand on her shoulder.

She flinched and shoved his hand away. The man—probably Hector—said something to her, and she looked up at Jay's car. Then she started rocking again, eyes darting down and resting her chin on her knees.

Jay opened his car door and pulled the black titanium

frame of his chair from the passenger side of the front seat across his body, setting it outside the car. Then he grabbed the wheels of the chair from the backseat and put it together—popping the wheels onto the frame, flipping up the backrest, and putting the special cushion that protected his ass from skin breakdown in the seat. The whole process took about a minute.

He transferred to his chair and wheeled up the driveway, then balanced on his back wheels and leaned forward to lift his front casters off the ground: They would only get stuck in the thick St. Augustine grass, so it was easier to roll doing a wheelie. He pushed hard across the lawn and soon reached Erin.

A flicker of surprise crossed the faces of the people around Erin at the sight of Jay's wheelchair, but no one said anything. The Hispanic man stepped forward and gave a crisp nod. "You Jay?"

"Yeah."

"I'm Hector." He turned to the women standing behind him near Erin. "This is my wife, Carla, and our two daughters, Isabela and Tina." The two pudgy daughters looked to be teenagers, while Hector and his wife looked to be in their forties.

Jay gave a nod of acknowledgment. He wasn't exactly in the mood for pleasantries, and neither was Carla, judging by the way she had her arms folded over her chest and her lips pressed tightly together in a belligerent pose.

Resting his elbows on his knees, Jay leaned forward

to get as close to Erin as he could get. He was shocked by her appearance: long brown hair mostly escaped from its ponytail and tangling wildly around her face, some of it sticking to her grimy cheeks. "Hey, darlin'. You okay?"

Erin's eyes were glazed over and bloodshot, their sea-hazel color too bright against red whites. They were almost glowing when she looked up at him, then they welled with tears. "Jay?"

There was so much infused in the way she said his name—relief, fear, despair—that it made his heart ache. "Yeah. I'm here," he said in a low tone.

Her face crumpled and the tears in her eyes slipped free.

"You ready to go home, darlin'?"

She nodded like a lost child, still hugging her knees.

He looked up at Hector. "Can you help me get her to my car?"

Hector's brows went up, his face doubtful. "Yeah, if she'll let me. She wouldn't tell us nothing or let anyone near her, just kept waving her phone like a crazy woman and yelling your name. That's the reason I called you. Found your name in her contacts. I found her passed out on our lawn earlier when I was leaving for work. I'm supposed to be there by 5:30."

It was almost six now. "Sorry, man," Jay said.

"Shit happens," Hector said philosophically.

"You're lucky we didn't call the police," Carla put in. She glared at her husband. "If it had been up to me, that's what we would have done."

"Shut up, Carla," said Hector. "Like you can throw the first stone. I seem to remember scraping your ass off the ground a time or two."

Carla rolled her eyes and pursed her lips.

Jay said to Erin, "Darlin', you need to get to my car. Okay?"

She lifted her gaze to his and nodded.

"Hector here is gonna help you."

She frowned and shook her head frantically.

"Erin, he won't hurt you. He just wants to help."

She shook her head again and started rocking.

Jay looked up at Hector, who shrugged as if to say, *See? I told you.*

When Jay reached forward and cupped Erin's cheek in his hand, she froze at his touch, wary, but didn't jerk away. He gently rubbed her cheekbone with his thumb. "You need to trust me. No one's going to hurt you."

Her eyes skittered to Hector and then she seemed to stare at nothing.

Jay let out a frustrated breath. Jesus Christ. What had happened to her? What had she been doing for the past week? Who the hell had done this to her? He wanted answers, but first he had to get her home and sobered up, not to mention cleaned up. She smelled foul, like vomit, pot, stale beer, and other things he couldn't identify.

It took a lot of coaxing, but Jay finally got Erin to let Hector help her to the car. When Jay got her home, she was too wobbly and disoriented to walk to the house, so Jay secured her on his lap, guiding her arms around his neck and awkwardly wheeling her inside.

He helped her shuck her soiled clothing and then removed the shower chair from his tub so she could bathe in it, since he could maneuver his wheelchair better in his bathroom. She was so out of it that she didn't make even a squeak of protest at undressing in front of him. Then again, he didn't think she even realized she was naked. She was so docile, obeying Jay's every command as if he'd hypnotized her.

His blood boiled with rage when he saw she was bruised on her arms, wrists, and other random places. He prayed to God she hadn't been raped and wanted to kill the son of a bitch who'd manhandled her.

His conscience told him he should take her to a hospital first, that he might be washing away evidence, but he wasn't sure what she might have gotten herself into. A trip to the hospital might attract unwanted attention from nosy doctors and social workers, might even get her in trouble with the police, and he didn't want to chance it.

That possibility, combined with his past experience with doctors who could do nothing to fix him and a lifelong distrust of police instilled by his dad, made him wary. He would deal with the rape issue later if he had to, but he wanted to talk to Erin first, after she'd detoxed, to find out exactly what had happened.

She was lying back in the tub now, her petite, slender body distorted a bit by the warm water submerging part of her. She had small tattoos in places that were usually hidden, like the inside of her thigh up near her bikini line and one just above her breast. He'd also seen one at the base of her spine when she'd clumsily undressed. The tats were just butterflies and cheesy shit like that, but on her, they were sexy as hell.

This wasn't at all how he'd pictured the first time he would see her naked. Just like any normal, decent dude, he wanted a woman to be a willing, eager participant when things got intimate, not barely conscious and coming off a bad high. Still, he couldn't stop his hand from trembling a little with need as he sluiced a warm, soapy washrag over her collarbone and breasts, between her thighs, and over her exquisite calves. Lust shot through him and he instantly felt guilty, especially in light of the evidence she'd been mistreated.

"Christ, Jay. Get a grip," he muttered. He drew in a shaky breath and tried to be more clinical in his touch. The long, raised, dark pink scar that ran along the outside of her right ankle, a souvenir from her car wreck, helped to squelch his desire a little, but not because it marred her otherwise perfect body. It was because the thought of her small bones splintering and having to be screwed back together, of her being seriously hurt, made him queasy. He wanted to protect her, to never let anything bad happen to her again.

The scar didn't detract from her loveliness, though, and he still wanted her. Badly.

Erin, on the other hand, was only half-conscious, her eyes hooded and glassy. It was like she had one foot in this realm and one in a place only she could see. One thing was for sure: Wherever she was, Jay's touch had no effect on her.

Chapter 17

Someone was squeezing her. It wasn't unpleasant, wasn't cutting off her breath. It was just a heavy weight resting on her waist and hip that felt safe and protective.

She was home. She knew by the softness and just-right puffiness of the pillow beneath her cheek and the familiar scent of the fabric softener—lavender Bounce—in her sheets. The fake lavender mingled with other scents: the natural smell of her own body (not unclean, just there, just normal), and a male spiciness that she knew without a doubt belonged to Jay. Tentatively, she moved her hand until she felt a warm, masculine hand and then an arm lightly dusted with wiry male hair. Her heart instantly beat faster, a flashing beacon seeking a response.

Why was Jay's arm around her? Why was he in her bed? She knew she should open her eyes, but she waited just a few more blessed seconds. She wanted to savor the fact that she finally felt clear-headed again, that the nausea, the headache, and, worst of all, the terrifying paranoia she'd felt had subsided. And then there was Jay's body heat wrapped around her like a warm blanket.

She didn't remember much. She'd smoked the A-bomb and then drunk way too much at Lars Bar before leaving at the end of her shift with Duncan and some of his friends. They'd done more drinking and drugs, and everything after that was spotty. She remembered Duncan on top of her, trying to get her clothes off. She remembered terror and hands gripping her too hard and not letting go. She remembered walking but going nowhere. She remembered hands again, flapping around her like crazy white doves. She remembered more fear, more sickness, more shame.

She remembered a familiar face—a handsome, chiseled face with dark, blue-gray eyes—a whiskey voice, strong soothing hands, cool water easing down her throat, back rubs, fingers tenderly holding her hair back to get it out of her face as she threw up. She remembered peace.

How long had she been out of it? Had Jay taken care of her the whole time? She was horrified by the thought. There was no telling what he'd seen. She must have been at her worst, like shitty-butt-wasted worst. Guilt squeezed her belly, along with the embarrassment and fear of what she might have done or said. She suddenly felt tense all over, her shoulders stiffening.

The arm around her waist tightened and pulled her closer, and then Jay's voice was there, a rich, sleepy vibration in her ear. "What's wrong, darlin'? You need something?"

She closed her eyes, almost groaning with pleasure

at the sound of him. "Um, no. Thanks. I'm okay." Her voice sounded like someone else's, kind of froggy and craggy; her tongue and throat felt like they'd been sanded and Spackled.

Jay's arm relaxed but still held her close. It was a nice feeling, but her need to fill in the blanks was overwhelming. Erin rolled over to face him, his arm remaining steady as her body twisted beneath it. When she was settled, he rubbed lazy little circles on her back with his hand. It felt divine and reassuring.

He was lying on his side, his thin legs covered by loose gray sweatpants, a pillow between his bent knees. She knew the pillow was there to prevent pressure sores from developing where his legs rubbed together—so he must have planned on lying there with her for a while. The sheet and comforter were all bunched up and had been pushed down to the bottom of the bed.

"You kept getting hot," he said, seeing where her gaze had stopped. "You finally shoved all the covers off of you." His mouth was curved into the ghost of his usual smirk, his blue eyes unreadable and unwavering from her face.

His scrutiny made Erin self-conscious. She glanced down to escape it, but she didn't get any farther than his broad chest. The white T-shirt he wore hugged every muscle. "Why"—she cleared her throat because her mouth seemed to get drier by the minute—"are you sleeping in my bed?"

"You slept better when I was here."

"Oh." She let that soak in for a second, tingling warmth curling through her at the thought of him watching over her. "So, um, how long have I been out of it?"

"About two days."

Not good. So not good. She closed her eyes and then forced herself to open them and meet his gaze. "And you . . . " She paused, trying to fight off a blush. "You've been taking care of me?"

He nodded. "Good to see you're coming back to the land of the living."

She felt heat rise up her neck to her cheeks. "I'm sorry. I guess I was pretty messed up."

"Yeah, you were." After a beat, he asked, "You wanna tell me what happened?"

"Just overdid it, I guess."

His gaze burned into her. "Just overdid it? Erin, you were sick as a dog, incoherent, and having a full-on paranoid psychotic freak-out. Some dude that lives in the neighborhood behind North Star Mall found you passed out on his front lawn at five in the morning."

Erin cringed inwardly.

"You've been coming down for two days from whatever got you so fucked up. So, yeah. I'd definitely say you 'overdid' it."

Shame blasted through her, making her wish that she could just disappear, that the bed would swallow her up. "I'm sorry," she said quietly. When he didn't respond, she added, "Thank you for . . . helping me."

He tilted her chin up with an index finger, as if making sure he had her full attention. "I want to know what happened."

"It's really not that big of a deal."

A flare of his nostrils told her that was the wrong thing to say.

"To be honest," she rushed on, "I don't remember that much. I'm sorry. I'm sorry that guy called you and sucked you into my shit."

"You'd better be glad that guy called me instead of the police. You could be detoxing in a hospital or the clink right now instead of here with me."

She got a cold, sick feeling in the pit of her stomach. He was right. She could have gone to jail for public intoxication or something much more serious if the wrong person had found her. There were definitely worse things than having to detox with Jay.

"Erin," he said, "you have bruises all over you." Her hand was resting on her pillow, near her chin, and he caressed her wrist with his fingers. Without looking, she knew he was touching one of the bruises, underscoring his point.

Jay's touch was gentle and so different from when Duncan had pinned her wrists down, his hands like steel bands. She didn't remember a lot of what had happened the past couple of days, but she would never forget that horrible helplessness or the feeling of stark terror that had cut through her drugged stupor with razorlike clarity.

"I want to know what happened. Who were you

with? Did he . . . " Jay swallowed hard and then spoke with slow, succinct words, overenunciating to make sure she heard him. "I need to know what happened. I need to know if you were . . . forced."

He was talking about rape, and she'd come damn close to it. This time, a memory of Duncan sitting on top of her, trying to undo her jeans and get her shirt off, flashed through her mind. She stared at a spot just above Jay's shoulder, unable to look him in the eye. "No. No one raped me."

He studied her face, as though trying to figure out whether she was telling the truth. "Then where did the bruises come from?"

"Things got a little rough with the guy I was with. It's not a big deal. It . . . was consensual," she lied.

"Bullshit," retorted Jay. "I don't believe you like it rough. You're not the *Fifty Shades* type."

"Really?" she challenged. "How do you know? How do you know experimenting with the whole freaky dev thing wasn't just the tip of the iceberg? Maybe I'm all kinds of depraved and kinky."

Jay's brow creased in irritation "You're not, so tell me who hurt you."

She didn't want him to know what had happened, didn't want him to know what a loser and a slut she was or that, although her issues ran deep, the main reason she'd smoked heroin and gotten so fucked up was to escape her feelings for him. It was so juvenile, so high school, and she'd be mortified if he knew. She just wanted to pretend none of it happened. "Let it go, Jay. It's none of your business."

His lips pressed together in a grim line of disagreement.

"Please," she added.

He hesitated. Then, as if making a decision, he pulled the pillow out from between his legs, chucked it to the floor beyond the foot of her bed, and reached over with one hand to grab the edge of the mattress on his side of the bed, pulling until he was lying on his back. His legs were still angled toward her, so he had to shove his knees over with his other hand before getting his elbows braced under him to lever himself, inch by inch, into a sitting position.

It was something Erin took for granted, the simple act of turning over and sitting up, but for Jay, because some of his abdominal muscles were paralyzed just like his legs, there were all these extra steps involved. A lot of things were like that for him, but he made it all seem normal, like it wasn't a struggle at all. There was something very admirable—and very sexy—about that.

Once he was upright, he transferred to his chair, which was next to the bed, and lifted his legs at the knees to maneuver his bare feet onto the footrest. His feet were sort of puffy-looking and limp, and because they were never used for walking, they were devoid of any calluses Erin could see. It was the first time she'd seen him without socks, and the sight sent a little thrill to her special parts.

And there she went again, being a freak, getting turned on by something any non-creepy person wouldn't be turned on by. She added that to her growing mountain of guilt, her stomach going all wrong and tight. Even so, she felt bereft and cold without Jay by her side and didn't want him to leave. Sitting up, she said, "Where—where are you going?"

His shaggy blond hair was mussed and kind of smooshed in on one side, and the usual daily allotment of hot-guy, blond stubble shaded his jaw. He looked adorable, despite an abruptness to his movements and a set to his mouth that told Erin he was pissed, that he didn't want to just let things go. Biceps bulging under his T-shirt sleeves, he gripped his wheels and drew his shoulders back as if about to swivel his chair around.

"Where are you going?" she repeated.

"To get you something to eat," he said gruffly.

Relief that it was something so innocuous almost made her smile, not to mention it was really nice of him. She was glad he was letting her off the hook for now, even though he was clearly annoyed with her.

But her relief was short-lived. He lifted his head and looked straight in her eyes, direct and steady, and said, "And then we're gonna have a talk, darlin'—one where I ask you questions and you give me actual answers."

Chapter 18

The doorbell rang while Jay was heating up Campbell's chicken noodle soup on the stove. The soup was the very basic version, just broth and a few paltry noodles, but he didn't figure Erin's stomach could handle anything fancier yet. If she kept this down okay, he'd make her something heartier.

He reached up to turn off the burner, wiped his hands on a nearby dishtowel, and wheeled through the living room to answer the door. When he opened it, a guy of average height and long, dark hair was standing on the porch, holding something black in one of his hands, down by his side. He wore a faded black T-shirt and skinny jeans so tight they must be cutting off the circulation to his balls. He had the same rocker/musician vibe as Erin's brother.

Jay raised a brow in inquiry.

"Uh, hi," the guy said, looking down at Jay. His demeanor was cautious. "Uh, is Erin here?"

Remembering a chat with emanomaly where she'd told Panhead what traits she found attractive in a guy, Jay felt a stab of jealousy. This guy looked like he fit the bill: dark-haired, most likely a musician, and, from Erin's miniature perspective, tall. Jay guessed the guy could be called good-looking, which made Jay instantly dislike him. At least this guy didn't have an Australian accent.

"Now's not a good time," Jay told him. "She's been sick."

Frowning, the guy ran a hand through his hair and looked away. He was fidgety and hardly made eye contact, like someone who was guilty of something. And then Jay realized the black thing in the guy's hand was Erin's ankle brace. Jay instantly wanted to kill him.

The guy began, "But is she . . . ," and then trailed off, giving Jay a sideways look, like he wanted to know more but didn't want to say too much. "I mean, she's okay, though?"

Jay crossed his arms over his chest. "That depends. You the one who got her so fucked up? You the one who put those bruises on her?"

The guy's eyes widened and the color drained from his face. "Bruises? I—"

"Jay," Erin interrupted in a flat voice, coming up behind him. She took the door from Jay's hand and stepped back, opening it wider and indicating with a slight tilt of her head that he should leave. He ignored her. He wasn't going anywhere.

She exhaled and pursed her mouth but didn't argue. As she turned her attention to Rocker Boy, Jay studied her. She was gaunt, but at least she was vertical and seemed steady on her feet. Her long brown hair was in a loose ponytail, and she'd changed into tight black yoga pants and a long-sleeved gray T-shirt that hid the bruising on her wrists. Her eyes were lit by the morning sun, making their hazel tint even lighter than usual.

"What are you doing here?" she said to Rocker Boy. Her voice sounded kind of hoarse, although it still had that unusual doll-like quality that Jay found so hot.

"I wanted to bring you this," he said, handing her the ankle brace. "And I, uh . . . " The guy's eyes darted down to Jay and then back to her. "I just wanted to make sure you're okay."

"I'm fine."

Rocker Boy shoved his hands in his jeans pocket and hunched his shoulders. His jeans were so tight, Jay was surprised the guy could even fit his fingers in the pockets. "Can we just talk—"

"No," she said, cutting him off.

"I'm, you know . . . " Again, a quick dart of the eyes toward Jay. "I'm sorry."

She didn't respond, just stared at him.

This time his eyes traveled more slowly over to Jay, the action significant, before he said to her, "You didn't—"

"No."

She didn't what, Jay wondered. Rat him out?

The guy nodded and cleared his throat. "Uh, thanks . . . and, just, you know, I'm sorry."

She continued to stare at him, which made the guy

squirm more.

"It won't happen again," he said. "I didn't—I mean . . ." Another swipe of his hand through his hair. "That's not who I am. I don't—"

"You should leave now," said Erin.

The guy's mouth clamped shut. Then, with a nod, he mumbled, "Right," and retreated down the front steps, making his way down to an ancient white Mercedes station wagon parked at the curb.

Erin's hand fell away from the door and she disappeared, leaving Jay to sit alone in the doorway. He shut the door and swiveled his chair around to see her heading for the kitchen. By the time he reached the kitchen himself, she was pulling a bottle of Ozarka from the fridge. Maybe she'd be able to keep this one down.

She went into the living room and plopped down on the couch, wedging the insteps of her feet on the coffee table, her knees bent. Her bad ankle looked slightly swollen.

Jay finished warming up her soup, ladled it into a bowl, then loaded it onto his wooden lap tray, along with a paper towel, a spoon, some saltine crackers, and the ankle brace Erin had left on the kitchen counter. He pushed himself over to her and handed her the tray.

"Thanks," she said, setting it beside her on the couch. She put her bottle of Ozarka next to the soup bowl.

"So," he said, keeping his tone casual, "who's the shithead with the nut-huggers?"

The corners of her mouth lifted into a reluctant smile.

"Nut-huggers?"

"You gotta admit, his beanbag was packed in pretty tight."

"You always notice the crotches of strange guys?"

Jay shrugged. "One of the perks of living in a chair. You're always eye level with belt buckles, zippers, and crotches." He cocked his head. "Don't worry, darlin'. I stare at plenty of ladies' crotches, too."

She gave an amused snort and rolled her eyes. "They were skinny jeans," she said, like that explained Rocker Boy's blatant testicle abuse.

"I think that's a style I'll let pass me by," Jay said dryly. In a more serious tone, he asked, "Who was he?"

She picked up the plastic sleeve of saltines from the tray, selecting a cracker with her slender fingers. Before popping it into her mouth, she said, "His name is Duncan. He's a friend."

"A friend. The friend you been playing slumber party with for the past week?"

"Yeah."

The jealousy Jay'd felt earlier morphed into something darker and spread through him like thick, black oil. He gripped the tires of his chair until the treads dug into his palms, trying not to show how much the thought of Erin with another guy bothered him. Still, he couldn't resist saying, "Where did you find him, Chuck E. Cheese's?"

She shot him a don't-be-an-asshole look. "He's not that young. He's twenty-one."

"Twenty-one? Oh, sorry, my mistake. He's probably a fucking paragon of maturity and wisdom."

"Yeah," she said, undaunted. "He's a regular Buddha."

Jay folded his arms over his chest, frustrated he couldn't get anything out of her. She turned her attention to her soup, cupping the bowl in one hand and holding the spoon with the other.

Jay loved her small hands and her short fingernails, which were painted their usual midnight blue. He liked that she didn't have those long, fake claws so many women sported, including his ex-wife.

After taking a few careful bites of soup, she set the bowl down and bit off one corner of a cracker, giving him a glimpse of those slightly uneven teeth of hers. Somehow their imperfection made them more attractive to him.

She was so pretty, even when she wasn't wearing any makeup. Jay liked her better without it. She wasn't a classic beauty, but there was something so striking about her, so mesmerizing, so cool. And those eyes. Jesus. Even bloodshot and plain with no dark eyeliner to accentuate them, they were stunning, compelling.

She gave off something that drew him in, and he wanted to be closer to her—physically closer, like sitting next to her. Maybe she would open up more and be less aloof if he could touch her. "Scoot over, darlin'."

"Why?"

He eyed the space where he wanted to sit on the

couch, near the end. "Scoot over. Make room for me."

She narrowed her eyes. "Only if you promise not to grill me."

Jay leaned forward, resting his elbows on his knees, and looked up at her, speaking gently. "You were in pretty bad shape, darlin'."

Her lashes lowered.

"I don't think wanting to know what happened to you is too much to ask."

She paused, then said, "They shouldn't have called you and gotten you involved. I'm sorry."

"Would you stop saying that? I'm glad Hector called me."

She looked at him, frowning a little. "Who?"

"The Hector whose lawn you pulled a Goldilocks on."

"Oh, right," she said, pressing her lips together and closing her eyes. "Not one of my prouder moments."

Jay waited until her eyes opened and met his. "Hey. It's over now. And you can call me anytime you need help, darlin'. Always. Anytime." When she didn't respond, he said, "You hear me?"

She nodded reluctantly. "Yeah."

"So, you gonna scoot over or what?"

With a faint quirk of her lips, she moved the tray of soup to the coffee table and scooted over.

Jay's wheelchair was at an angle to the couch, the way he liked it for a transfer. He grabbed his leg that was closest to the couch and flopped it off the footplate so it wouldn't get in his way, then grabbed the outer frame of his chair with one hand and placed his inside hand on the couch cushion. In a quick, efficient move, he shifted his weight from his outer hand to his inner one and swung his butt onto the couch, then adjusted his legs with his hands, looking down at his feet to make sure they weren't twisted.

"You make that look so easy," said Erin offhand. "It almost looks like you're using your legs."

"Huh." He heard what she was saying but wasn't really comprehending it because he could feel the warmth of her body and smell the tantalizing scent of her now that they were shoulder to shoulder.

She glanced furtively at him and leaned forward to grab her water bottle off the tray. Her shoulder brushed his as she flopped back against the couch. She didn't take a drink, only tore idly at the bottle's red label, but her focus on it became too intense, like all of a sudden it was the most fascinating thing she'd ever seen.

Jay wondered what was wrong. Was she embarrassed about calling attention to his legs? Hoping that talking about his disability would make it less of a big deal, less awkward, he said, "Transfers like that are easy now. When I first got injured, though, they were a bitch. Busted my ass a few times before I got it down."

She didn't say anything, just kept staring at the Ozarka bottle.

He cupped her chin and turned it toward him so she would look at him. "Hey. It's okay. It's okay to talk about it." When she didn't say anything, he said, "I won't think it's weird. I understand it all—you—more now, Erin. That stuff I said about devs—that was me being a judgmental prick. I didn't know what the fuck I was talking about."

She jerked back her head, breaking his hold. "Just like that, you've had a change of heart?" She shook her head. "Uh-uh. I don't believe it. You can't change deep-seated . . . ," she looked around, as if searching for the right word, " . . . revulsion like that overnight."

"It wasn't overnight. I didn't know any devs then. Now I do. I've lived with one for the past three months."

"I'm not a dev," she said, looking obstinate.

"You can't change something like that overnight either," he said.

"I'm not a dev," she insisted.

He was still skeptical. "Why are you denying it?"

"Why do you care?"

"Because I like you."

"Oh, please."

"I do like you," he insisted. "Do you think I would've taken care of your ass for the last two days if I didn't care about you?"

She assessed him for a long moment. "Yeah," she said softly. "I think you would have."

That surprised him. "Why do you think that?"

"Because maybe you're not the asshole I thought you were."

He grinned. "Thanks. I think."

There was the barest smile on her lips.

"I like you, Erin. You don't have to deny the dev thing with me. I'm okay with it."

"Yeah, right." Her tone said she was still far from convinced. She held the water bottle to her mouth and took a sip.

"Let me show you how much I'm okay with it." Before she could do anything to resist, he cupped the back of her neck with his palm, then leaned toward her and grazed his mouth across hers. It was innocent as kisses go, but when their lips touched, an instant buzz of electricity made Jay's heartbeat stutter.

Abruptly, Erin crunched the plastic bottle in her hand and broke away. "Don't."

"Why?" he asked, sure she must have felt the same buzz he had.

"How can you—God." She tossed the Ozarka to the side and scrubbed her hands over her face. "You don't even know where I've been or what I've been doing."

Jay hated the reminder she'd been MIA for over a week with Rocker Boy, aka Duncan. "I just met Duncan, remember? And I got you through the worst hangover in human history. I've got a pretty good idea what you've been doing."

She hung her head. "How could you possibly want to kiss me?" She turned to him. "You were right, you know, that day in Luis's apartment. I am a bottom-feeder."

"Goddammit. I never should have said that." He ran his hand roughly through his hair, close to pulling out a good chunk of it in frustration. "I wish I could take it all back, Erin. Every single word. You are *not* a bottom-feeder."

She didn't respond, just stared at nothing.

Jay ached to tell her so much more—for starters, how good he thought her novel was. She was a smart and talented writer, but he couldn't tell her because it was a part of herself she hid from him so thoroughly. He should tell her anyway. He should come clean and tell her he was Panhead, but he felt like they were about to turn some kind of corner here, like maybe if he could say the right thing, she might begin to trust him—trust *him,* Jay Bontrager, not Panhead.

"You are not a bottom-feeder," he repeated.

"Okay. Just a slut, then."

He felt like a hot branding iron had just gouged his gut. "What happened to you, darlin'? Why would you say that?"

"Nothing happened."

He knew that was a lie. There was a hollowness about her now, like some of the life had been sucked out of her. It was like she was giving up, and Jay didn't like it one bit.

He put his arm around her shoulders and hugged her to him. To his relief, she didn't stiffen or pull away.

Instead, she sighed and laid her head on his shoulder. "This doesn't mean we're having a heart-to-heart," she murmured.

"Why not?"

"Because you're the last person I should talk to."

"Why? Like you said, I'm not such a bad guy."

She was quiet.

"Come on. Let's start with this Duncan dude. How do you know him?"

She waited a full minute to answer, but she must have finally decided it was okay. "He's the bass player for The Poonmatics."

"'Poonmatics'?" Jay snorted derisively. "Brilliant."

She gave his leg an admonishing nudge.

"You know I can't feel that, right?"

She lightly pinched his arm instead.

"Ouch."

"The Poonmatics sometimes open for my brother's band—our band, I mean. I've sort of known Duncan for a while."

"Don't tell me. You used to change his diapers?"

She pinched Jay again, this time hard enough to sting.

"Ow!"

"Enough with the cougar references. I'm not that old."

Jay smiled and rested his chin on the top of her head, getting a whiff of the apple scent of her shampoo. "So anyway. Keep talking."

"There's not much to tell. I've been hanging out with him. A few nights ago, things got . . . out of hand."

Jay steeled his jaw. "And he hurt you?"

"He . . . he just did what any guy would do, what any guy would expect."

Jay took a deep breath, trying to control his temper. "What's that supposed to mean?"

She hesitated. "I'm not known for being chaste, Jay. My reputation preceded me."

He got a sick feeling in the pit of his stomach. "And that gave him the right to put bruises on you? I don't think so." He hugged her tighter. "Erin, are you sure he didn't force you?"

She stiffened. "Yes. It's nothing that dramatic. He's a dickhead, but he's nothing I can't handle."

"What if . . . " Jay trailed off, not sure how to say what he wanted to say without pissing her off. "Erin, you were really out of it. I mean, what if—"

"What if he raped me and I don't remember? Don't worry," she said, her tone filled with bitterness and self-disgust. "He didn't. He told me he was tired of waiting, that it was time he got his reward. He wasn't so gung ho for his reward after I threw up on him, though."

She tried to sit up, but Jay kept his arms around her.

"Still want to kiss me?" she asked. Her words were barbed, cynical.

"Yeah," he said simply. "I do."

She pulled back and looked up at him like he'd lost his mind. "You can't be serious."

"I am. And I want to kill that son of a bitch Duncan."

Guilt twisted her features and she shook her head. "Duncan hasn't hurt me any worse than I've hurt myself."

He had a feeling she was referring to something more than what had happened with Duncan. "What are you talking about?"

She wrenched away from him and put a couple of inches between them. "Nothing. It just means Duncan didn't force me to get fucked up. It was my decision."

"What did you do? What did you take?"

"Smoked heroin, among other things."

Jay let his head fall back against the couch. "Jesus Christ."

"It wasn't straight heroin. It was an A-bomb. You know what that is?"

"Yeah. I know what it is." Fury roared through him, but he reined it in. Erupting like a volcano right now would just make Erin clam up. That didn't mean the need to rip that little shithead Duncan apart wasn't eating him alive. Even if Duncan hadn't raped her, he'd been rough with her, and he'd let her do heroin, for fuck's sake. Maybe he'd even talked her into doing it.

"Why did you do it?" Jay asked, forcing his voice to remain calm.

"There doesn't have to be a reason."

"Yes, there does. For you, there does."

She rolled her eyes. "You don't know me, Jay. I think I just proved that with all this Duncan crap. You don't really know anything about me."

"That's not true," he said. If she only knew how much it wasn't true.

A stray strand of her hair had escaped from its ponytail, and he reached forward on impulse and tucked it behind her ear. His skin thrummed when his fingertips made brief contact with the shell of her ear.

She glanced down shyly and ran her tongue over her top lip.

He wondered if it was in reaction to his touching her. He didn't think she was trying to be provocative, but the action made his mouth go dry.

Christ, Jay. Focus. Here he was, having a serious conversation with her, and he was getting all horny because she'd licked her lip.

He drew in a breath to clear his head and looked her in the eye. "I know you're smarter than this, Erin. You're not a druggie. Why did you do it?"

She shook her head, and a couple of tears slipped out from underneath her lashes. Jay pulled her onto his lap, enveloping her in his arms, and gently pressed her head onto his chest. It felt like she belonged there, like two puzzle pieces coming together.

She stayed in his arms for a few minutes, until she tipped her head back to look at him, more composed. "You can't keep rescuing me like this. You're supposed to be the angsty, surly cripple, and I'm supposed to be the one who comforts you and shows you life is still worth living."

He chuckled. "Sorry."

"Just try not to have your shit together so much."

He smiled and ran the pad of his thumb over her soft lips. "Hmm," he said idly. "I'll try to remember."

"Please," she groaned, "tell me you're not thinking about kissing me again."

"I'm not thinking about it. I'm going to."

"Don't," she said, pushing her palm against his chest in warning.

"Why?"

"It's just a really bad idea."

"Why?" he asked, frustrated. "Why is it a bad idea?"

"Aside from the fact that you hate devs—"

Jay's nostrils flared. "I don't—"

She put a finger over his lips to shush him. "—and aside from the fact that I swore I'd never date a wheeler again, it has to do with holding on to what's left of my self-respect."

Jay was incredulous. "Oh, really? Let me get this straight. Smoking heroin and almost getting raped is okay for your self-respect, but kissing me isn't?"

He knew by the way her features hardened he shouldn't have thrown her mistakes in her face, no matter how much her reasoning sucked. "I'm sorry. I'm sorry," he said. He placed his hand on her cheek. "I'm sorry."

She shoved at his chest and started to get up.

"No." He grabbed her arms, not tight enough to hurt her but just enough to keep her on his lap, and growled, "Stay, dammit."

"You don't understand."

He struggled to keep his emotions in check, but he knew the look he gave her was intense. "What I understand is there's something between us that's driving us both insane. Don't go."

Her body was still stiff with resistance, but the air

between them was crackling. He was positive she wanted to kiss him as badly as he wanted to kiss her. "Come on, Erin. Don't fight it. I know you feel it, too." He gave her arms an imploring squeeze. "Stay here with me."

She grimaced. "I'm broken, Jay. You of all people know there's something wrong with me."

"Bullshit."

She swallowed thickly and shook her head. "I can't risk getting hurt. I can't take it anymore." After a hesitation, she added, "That's why I smoked the heroin."

"That doesn't make sense," Jay said, frowning.

She looked at him. "I smoked the heroin because I was trying to stop thinking about you."

"What?" He thought he couldn't have heard her right.

"I couldn't stop thinking about you," she said, her features twisting with torment, "and I—I needed relief."

Jesus. Jay was torn between elation she'd been thinking about him and horror she'd gone to such an extreme to get him out of her mind. Loosening his hold on her arms, he slid his hands up to her neck and rubbed the delicate line of her jaw with his thumbs. "Thinking about me is not a bad thing," he said gently.

Erin put her hands on his wrists. "Yes, it is," she said, her voice filled with anguish.

"Why?" With a small smile, he confessed, "If it helps, I've been thinking about you, too."

"It doesn't help. It gets my hopes up and sets me up for a bigger fall."

His chest tightened, and he wanted to murder every

bastard who'd ever hurt her, including himself. "I swear to you, darlin'. The last thing I want to do is hurt you."

"But you will, even if you don't intend to. Trust me. In my case, history always repeats itself."

He shook his head. "We'll take things slow. Let me prove myself. Give me a second chance."

"I never give second chances," she reminded him, but now she sounded doubtful, and her eyes touched him in a way that ignited a bonfire inside him.

"You know what they say about never," Jay said huskily. Working his fingers around to the nape of her neck, he pulled her to him. This time there was nothing light or tentative about the way he kissed her. He was hungry, and he crushed his mouth to hers, wanting to devour her.

Her lips fit perfectly with his, and when he probed with his tongue, she let him in and mingled with him, her tongue and mouth hot and moist. She tasted like chicken soup and toothpaste, and he'd never tasted anything so intoxicating.

She straddled his lap and melded herself to him, wrapping her arms around his neck, and he felt like his soul was about to take flight. She was sexy and soft and warm in all the right places. He wanted more of her but knew he'd never get enough, not in a million years.

A moan of pleasure escaped her throat, stoking the lust inside him. He loved the sound of that little moan, loved knowing she was enjoying this as much as he was.

Finally, when they started to taper off, Erin nipped

at his bottom lip with her teeth and rested her forehead against his. "Wow," she whispered.

Jay pressed his lips together to keep from grinning like a fool and tried to catch his breath.

"Are you sure you want to do this?" she asked. "Start something with me?"

Joy flooded through him so fast he couldn't find his voice, so he brushed a kiss across her lips to give himself a second. When he did speak, his voice was filled with emotion. "I don't want to do this with anyone but you."

"You deserve better, Jay."

"No," he said, closing his eyes and shaking his head. Now was the time. He should tell her he was Panhead, but he didn't have the balls to do it. All he could think about as he breathed her in was that she was finally in his arms, and he wasn't about to do anything that might make her leave. But he knew the truth. He wasn't the one who deserved better. She was.

"We'll take things slow?" She sounded so vulnerable.

He groaned, his body still begging to be with her. "What moron came up with that bright idea?"

Amusement sparkled in her eyes. "That would be you."

He smiled but then turned serious. "We can take things as slow as you want, as long as you promise you'll give me a chance. Just get to know me and let me get to know you. No more Jay the wheeler; no more Erin the dev. Just you and me," he said, pointing to her and then to himself.

She grabbed his finger and kissed the tip of it, making his heart jump, and said, "I promise."

Chapter 19

Erin loved watching Jay cook. His large, strong hands were nimble and skillful when he was chopping, and he could dice an onion at warp speed. The ripped shoulder and arm muscles under his plain navy T-shirt flexed and bulged with every little movement, the same way they did when he worked on his motorcycle.

He was one of those cooks who never measured stuff out, just went by taste and instinct. Whatever he did worked, though. So far he hadn't concocted anything that didn't delight Erin's taste buds.

It was beyond sexy. Who knew a guy at ease and confident in a kitchen could be such a turn-on? Then again, Jay would probably ooze masculinity even if he were wearing capri pants and a fanny pack.

Jay had to turn his wheelchair sideways to get as close to the counter as possible and stretch his arm up to the sink or stove to reach the knobs, since he couldn't stand. It was one of the few differences between him and an able-bodied cook. He also did most of his chopping and mixing and so forth on an all-purpose, sturdy wooden tray on his lap or at the table instead of at the counter.

The pots, pans, and dishes he used were in the lower cabinets within his reach, and most of his ingredients were on the lower shelves of the kitchen's small pantry.

Erin studied him as he concentrated on his latest concoction, stirring it with a wooden spoon at the stove. Blond stubble covered his jaw (no shock there), giving him a roguish appearance. He was wearing his Oakland A's baseball cap backward, his blond hair sticking out the back and flipping upward—but not in a girlie way— wherever it brushed his shoulders. He always wore a cap when he cooked as a precaution. Nobody liked hair with their meal, he said.

He had on loose jeans and white socks, and his thin legs were hugged in close to his well-engineered chair, designed to minimize ramming his feet into things. Erin liked how Jay's chair seemed a part of him, how it fit his personality. It was black and sporty, made with titanium parts that promised power and speed.

His feet rested perfectly together on the solid metal footplate. Their stillness made them look unnaturally prim and proper, but they didn't detract from Jay's appeal. Like everything else about him, the sight made Erin feel hot and restless low down in her belly and stole her breath for an instant.

She wondered if his newly found acceptance of her would last if she told him she'd just been perving on his paralyzed feet. He'd said he wanted to get to know *her*, not Erin the dev, but the harder she tried to separate the two, the less she succeeded. So much for ever being normal.

Disheartened and embarrassed by the direction of her thoughts, she shoved them away and said, "You ready for me to set the table?"

"Yeah," Jay replied absently, reaching up with a dish towel in his hand to grab hold of the handle of the stainless steel saucepan simmering on the stove.

He set the saucepan on his lap tray, which was not only handy but also protected his insensate legs from the pan's heat. He used his index finger to wipe up a bit of homemade red pasta sauce that had sloshed over the side, then popped it into his mouth.

It was a quick, totally unconscious gesture, but, again, Erin got a heated reaction in her nether regions— and was relieved that this time the cause was something normal. Jay's hands were big, masculine, and callused from years of pushing the wheels of his chair, yet they were also surprisingly elegant, and this wasn't the first time she'd wondered what those lean, graceful fingers of his could do to her.

She thought of the way her spine had prickled when he'd brushed his callused thumb over her cheek a week ago, then ever-so-lightly touched his lips to hers and told her he liked her.

Just get to know him, he'd said. Just give him a chance.

And then there was that second kiss, the one that made her toes curl and sent a zing through her veins. There had been other kisses since that one, kisses that pulled her deeper and deeper into the possibility of unequaled bliss . . . or unequaled despair. The more she was around Jay and got to know him, the more she liked him. He was everything she'd ever wanted in a guy: funny, intelligent, thoughtful, and affectionate, not to mention heart-stoppingly gorgeous.

He was also the perfect gentleman. Jay had kept his promise to take things slow. He'd never put any pressure on her to have sex, but even without that level of physical intimacy, they'd grown close in a very short amount of time.

Already Erin's feelings for him were intense, and she wasn't sure she could hold up her end of the bargain to take things slow. Sometimes she wanted Jay with a desire that was literally painful, and it was all she could do not to give in to her slutty side and drag him to the first bedroom she could find.

She felt like she was on a runaway train that wouldn't stop barreling down its tracks, no matter how hard she applied the brakes, sparks flying. She had the constant need to always be touching Jay in some way, to breathe in his clean maleness and feel his deep, buttery voice glide through her. She craved him more than she'd ever craved any guy, and it terrified her.

Not for the first time, Erin wondered what the hell she was doing. She was playing with fire by letting her guard down. Her brain screamed that trusting Jay was a bad idea, that it would only lead to heartache, but her heart countered that it ached painfully whenever he wasn't around.

Her track record when it came to relationships sucked, but maybe, for once in her life, she would catch a break and things would work out with Jay in spite of their rocky start. She'd decided to take the plunge, to let herself have a chance at happiness, because staying away from him definitely didn't make her happy.

After she finished setting the table, she dug out two of her grandmother's crystal wine glasses and added them to the settings as a finishing touch. She wasn't a wine person, but Jay—this rugged man who owned a Harley, a muscle car, and a huge Rottweiler-ish dog—had insisted the dish he was cooking needed red wine to go with it.

Erin kept discovering these things about him. Just when she thought she had him figured out, he surprised her with some new (sometimes incongruous) facet of his personality. She shouldn't be surprised by the wine, though. As much as he knew about cooking, it stood to reason he would know about wine, too.

Jay wheeled up to his usual spot at the table and removed his baseball cap, tossing it to the nearest empty dinette chair. His blond hair was flattened a little, but on Jay even hat-hair could be charming.

When Erin sat down and joined him, the aroma of the homemade sauce sitting on the table made her mouth water. Jay quickly plated their pasta, covered it with sauce, and then poured them some wine. Erin took a bite of the pasta and rolled her eyes with ecstasy as the heavenly flavor filled her mouth. "Oh, my God, Jay. This is awesome."

He smiled with satisfaction, his blue-gray eyes trained on her. His mouth was too full of his own bite to speak.

"You're a freaking genius." Erin wondered if he had some Italian mixed in with his blond-haired, blue-eyed, German-and-maybe-Viking ancestors. "Do you have some special, secret ingredient?"

He sat back and shrugged. "Just the stuff you saw me chopping. Fresh tomatoes, onion, peppers, garlic, and a bunch of other shit I threw in—spices and herbs. I like to experiment."

That made Erin think again of Nana, and she smiled. "My grandma cooked like that. She never used a recipe for anything. Zac and I tried it a couple of times—you know, experimenting."

Faint crinkles at the corners of Jay's eyes deepened. "Let me guess. It didn't turn out so well?"

"No." The memory turned Erin's smile rueful. "We almost burned down the house. Apparently," she said with feigned gravity, "water is bad for grease fires."

Jay chuckled, and the sound of it rippled through her, like someone was tickling the back of her neck with a feather. Suddenly feeling self-conscious and trying not to blush, she rolled another bite of pasta onto her fork and said, "What about you? How did you learn to cook?"

"I don't know. Just started messing around in the kitchen." He picked up the napkin on his lap and wiped his mouth. "I had to change the way I ate after my injury.

It's better if I'm careful about what I eat and drink and stay on a schedule, if I can. Sometimes it doesn't always happen because life gets in the way."

He looked down for a second, and then, as though he'd made a decision about something, he looked up at her, his expression frank. "The schedule helps, you know, with my bladder and bowel management." He cleared his throat. "Do you . . . know about all that?"

"Yeah," she answered with a nod. "I know."

He colored a little, which was unusual. He was usually so confident. "Sorry. Probably shouldn't bring that up during dinner."

"It's okay. It's not a big deal." She thrust the pasta still waiting on her fork into her mouth to emphasize her point. She knew he probably had to use a catheter to pee, and she knew what "bowel management" entailed: He had to use his fingers or a suppository to stimulate his bowel. She didn't care, and she didn't want him to be embarrassed or feel awkward about it. Everyone had to go somehow.

Jay seemed relieved he didn't have to go into more detail on the subject, and his shoulders relaxed. "When I was married, before I got hurt, my diet was crap, and Jennifer wasn't any help. She wasn't exactly Betty Crocker. Her idea of cooking was Hamburger Helper and asparagus from a can."

Erin scrunched her nose. "Canned asparagus is disgusting. But what's wrong with Hamburger Helper?"

"It comes from a box," he said, like the answer was

obvious.

"Don't knock the box."

He tilted his head a bit and shook it. "That shit is all preservatives, darlin'. It's bad for you. You should be more careful what you put into your body."

It warmed Erin from the inside out that he cared, and she smiled. "I'll keep that in mind, Dr. Oz."

"I'm serious."

"Trust me," said Erin. "My body will go into convulsions if I put too much healthy stuff in it."

Jay rolled his eyes and pursed his mouth disapprovingly, but then he studied her, the ghost of his trademark smirk telling her he wasn't really annoyed—far from it.

Her skin tingled when she noticed the intent way he was looking at her, and she grinned for no real reason, other than she couldn't hold it in anymore. God, what he did to her. She had to look down for a second to keep yet another blush at bay.

"So, after Jennifer split," she prompted, getting back to the original subject, "you got into cooking?"

He traced his jaw with his fingers, making a rasping noise against his stubble. "Yeah. It wasn't like there was anyone else to do it, and it was kind of therapeutic in a way. Cooking relaxes me, gets my mind off things. It's a lot like science, like chemistry. It's all about discovering what ingredients work together and which ones don't."

"No wonder I'm so bad at cooking." She made a face. "I suck at science, and I got a C in high school chemistry."

She took a sip of her wine and liked the way it went down her throat, warm and spicy. Jay had been right. It enhanced the taste of the pasta, made the flavors more intense. She vaguely remembered this from another life, when she'd been a different person, before things had gone all wrong. It was something pleasant she'd forgotten, like a really good pedicure. Or the era when MTV actually showed music videos.

"It's not that hard," said Jay, breaking into her reverie. "Once you know the basics of cooking, you can get creative. But the biggest thing I've learned? The ingredients have to be fresh, not from a box."

"Yeah, yeah," Erin said, but she was smiling. "Whatever your secret is, you're awesome at it. You should be proud."

He broke eye contact with her and muttered a sardonic "Yeah" before forking a bite of pasta.

Erin frowned. "Why did you say 'yeah' like that?"

He looked up at her. "It's nothing. Just something you said made me think of my old man."

"Oh," she said. "I take it that's not a good thing."

Jay wiped his mouth and sat back. "He thought I was a pussy for taking up cooking. When it was clear I wasn't ever gonna walk again, he thought I should man up and try to overcome my disability—you know, do something macho like snow ski in the Paralympics or drag my ass up fucking Mount Everest. Needless to say, the cooking was a disappointment."

"God. I'm sorry."

Jay shrugged as if to dismiss it, but she could sense the pain behind it. "You know," he said, "I used to be a mechanic in his garage. The original plan was I'd eventually become his partner, but he never wanted me back after my accident."

Her heart twisted.

"I still could have done it—worked with him. I just needed to adapt a few things, mostly just get things within my reach, because everything's about height when you're in a chair, you know? But he wouldn't have it." He stared out the kitchen window at the dark backyard, a muscle ticking in his jaw.

Erin's whole body tensed with biting fury. "Your dad's a jackass."

"No argument there," Jay said, turning back to her and giving her an ironic version of his smirk. "But there's always a silver lining, right? At least the asshole never tried to hit me again."

Erin was disgusted by that and sorry for Jay, and it must have shown on her face.

"Come on, darlin'. Don't look at me like that. I don't even know why I was thinking about it. It all went down years ago."

"How long ago was it?"

He glanced away for a second, seemed to think about it, and said, "2005."

"That's . . . a long time."

"Yeah."

Something disturbing niggled at the back of Erin's mind. "How old are you?"

"Twenty-nine," he said, watching her.

Her stomach clenched. Jay was twenty-nine, and 2005 would make it eight years since his accident. Just like Panhead.

No, no, no. It couldn't be. Was she the biggest dumbass on the planet or just paranoid?

Jay said something to her, but she had no clue what it was. "Um, what did you say?"

He smiled, and there was nothing suspicious about it. It didn't shout, *I've been Panhead all along, and you've been duped.* "I asked how old you were," he said.

"Oh. Twenty-six," she managed to answer, but her mind was still on Panhead.

No. Stop. She wouldn't go there. It would be mortifying, and she didn't want to ruin whatever good thing was developing between her and Jay by bringing up Panhead.

So there were similarities. He *wasn't* Panhead. Jay wouldn't do that to her. He would tell her. And she didn't want to creep him out by admitting she was chatting from time to time with a wheeler from a dev website— which she would have to do if she asked him about it. She realized she was the one deceiving him, not the other way around, and she felt guilty. She would have to end her chats with Panhead.

"Tell me about your bike," Erin said quickly, changing the subject before Jay picked up on the fact that she was having an internal freak-out.

He watched her for what seemed a second too long and said, "What do you want to know?"

She half-shrugged. "I don't know anything about motorcycles. Are you rebuilding it from scratch?"

"Yeah. Pretty much."

"It's a Harley, right?"

"Yeah." He sipped his wine.

She hesitated, not sure if she should ask him the question she'd been wondering about since the first time she'd seen him working on the bike.

He grinned wryly. "Let me guess. You want to know why a dude with paraplegia is restoring a bike he'll never be able to ride?"

She was a little embarrassed but curious enough to admit the truth. "Yeah."

"It's okay." He spoke with a bit of his usual smirk but then grew pensive. "I don't know. It's symbolic, I guess."

"The bike's symbolic?"

"Yeah." He sat back in his chair and loosely gripped his tires. "It's the bike I broke my back on."

"Oh."

"I figure if I can rebuild it, I can rebuild my life, too."

"Oh," Erin said again. What he'd just said was kind of profound, and she was moved by it. She wasn't sure what to say.

"It's stupid, right?" He sounded uncertain—a rare thing for Jay. He ran a hand through his hair. "Jesus, I sound like a pussy. Maybe my old man was right."

"No, he wasn't," Erin said softly, a little in awe of him. "I think it must take a lot of strength to face something so painful. But I don't get it. I mean, it looks to me like you've done a pretty good job of rebuilding your life. You make a decent living. You've moved on and done well for yourself."

He nodded. "In some ways, yeah. But I've been injured a long time, and it's still taken me all this time to even be able to look at it—the bike."

"I would think that's normal. I can't believe you even kept it."

"Yeah. I guess that is kind of strange."

"Maybe a little," she said with a smile, "but I get it. It's a symbol of your survival."

He nodded again. "I started restoring it last year, and it gives me this feeling of satisfaction to see that I'm making progress. It was pretty much a hunk of scrap metal."

Erin tried not to wince. The thought of Jay being on that bike when it was turned into scrap metal made her feel ill.

"Restoring it is just something I have to do, like a personal quest or some shit like that."

She smiled. "So, what will you do with the bike once you're finished?"

He shook his head. "I don't know. I thought about giving it to my little brother, but it's got bad mojo now, you know?"

Erin nodded. "You could sell it."

"Yeah, but I don't know that I could sell it to someone in good conscience without telling them about the bad mojo. It would be sort of like trying to sell a haunted house." After a beat, a slow, caustic smirk spread across his handsome features. "Maybe I'll give it to my dad."

She laughed. "That's a great idea."

His smirk softened into a grin that made her stomach flutter. God, he was a gorgeous man, and she wanted to be closer to him. As if he had read her mind, his grin disappeared, his face became intense, and his eyes locked onto hers. He pushed his chair out from the table and held out his hand. She placed hers in his warm rough one, and he pulled her onto his lap in one smooth move.

Erin put her arm around his shoulders and looked down at him. With her free hand, she cradled his face. She loved the feel of the soft-yet-scratchy golden stubble on his jaw that tickled her palm.

"I'm gonna kiss you now, if that's okay," he said, his blue eyes darkening sensually.

Her heart did a somersault. "Um, yeah. A kiss would be good."

He smiled and worked his fingers into her hair, making her scalp tingle. Then he brought her mouth to his. Her senses were overwhelmed: his spicy, clean scent mixed with the aromas and flavors from their dinner, his thick, soft hair brushing against her arm, and his hard, muscular chest against her breast. His mouth was hot, and his tongue played with hers in a dance that seared her insides.

When they came up for air, she hugged him tightly, burying her head in the curve of his shoulder. Her heart was beating wildly, and she felt flushed and breathless. "Thank you," she whispered next to his ear, and then she pulled back a little to see his face.

His eyes were still hooded and filled with the heat of their kiss. "For what?"

She grazed her fingertips over his lips. "For . . . " She trailed off and looked down, feeling shy all of a sudden. Reminding herself she wasn't a sixteen-year-old girl, she looked him in the eye and gave him a tender smile. "For being such a gentleman. For respecting me. For—I don't know—courting me, I guess? And for being patient."

He pulled her in for another kiss, this one short and deliciously sweet. When he spoke, his voice was silk against her skin. "Trust me, darlin'. You're worth the wait."

Chapter 20

emanomaly: So, I'm sorry, but I can't chat with you anymore.

Panhead: Why not?

emanomaly: You're not going to believe this, but it has to do with my roommate.

Panhead: The wheeler? What does he have to do with it?

emanomaly: Things have changed with him.

Panhead: Changed how?

emanomaly: How to say this without jinxing it . . .

Panhead: Say what? Are you starting to like him?

There was a pause.

emanomaly: Yes.

Jay's heart expanded. He worked the wheels of his chair back and forth as he stared at the screen of his laptop, trying to keep from pumping his fists in the air like a dork. Chopper, who was lying on his papasan cushion next to Jay's bed, pricked up his ears and opened one eye.

"She likes me," Jay said to him, arching a brow. It wasn't like he didn't already know, but it was nice to have definite confirmation.

Chopper was unimpressed and closed his eye. Grinning, Jay shook his head and got back to typing.

> *Panhead:* Wow. You like him?
>
> *emanomaly:* It's a bad idea, I know. I'm an idiot for getting involved with him, but I can't help it.
>
> *Panhead:* Why does that make you an idiot?
>
> *Emanomaly:* Because every single relationship I've ever had has ended shitty, especially the ones with wheelers.
>
> *Panhead:* That doesn't mean this one will.
>
> *emanomaly:* True. But the odds are stacked against me. You'd think, at some point, I'd see a pattern and stop.
>
> *Panhead:* You can't be alone forever. It goes against human nature. You should take the risk and go for it.
>
> *emanomaly:* Yeah, well, I guess I'll see where it goes. That's why I can't chat with you anymore.
>
> *Panhead:* He doesn't want you to?
>
> *emanomaly:* He doesn't know, and I don't want him to. I would be embarrassed if he knew I was chatting with someone from the dev website. He says he's okay now with the dev thing, but I don't feel right about it. And I don't want to lie to him.

Yeah. Lying was bad. Jay shoved back the guilt jabbing at his conscience and let relief trickle in. This was the perfect solution. He wouldn't have to tell Erin anything. The Panhead/emanomaly thing could die a quiet death, both sides mutually agreeing it should end, and Erin never had to know he was Panhead. He'd been trying to find a way to tell her, but it never seemed to be the right time.

Things had been going so well with her. She'd even opened up to him about a few things, but the fact that she'd never mentioned her writing told him she still didn't quite trust him. The last thing he wanted to do was tell her he'd been lying to her for weeks. She already had trust issues. Maybe she would understand; maybe she wouldn't. But he didn't want to do anything to ruin what was budding between them. Why take the risk if he didn't have to?

> *Panhead:* I understand.
>
> *emanomaly:* I'll miss chatting with you.
>
> *Panhead:* Me, too. I guess this means I won't get to read any more of your writing?
>
> *emanomaly:* Oh! I forgot. I got the comments you e-mailed about my novel. Thanks. They were REALLY helpful.
>
> *Panhead:* It's a great story. There's only a few things I would change from the wheeler's perspective. Most of the stuff, you nailed. The wheeler dude is believable and realistic, and the mystery part is good, too.

emanomaly: Thanks!! You don't know how much that means to me.

Panhead: It's just the truth.

emanomaly: So . . . I have other stuff I've written.

Panhead: About wheelers?

emanomaly: No. Nothing like that. Just stuff I've started but never finished because I thought it was crap. One is a thriller. One is a romance.

Panhead: Can I take a look?

emanomaly: You really want to, or are you just being nice?

Panhead: I really want to.

There was another long pause, and then, finally, something popped up.

emanomaly: I'm grappling.

Panhead: With what?

emanomaly: Well, in order for you to read more of my writing, we have to keep chatting.

She was right. What the hell was he doing? He'd been given a reprieve, a painless way to end the chats where Erin would never have to find out, and he'd just screwed it up.

Panhead: Now that things are going well with your roommate, maybe you should show your stuff to him and let him read it instead of me.

emanomaly: I'm not ready for that yet. He doesn't even know I'm a writer.

Panhead: You live with the guy. How could he not know?

emanomaly: It's not something I advertise. My last boyfriend who knew about my writing didn't take it seriously and thought it was a waste of time. I'm not ready to go there with my roomie.

Panhead: Don't you trust him?

emanomaly: Everything's still new. We're gradually revealing things to each other, and I'm going to have to really, really, really, really trust him before I let him see my work. Plus, right now, it's about him and me and nothing else. I don't want to complicate things with my hang-ups about my writing or my devness or anything else. That's the way he said he wants it, too. Just him and me.

Before Jay could respond, she added something else.

emanomaly: You don't have to look at my other stuff. I understand if you don't want to or don't have time or whatever. It's not even finished.

He couldn't stand to let her think he didn't want to, although he was stupid for keeping Panhead alive. Blowing out a frustrated breath, he started typing.

Panhead: Did I say I didn't want to?

emanomaly: No.

Panhead: I really want to.

emanomaly: You sure?

Panhead: Yes.

emanomaly: You're the shit. You don't have to read the romance. I know guys aren't into that sort of thing.

Panhead: I like romance. *Transformers* is one of my favorite movies.

emanomaly: *eye roll* Sorry to break it to you, but *Transformers* is not a romance.

Panhead: Shia LaBeouf has the hots for Megan Fox. It's a romance.

emanomaly: Right.

Panhead: Are you rolling your eyes again?

emanomaly: Yes.

Panhead: I'll read your romance anyway. I'm a sensitive guy.

emanomaly: I'm sure. :) I can't believe I'm letting you read my raw stuff. What is it about you?

If she only knew.

* * *

Erin studied Jay's hand. They were lying on their backs in the backyard on a blanket, soaking in the sun. The temperature was relatively mild in San Antonio for the last day of May. It had been a hot spring, but today there was a blue sky, a nice breeze, and it wasn't too hot—sort of a reprieve before the real heat of summer kicked in.

They'd just taken Chopper for a walk and weren't ready to go in yet. Jay had taken his T-shirt off to cool down. His eyes were closed, but Erin didn't think he was asleep.

She was wearing knee-length yoga pants and a racer-back purple tank top that accentuated her boobs, which Jay seemed to do a lot of staring at when he thought she wasn't paying attention. She smiled to herself.

Their elbows rested at their sides on the blanket and their hands were suspended in the air between them, so Erin had a good view. His hand was warm and beautifully male, and she liked the way his long fingers interlocked with her smaller ones, making her feel safe. As happened often when she was with Jay, she got a tingle in her belly that made its way down to parts unmentionable.

Inhaling a deep breath to get her hormones under control, she squinted at a wispy cloud overhead. How long was an appropriate time to wait for sex when you were taking things slow?

She and Jay spent every moment together they could when they weren't working. They took Chopper for walks and both loved to be outdoors. If she was off from the bar, she would hang out with Jay while he worked on his Harley in the evenings. Sometimes they would talk about anything and everything, and sometimes they sat in companionable silence—Jay working on his bike, Erin reading a book or a magazine, content to be near him.

They had different tastes in music. He was into classic rock and heavy metal (but not any cheesy '80s hair bands, thank God), and she was into more obscure indie and alternative rock. Jay was open-minded, however, and she'd introduced him to some of her favorite bands. Some he liked; some he didn't. Some of it was too weird or too mellow for him, and they would playfully argue over whose iPod got plugged into the living room speakers.

They liked a lot of the same movies and TV shows and had the same sense of humor. He took her on real dates, like out to dinner or to see a movie, not just to Lars for beer with a side of weed like Duncan.

He treated her like a man should treat a woman, something she hadn't experienced since she'd been engaged to Trynt. And, although Trynt had taken her to fancy restaurants and such because that's what someone of his social standing did (because keeping up appearances was everything), he'd never really respected her or her opinions. Jay did.

Maybe she was ready for the next step, but she felt nervous about it, like she was a freaking virgin or something. Jay had never said anything to pressure her, but she knew he was ready. All she had to do was say the word. It was just that she wanted so much for things to be perfect with him and dreaded the inevitable awkwardness that would come with sex.

In the past, when she'd been with wheelers, most of them had made it about her from the get-go. That might seem like a good thing to most women, to be the sole focus of a guy's attention, but it wasn't as great as it sounded. Because wheelers couldn't feel anything below the belt and didn't expect to get anything out of it themselves (at least the ones Erin had been with), by the time she came (if she did), they were over it, easily getting bored with the whole thing.

One guy had actually checked his watch while she'd been on top of him, about to come. Needless to say, she hadn't. She'd been humiliated; he'd been an asshole.

Erin didn't want it to be that way with Jay. He seemed to genuinely care about her, though, so maybe it would be different with him. She hoped that was part of it, that being with someone he liked would help with his pleasure.

She reminded herself he'd been injured a long time and should know what to expect. But he'd never been with a dev. What if he expected more than she could deliver? She didn't know any special secrets to make him orgasm if he couldn't feel anything in his southern parts, although she was willing to try just about anything. She wanted him to experience mind-blowing pleasure, and she wanted to be the one to give it to him.

Maybe Panhead was right. Erin felt comfortable around Jay and liked the easy, bantering relationship they'd fallen into. Maybe she should trust him completely—not just about the sex, but with her writing. Maybe she should at least let him read the novel she'd finished, if nothing else.

Her stomach contracted into itself at the mere suggestion. She felt exposed—stripped—at the thought of Jay reading her writing. Panhead had liked her portrayal of the wheeler in her novel, but what if Jay thought it was stupid? What if she'd botched it horribly and Panhead was just being nice by saying it was good? What if parts of it reminded Jay of her devness? She wanted to downplay that with him, not emphasize it.

If it came down to it, she'd rather take a chance at having bad sex with him than let him read her work— and that was saying a lot. The thought of him reading her stuff was like having severe stage fright—the worst, most immobilizing kind imaginable.

She studied Jay's silhouette. His eyes were still closed, and his lashes, which looked more brown than blond, skimmed his cheek. His nose was straight and nicely shaped, his cheekbones broad and chiseled; his jawline, which was covered with blond stubble that could pretty much be called a beard at this point, was firm and masculine. She was eating crow for insisting she didn't like blonds. Jay was blond, and he was a god.

Lying on his back as he was, Erin could see how long his legs were. If he could stand, he would dwarf her. Because he was lying flat, his slight paunch had disappeared, and his loose gray sweatpants (apparently he didn't own any other color) rode low on his narrow hips. The black waistband of his boxers peeked out above his sweats, and even that little detail was unexpectedly sexy.

Wiry, blond-brown hair dusted his muscular chest—not hairy-as-a-gorilla, old-geezer hair, but still enough to be manly—and it tapered into a thin trail that traveled down his belly and disappeared into his boxers.

Erin couldn't resist. She carefully laid his hand, which was still entwined with hers, onto his stomach, then turned onto her side, propped up her head with her elbow, and lightly ran her fingertip over the hair on his chest.

His lids popped open, and she found herself looking into a pair of silvery blue eyes, made lighter by the sun.

She leaned in close to him and kissed the tender spot just below his ear. "Hi."

His mouth curved up on one side. "Anyone ever teach you about personal space, darlin'?" he teased in his easy California drawl.

She ran her hand along his soft beard and smiled. "Anyone ever teach you how to use a razor, darlin'?"

"You want me to shave?"

She raised her brows. "Would you if I asked?"

His eyes got sultry. "I'd do anything for you."

Holy horny toad. He had an uncanny ability to disarm her with a few simple words. A lump of emotion clogged her throat, leaving her speechless for a second before she said, "You don't need to shave. I like you any way you come."

He reached toward her face as if to touch it but stopped in midmotion. Grimacing, he closed his eyes and dropped his hand.

Her heart sank. "Your back is hurting again?"

He grunted noncommittally. The grimace went away, but there was still a tightness around his closed eyes, and he looked drained.

She placed her palm on his face and gently turned his head toward her. "Jay, how long has it been since you had a good night's sleep?"

"1987."

"I'm serious."

He opened his eyes. "So am I. That's how long it feels like it's been."

"Would a back rub help? If you turn over onto your stomach, I'll give you one."

His jaw tensed and his tone grew harsh. "It won't help. Nothing does, so why fucking bother?"

Erin didn't know how to respond. She knew his anger wasn't directed at her and she hated that he was hurting, but she knew he wouldn't want her pity.

His irritation fizzled as quickly as it surfaced, and he let out a sigh. "I'm sorry. I didn't mean to be a dick. I just get so damned tired of it sometimes, and I haven't slept in days." He brushed his knuckles along her cheek. "I'd have to be insane to turn down a back rub from you. I'd appreciate it, if you still want to."

Still want to? She had visions of running her palms all over the sun-warmed skin of Jay's broad, powerful back. The pleasure would be all hers. "I think I could still be persuaded."

Cupping the nape of her neck, he pulled her toward

him to give her a kiss. It was one of the toe-curling ones, the kind that scrambled Erin's brain and made her forget to breathe. When they broke apart, she stared into his eyes, hypnotized by them.

"How was that?" he asked, his voice sounding a little gravelly.

"How was what?"

"The kiss."

Her brain still wasn't firing on all four cylinders, but she knew he was getting at something. "Um, great?" she hedged.

He flashed his white teeth in a smile. "I mean, was it persuasive enough?"

"Oh, my God. *Yes.*"

Jay chuckled at her heartfelt response, and the smooth rumble of it was contagious. Erin snickered. "Um, so, what was it I was supposed to be persuaded to do?"

"Back rub."

"Oh, right."

Erin sat up and, after Jay rolled onto his belly, she helped him put his long legs in the right position. Only the upper half of his torso moved whenever he turned over, so his legs had to be manually untwisted. He could do it himself, of course, but Erin liked that he was letting her help and that he didn't seem self-conscious about it. The small squeeze of lust she got while touching his heavy, thin legs, she fiercely and doggedly ignored.

Once he was settled, head turned toward her and resting on his bent arms, Erin got to work. She ran her hands over the steely sinew of his back and shoulders in a cursory rubdown and tried not to drool. Then, starting with his neck, she rubbed and kneaded at the knots there. She wasn't a professional masseuse by any means, but even she could tell he was wound way too tight. "Tell me if I do anything that hurts. I don't want to make the pain worse."

"Mmm," he groaned with pleasure. He turned his head forward, resting his forehead on his forearm and exposing more of the back of his neck. His words were muffled when he said, "Trust me, darlin'. There's no way you could ever make it worse."

Erin's hands glided over his warm skin easily as she moved down to his inked shoulders, and it was every bit as good as she'd imagined. No gross back hair, just smooth, bronzed skin that got warmer and warmer with her touch. She ran her hand over his tattoo, the one on his left shoulder with the intricate lettering. "What does your tat say?"

He snorted. "It used to say 'Jennifer.' Now it says 'loyalty' if you look at it one way and 'betrayal' if you look at it upside down."

Erin paused and studied the tat, cocking her head to one side. Now that he'd explained it, she could see the hidden words. "Oh, my God," she said, widening her eyes. "That is so cool. It's amazing the tattoo guy could do that."

"Not tattoo guy—tattoo girl," he corrected. "She was a fucking genius."

"Apparently. That's some of the coolest ink I've ever seen. And she completely covered up the 'Jennifer' part." *Thank God,* Erin added to herself, feeling a twinge of jealousy. "I don't have anything that good, but I have a few tramp stamps I got when I was drunk."

Jay turned his head slightly more toward her, a sudden mischievous gleam in his eye. "I know."

"How would you know?"

"You were a mess that night—or morning—I got you home from your brush with the A-bomb, so I helped you take a bath."

"Oh," she said, pressing her lips together to hide a smile. She was a little embarrassed and a lot intrigued that he'd seen her naked. The realization gave her goose bumps. "Sorry about that."

He grinned, then closed his eyes as she resumed the massage. "Trust me, darlin'. You have nothing to be sorry for."

For that, he got a kiss on the spot behind his ear again, and it made his grin grow bigger.

Erin worked methodically down his back and was glad he couldn't see when she winced at the long, vertical surgical scar from his SCI that ran along his spine.

After a few minutes, he looked over his shoulder at her. "Erin?"

"What?"

He glanced pointedly at her hands, which were massaging his lower back. "I can't feel that."

"Oh. Sorry. But your muscles are doing weird things

down here. They're spasming or something. I think it would help to get out the knots."

He didn't say anything, just turned his head and rested his chin on his arm, but Erin didn't miss the annoyed tic in his jaw.

She felt like she was doing some good, but first and foremost, her purpose was to soothe Jay, and it was clear he didn't like her touching where he couldn't feel. When she moved her hands back up above his waistline, he flinched as if she'd tickled him, but then he relaxed. "That's better. Thanks."

She massaged for a minute in silence, trying to decide if she should pursue the subject of his back pain. Her concern won out. "Jay, why do you live with the pain? Maybe you should see a doctor."

"Wouldn't do any good."

"Why not?"

"Some things a doctor can't fix."

"But—"

"Look. My back hurts because three of my vertebrae were shattered, my nerves are all fucked up, and I've got enough hardware in me to open a Home Depot."

She cringed. "I'm sorry."

"Don't be."

"I didn't mean . . . That wasn't pity."

"I know. I didn't take it that way. But there's no reason you should be sorry. 'S just how it is."

"The pain's been worse lately, though. Right?"

He didn't respond, but his silence was answer enough.

"You should go to a doctor, Jay."

His shoulder lifted in a half-shrug. "You think I haven't? There's nothing a doctor can do. That's what the last three I went to in California said. 'Sorry about ya, Jay. You're shit outta luck.'"

Erin didn't want to believe nothing could be done. "Then go to someone here in San Antonio. There has to be something to make it better. What about surgery?"

Jay scoffed. "There's always some doc willing to cut into me, but the payout is shoddy at best."

"What do you mean?"

"There's a lot of shit involved with surgery—hospital stay, recovery time, possible complications—and I would need . . . help . . . afterward."

Her heart clutched, knowing it was hard for him to admit that. "I would help you."

"No. I wouldn't ask you to do that. I'd have to go back to California, and I sure as hell don't like the thought of having to rely on my old man. Besides, there's no guarantee surgery will help when it's all said and done. Most SCI pain has to do with nerves and neurological problems that can't be fixed. Might as well stick with the status quo."

"But what if it keeps getting worse?"

"I'll deal," he said stubbornly.

"That's ridiculous. Maybe—"

"Erin," he said, turning to look at her, "just let it go."

She bit her lower lip, wanting to argue, but his unbending tone told her this wasn't an argument she would win anytime soon.

Chapter 21

An enormous, slobbery, foul-breathed water buffalo was licking her ear. When Erin opened her eyes, she realized it was just Chopper, who took up a large portion of her queen-sized bed. "Gotta get you some doggy breath mints," she grumbled.

Chopper's response was a direct lick to her mouth.

"Blech!" She turned over to escape her amorous companion.

Daylight streamed in through slim openings in the slightly tattered curtains of Erin's room. She looked toward the door, expecting to see Jay wearing the playful smirk he always wore when he let Chopper in to join her in the mornings, but he wasn't there. That was strange. She must not have shut her door all the way last night and Chopper had let himself in. But where was Jay?

Still not fully awake, Erin clumsily patted Chopper on his huge head and sat up, then swung her legs over the side of the bed.

Chopper jumped off the bed, went to the door, then circled back to put his meaty front paws on the mattress. He began wagging his bushy tail so hard the entire back half of his body moved, causing the bed to shake.

"You need to go outside?"

"Woof!" Chopper's tail wagged even more frantically, and he went back to the door. He sat down, giving Erin a woeful look.

Had Jay not let him out yet? Surely he had.

Erin eased off the bed and padded barefoot out into the hallway, where she stood by Jay's door to listen. She didn't hear anything, so she carefully opened the door a crack and peeked in. Jay was lying on his stomach, his face toward her, sound asleep for once.

No wonder Chopper had woken her. He was probably about to burst.

Erin frowned. This wasn't like Jay. It was a weekday. Usually, by this time, he'd been up for several hours, working either at home on his laptop or at his office with Luis and a couple of other IT guys.

She knew his back was the reason he'd overslept. Erin had broached the subject of seeing a doctor a few other times since her original conversation with him about it, but he always cut her off and changed the subject. No matter what he said, however, it was clear the pain was still keeping him from sleeping and was starting to affect his work. He'd been awake at one-thirty last night when she'd gotten home from her shift at Lars, and she'd heard him in the living room moving around when she fell asleep around two-thirty.

Jay would probably want Erin to wake him, but she decided to wait a bit. He needed the rest, and he looked so peaceful in sleep, kind of like a really hot fallen angel.

She rolled her eyes at her own cheesiness. God, she was turning into such a sap. She shut his door, then headed down the hall toward the kitchen to let a now-dancing Chopper outside.

While Chopper was in the backyard doing his business, Erin started coffee brewing and checked her cell phone to see if she had any messages. There was one from Zac. He'd called earlier that morning, at 3:47 a.m.

Erin shook her head. Her brother had no concept of time. His days and nights were completely turned around, not that she could talk. Had it been a few weeks earlier, she probably would have been up at that time, too. Last night, though, she'd gone almost straight to bed, exhausted from work. She was glad the phone had been on the kitchen counter and hadn't woken her.

Since she'd been seeing Jay, she wasn't drinking as much on the job anymore—in fact, hardly at all—and without the beer and shots to give her false confidence and energy, she found she was ready to go to bed most nights when she got home instead of being wired.

This was better all the way around. She slept more soundly without the alcohol coursing through her veins—no beer wakies—and she'd been writing more first thing in the morning after she got up. What a shocker: She found she was more creative and positive about her writing after a good night's sleep.

For the first time in a long time, she was motivated to make something of herself. Most of all, though, she wanted to be worthy of Jay.

Zac didn't leave a voice mail. He never did. After pouring herself a mug of coffee, Erin tapped his name from the favorites list on her phone. His phone rang and then went to voice mail. She glanced at the microwave clock and saw it was 10:12 a.m.—an ungodly hour for Zac. She smiled wickedly and texted "wake up" over and over until he called her back.

"Hello?" she answered.

"What the fuck, Erin!" he griped. "What's with the text abuse?"

"I wanted you to answer your phone."

"What time is it?" Zac's voice was thick with sleep and scratchy, probably from singing and smoking the night before.

"Midmorning," she said, feigning innocence.

There was a shuffling noise, and then he sounded indignant. "It's ten fucking—this is cruel! Call me back in four hours."

She laughed. "I saw you called last night. Were you drunk-dialing, or did you actually need to talk to me?"

He sighed heavily, conveying his annoyance. "Both." Then the grumpiness left his voice and it softened. "Mostly, I had the beer blues and was missing my sister."

Erin was touched. Zac could be sweet sometimes. They had their ups and downs, like any siblings did, but they had a strong bond that could never be broken.

A sudden pang of remorse slid through her. She'd tried to end her life, and it would have devastated Zac. It was the stupidest thing she'd ever done in a long line of stupid things. Sometimes the weight of it, the profound shame of it, threatened to eat her up from the inside out.

It was ironic Jay had triggered the suicide attempt because he was now a huge reason Erin was glad she was alive. And then there was Zac. It would have been such a shitty thing to do to her brother.

She cleared her throat to get the guilt out of her voice and tried to sound normal. "I miss you, too, Zacky."

He sucked in a horrified breath. Knowing how he hated that nickname, Erin shook off her morose thoughts and smiled. Ah, the joys of tormenting her twin.

"Dude, I'm taking the high road here," Zac said in a lofty tone. "I did *not* just hear you call me that."

"So what did you want to talk about?"

"Just wondering how the ankle is."

Erin was wearing a tank top and short pajama boxers, so her legs were bare. She looked down at her bad ankle. Her physical therapy had ended almost two weeks ago. Sometimes her ankle was still stiff and swollen if she was on it too much, but, for the most part, it was much better. The scar from her surgery, however, was a different story. It would always be a reminder of something she wanted desperately to forget. "It's fine," she answered cautiously.

"Good. Get this," Zac said, excitement evident in his voice. "The response to us has been excellent, so our sponsor wants to extend the tour through the rest of the summer and into the fall."

Erin laughed with genuine happiness for her brother. "Oh, my God, Zac. That's awesome."

"Yep. So now that your ankle is better, you can join us. We'll be in New Orleans in a week. You can catch up with us there. Bryan will get you a ticket on Southwest." Bryan was the band's manager.

Erin pressed her lips together, thinking about the last couple of weeks she'd shared with Jay. She didn't want to leave him. Who would rub his back and bug him about seeing a doctor if she wasn't here? Then again, who was she kidding? Jay didn't need a nurse. Even though he was being stubborn about the doctor thing, he was one of the strongest, most capable people she knew.

The simple truth was, Erin would miss him horribly. Who would kiss her breathless and make her heart do pleasant, flippy-floppy things? The thought of leaving him was . . . well, she just didn't want to think about it.

"Erin?" prompted Zac. "You still there?"

"Yeah. I'm here."

"So, what do you think? You ready to come back?"

"What about the house?"

"What about it?"

"Jay's lease is almost up."

"Uh, like at the end of next month, and we just started this one." Zac sounded annoyed that she'd mentioned it, like it wasn't a big deal. "Hopefully, Jay will be willing to sign another lease. If not, we'll find another renter."

"What if it's not that easy?"

"We'll deal. What does that have to do with you

coming on the tour?"

Erin shrugged, even though she knew Zac couldn't see her. "I just think one of us needs to be here to take care of all that."

"Has Jay hinted that he's not going to renew?"

"No."

"Then why are you worrying over something that might not even happen?"

"I don't know." Erin searched for another excuse. "Don't you think it'll be unfair to Nate to kick him off the tour after he was cool enough to take my place at the last minute?"

"Nate's the problem. He's got a family. His baby mama is bitching at him to get back home because she's tired of taking care of their kid by herself. Personally, I think he's a wuss. I think he's just using his girl as an excuse because he's getting sick of the road."

Imagine that. Getting sick of sleeping in a tiny, cramped RV with three other people and only one minuscule bathroom where showers were iffy to nonexistent; playing mostly small dingy venues that reeked of stale smoke and beer; waking up every day in a different city, usually with a hangover. It got exhausting and old after a while, and Erin hadn't really been looking forward to it, although she wanted the band to succeed for Zac's sake.

It wasn't the life she wanted for herself, but she hadn't drummed up the courage to tell her brother yet. The band was everything to him, and he assumed it was for her, too. The truth would hurt and disappoint him.

"Erin, what the fuck? Why all the roadblocks all of a sudden? I mean, come on," Zac coaxed. "The band needs you. Is it the ankle? I swear we'll be careful. I mean, hello. You'll be on it less on the road than you will be on your feet working at Lars."

Erin sighed, knowing she needed to come clean. If she was going to be a better person, she needed to start by telling her brother the truth, no matter how difficult. It was probably what Jay would do if he were in the same situation. "Zac, it's not the ankle."

"Huh?"

"It's not the ankle."

"Then what is it?"

She stalled for a second, tracing the rim of her steaming coffee mug with her finger. "The band—I mean, don't get me wrong. I'm really, really happy things are taking off for you."

"It's not just me, Erin. You're still a part of it. There will always be a place for you. It's your band as much as mine."

She rubbed the back of her neck with her hand and stared down at her bare feet. "Thank you for saying that, but . . . "

When she didn't finish, he prompted, "But what?"

She inhaled a fortifying breath and let it out. "Zac," she said gently, "the band has always been your dream, not mine."

"What the fuck are you talking about?"

"I—I don't want to do it anymore."

Silence.

"I'm sorry," she said.

"No way. Uh-uh."

"You don't need me."

"What?" He sounded outraged. "No one—*no one* can replace you, Erin. No one. I thought this was a family thing, that we'd always stick together. It's not the same without you."

The injured, betrayed tone of Zac's voice sliced Erin to the core. She started to waver. She loved her brother, and saying no to him was killing her, but she needed to be strong. This was about doing what was right for her for once and not living her life for someone else. "You'll be fine, Zac. Like I said, you don't really need me."

"That is such bullshit," Zac said angrily. "I hate being away from you. Do you know how much I've missed you? This is the longest we've ever been apart."

"Oh, please. You're just saying all this because Nate wants to leave."

"That's not true."

"Zac, you were fine with me not going before," Erin pointed out. "In fact, you were so fine with it, you left me with a total stranger just a few days after I came home from the hospital."

"Oh, so now you're gonna throw that in my face? I had no choice, Erin." Any trace of the laid-back, stoner flakiness Zac usually affected was gone. He sounded sharp and clipped. "This tour was the chance of a lifetime.

Don't put that on me to make yourself feel better."

She didn't know what to say. She'd known this would be a difficult conversation, but Zac was taking it really hard.

"Erin, don't do this," he pleaded. "You're just out of the loop. You've forgotten what it feels like, the high you get from being onstage, the thrill of it, the music pulsing through your veins. There's nothing that compares. You know that."

"I'm sorry, Zac. That's how it is for you, not me. My dream is writing."

His voice turned mocking. "Oh, really? That's your dream? You could have fooled me. You've been saying that for years, but what the hell have you got to show for it?"

Anger mixed with Erin's guilt, and she clenched her fist. "Oh, thanks, *Trynt*. Your support and understanding mean so much to me."

"Don't compare me to that douchebag," Zac snapped.

"Then don't act like that douchebag!" Realizing she was yelling, Erin took a breath and lowered her voice. "Everything's not always about you, Zac."

She could hear his frustrated exhale over the phone before he said, "Listen to me, Erin. We have a chance at something big with the band, a chance to make something of ourselves right now. What are you gonna do? Keep writing phantom novels no one sees but you and work at Lars until you're all used up? What kind of life—what kind of future is that?"

Her brother's lack of faith in her hurt, and she swallowed back the hard lump that had formed in her throat. "I've—I've had a lot of time to think these last few months. I want to try and get the novel I've finished published. I'm going to start submitting it to agents." Even to her own ears, she sounded too thready, too uncertain.

"Well, that's fucking great," said Zac, his voice oozing sarcasm. "And what am I supposed to do in the meantime when Nate leaves?"

"Guitarists are a dime a dozen, Zac. I'm sure you'll find someone else who's dying to go on tour with a national band."

"You know it's not that easy! I don't want to have to audition fifty million people and go through all that shit. I want you!"

"And I can't believe you're being such a selfish asshole." Her breath was ragged, and her emotions were all over the place—they kept flipping from guilt and regret to a righteous, hot fury that made her shaky.

"Yeah. That's me," he said. "I'm a selfish asshole. So, let me get this straight. You're passing up a chance at fame and fortune so you can wait tables and *maybe* publish some novel you say you finished."

"I think you're jumping the gun a bit on the fame and fortune," Erin said dryly.

He ignored her. "Which, by the way, why can't you write and mail letters to agents from the road?"

"Oh, and how would I do that, since I don't have a

laptop? There's no place for my desktop in that tiny RV."

Zac huffed. "If that's all it is, I'll buy you a damn laptop."

She clenched her fist. "It's more than just the writing stuff."

"Like what? Is it a guy? You fucking another random guy?"

Erin felt as if he'd just slapped her. Okay. Maybe she'd been kind of a ho in the past, but he'd never thrown it in her face before. This wasn't like Zac. He was normally the one who encouraged her and stood by her. He'd always been there for her and was the one person besides Nana who'd always understood her. She told herself he was just pissed off and lashing out.

She wanted to tell him about Jay, but now wasn't the right time. Given his current mood, he wouldn't take kindly to her choosing Jay over him and the band. She wanted him to like Jay and knew it would be better to tell him about their relationship after he'd cooled off.

"I think," Erin said, keeping her voice even, "we need to end this conversation before both of us say more we'll regret later."

Zac's voice was encased in arctic ice. "Yeah, like calling someone a selfish asshole."

She sighed. "I shouldn't have said that. I'm sorry."

"Whatever." The line went dead, and she knew Zac's cell hadn't dropped the call. He'd hung up on her.

A cold, sick feeling stole over her. She hated the thought of Zac being mad at her. Maybe she'd been too hasty. Maybe he really did need her and wasn't just being a self-centered jerk. Tossing her cell onto the counter, she scrubbed her trembling hands over her face.

"Morning, darlin'."

Despite the turmoil tying her insides into knots, Erin's body responded instantly to Jay's rich voice, the residue of sleep making it a little raspy. She looked up to see him wheeling with long, fluid pushes of his tires into the kitchen, moving with a natural male grace that was undeniably sexy. He had on a black Harley-Davidson T-shirt and his usual ensemble of loose gray sweatpants and white socks. His blond hair was mussed from sleep, but he looked better, more rested than he had the last few days. His broad shoulders were back and more purposeful.

Erin was heartened and hoped maybe today would be one of his good days, when his back pain wasn't so bad. "Hey," she said, and tried to manage a smile.

He wheeled over to her and tugged on her wrist, pulling her onto his lap and wrapping his strong arms around her. Then he gave her a slow, tender kiss that made her light-headed. When they parted, he studied her for a moment. "What's wrong?"

She shrugged. "Nothing."

His brows went up in a way that said, *Yeah, right.* "Who were you talking to?"

"You heard?"

One corner of his mouth curved upward. "Kind of hard not to."

She puffed out a breath that stirred her bangs. "Sorry. I didn't mean to wake you. It was just Zac."

"You two in a fight?"

"Yeah." Her stomach clenched again at the reminder. "He's being a shit."

Jay's forehead creased. "What did he say?"

"He wants me to join him and the band on the tour."

"Oh." Jay's expression went carefully blank and his arms tightened around her. "And what did you say? You gonna go?"

"No."

His shoulders relaxed and he rested his forehead in the curve where her neck met her shoulder. "Good."

Erin's heart leaped, and she had to restrain herself from doing a happy dance. He was relieved. He didn't want her to go. *He didn't want her to go.* In that moment, something clicked into place for her.

She'd wanted to believe it was all real, the way he seemed to be so into her, but a part of her had still been holding back, the part that had been burned too many times. She hadn't been able to give all of herself to him, but now the last vestiges of her fear were falling away.

Jay tilted his head back to look at her. "And now he's pissed?" he said, bringing her back into the conversation.

"Yeah."

He nodded and then asked casually, "So, why don't you want to go on the tour?"

She sensed the question held more weight than he let on, and she held in a smile. Angling her head to the side, she replied, "Why do you think?"

He gifted her with an easy, slow grin, then took her face in his hands and began to explore her mouth with his tongue.

Erin forgot about her fight with Zac. New Orleans? Going on tour? What was that? Her world was with Jay, and that's where she wanted to stay—where *he* wanted her to stay. "I want to be with you, Jay," she whispered, her heart pounding and her breath unsteady.

"I'm right here," he said, in between little wispy nips along her jawline.

"I mean *with you*, with you."

He went utterly still and looked her in the eye. "Are you sure?"

"Very."

Chapter 22

Jay's bedroom was closer, so that's where they ended up. Now that she'd made her decision, Erin felt shaky with anticipation. If she had to take it slow one more minute, she would explode. Why had she been so reluctant, so afraid? It suddenly seemed so right, so inevitable.

Jay transferred from his chair to the rumpled bed, his butt landing with an exaggerated thud that made the mattress springs squeak and Erin giggle. He smiled playfully, but his gaze was smoldering. As soon as he was sitting on the bed, Erin was standing in front of him and yanking his shirt off over his head. He did the same to her, pulling the bottom of her pajama tank upward as far as he could reach and exposing her bare breasts. She finished the job and flung the tank over her shoulder.

He closed his eyes and groaned. "Darlin', do you know how long I've waited for this?"

"Since you saw me naked?" she said wryly.

"No," he said, one corner of his mouth lifting as he looked up at her. "Since the first time you called me an asshole. Which I deserved, by the way."

"Oh, right. Being called an asshole is always a turn-on."

"I'm serious." Then he reached up and put his lean, callused hands on her hips, pulling her closer. "You're beautiful, Erin. I've always thought that, from the very beginning."

She wanted to believe him, didn't want to think of the things he'd said, of what he'd thought of her as a dev. If he wanted to sugarcoat it, she sure as hell wasn't about to argue.

He was in her blood, raging through her system. It was like she'd smoked a Jay-bomb. She leaned forward and kissed him, running her fingers through his soft, thick blond hair and then nibbling on his bottom lip until he took over, making the kiss hard and deep.

Lips still locked with hers, he fell back on the bed, his legs still bent and hanging over the edge, and pulled Erin with him. She landed on top of him, part of her legs and feet dangling over the side, too. He was so much bigger than she was, and his upper body was all hard muscle encased in warm bronzed skin.

"Scoot up for me, darlin'," he growled. "Let me taste your breasts."

She slithered up his body, letting her breasts sear his skin, and then placed them close to his mouth. The instant his tongue touched her nipple, a flame shot from there straight down to her lower abdomen. His tongue was wet and exquisite as it circled around her areola. When he took the rock-hard peak of her nipple between his teeth, the sharp, erotic pain of it caused her to moan.

After he'd thoroughly pleasured that breast, he moved to the opposite one and began to tease it as he had the other.

"Oh, my God, Jay," she breathed. "That feels . . . amazing."

His hands were still on her hips, and he put pressure on them to let her know he wanted her to move upward. She obeyed, and he began to lick her body, first between her breasts and then down her belly to just above the waistband of her pajama boxers. He hooked his thumbs inside them and began to pull them down, along with her lacy bikini panties, exposing her hips and buttocks until he couldn't reach any further.

She helped him by hastily pushing the garments off the rest of the way and letting them fall to the floor. She was totally naked now, her skin tingling and flushed. She had the vague thought that, thank God, she'd shaved and trimmed all her nooks and crannies last night.

Jay picked up where he left off, licking her with little circles of his tongue just above her pubic area and then lower, to that most sensitive, private place. Erin couldn't help but thrust her hips forward and arch her back. Holy God. The man was a magician with his mouth. He started to suck, and she nearly unraveled. She was on fire, every cell in her body pinpointed on what Jay was doing to her.

But it was too soon. She didn't want it to happen this fast, didn't want it to be all about her. She wanted to prolong the pleasure, and she wanted it to be mutual. No way was she ever going to let Jay get bored.

Although her body begged for the release that was

so near, she tore herself away from Jay's wicked mouth and began to kiss him on the stomach above his belly button, flicking her tongue over his moist, salty, heated skin, eventually making her way up to his cut pectoral muscles.

He massaged his fingers into her hair and, with a tug, urged her up to his mouth, giving her a kiss. "Why did you stop me? You were so close."

She loved the way his lips moved over hers as he spoke. "I don't want you to make it all about me," she replied, nibbling at his bottom lip. "I want you to enjoy this, too. I want this to be about both of us."

One of his hands was on her breast now, caressing it, his callused thumb tickling her nipple. "Trust me, darlin'. I'm enjoying it. I could spend the rest of my life tasting and touching your body and die a happy man."

She smiled.

His thumb traced her nipple, teasing it and then giving it a gentle twist between his thumb and forefinger, causing her to moan again at the lovely ache of it.

Trying to hold on to rational thought, Erin kissed him on his neck, just below his ear, and then took his earlobe in her mouth. "I want to taste you, too, Jay," she whispered. She gently pushed her tongue into his ear, in and out, in and out, and then skimmed the outer edge of it.

He sucked in a shuddering breath. "Jesus."

"You like that?"

His answer was a noise from deep in his throat that

was deliciously male and primal.

Encouraged by his reaction, Erin trailed her way down his body, making sure not to leave any swath of skin untouched. She kissed and licked and, at the same time, brushed her fingertips lightly over his chest, his stomach, his shoulders, his biceps, the inside of his elbows, his hands.

"I want you, Jay," she said into his palm as she kissed it. "I want to touch every inch of you." With her free hand, she hooked her finger inside the drawstring waist of his sweats and felt nothing but cool skin underneath—no boxers. He was going commando. How hot was that? She couldn't wait to get him naked.

Eyes hooded, he seemed lost in the sensual world she'd created for him, but when she said, "I think it's time we got rid of these," and started to untie the drawstring of his sweats, he seized her wrists.

"Don't."

Despite his grip on her, she pulled the loosened waistband down to just below his hipbone and kissed it. Knowing it was hard for him to see from his angle, and also knowing he couldn't feel it, she looked up and said seductively, "I just kissed your hip, Jay."

Nostrils flaring, he tightened his hold on her. "I said don't."

Erin was surprised by his vehemence but tried to keep things naughty and flirtatious. "All's fair in love and war. I'm naked. It's only fair that you are, too."

He didn't say anything, just shut his eyes, the features

of his handsome face going rigid.

"It's okay," said Erin. She didn't want him to be embarrassed. "I—"

"It's not what you think," he said in a rush. Letting go of her wrists, he dug his elbows into the mattress and levered himself up enough to see her better. "I can get hard." He let out a frustrated breath, his nostrils flaring again, his face tinged with color. "But sometimes—it's better if I take a pill . . . " He looked up at the ceiling, as if he didn't want to go on, and Erin felt bad for making him feel so uncomfortable.

Meeting her eyes again with purpose, he said, "I can still make it happen for you, Erin. There are other ways."

"I know that, Jay. I've never doubted that. Ever. But it will be more intimate for me if you're naked, too. Don't hide your body from me."

"I'm not hiding it, but what's the point?"

Defiantly, she pulled down the other side of his sweats and kissed his other hipbone. The skin there felt cold and dry to her lips compared to the skin above his navel, and she knew it was because blood circulation was more sluggish below the level of his injury. He wouldn't be able to sweat below that level either. Both issues were common side effects of paraplegia.

He watched the motion of her hand as she slid it inside his sweats and touched his cool thigh. Getting an immediate rush, she closed her eyes and drew in a breath, relishing the feel of him. "I don't care whether you can get hard, Jay. You are sexy to me in so many other ways, *every* part of you."

At first he didn't react, didn't move, his expression unreadable. Then he asked, "Are you saying—are you saying you're turned on by the paralyzed part of me, by my wasted legs?"

She paused, knowing she was at a crossroads. The answer was yes, but should she admit the truth—that, yeah, she was as pervy as he'd originally thought? The chance to come clean, to completely be herself with him, was tempting, but the possibility she might lose him made her queasy and filled her with dread. Touching his leg as she was now, though, she didn't feel like a perv. It was an expression of love, a connection, and it felt right. He was beautiful—all of him—and she wanted Jay to see himself the way she did. She hated the way he'd described his legs as wasted and with such disdain.

She looked at him boldly, wanting to reassure him, to liberate him, to make him see he didn't need to be inhibited with her—and prayed she wasn't about to make a huge mistake. "Your legs aren't wasted, not to me. They're part of you, Jay, and because of that, yeah. They turn me on. And I love the way your skin is cool on the lower part of your body. I want to feel it against mine."

His face contorted with disgust, and Erin knew she'd made the wrong choice. Shame slammed into her.

"That's fucking crazy," said Jay.

She wished to God she hadn't said anything. His instant withdrawal from her felt like a chunk of her soul was being ripped out.

"I thought . . . " he began, but didn't finish. Instead, he just stared at her like she was something he didn't recognize.

She didn't know what to do. She was still straddling him, nude and exposed. She felt unclean and wanted to cover herself, but there was no graceful way out of this. Humiliated, face hot and tears gathering in her eyes, she said, "I'm a dev, Jay. You knew that. You said it didn't matter."

A muscle ticked in his jaw. "Yeah, but I didn't think—I thought—I didn't realize . . . " He didn't finish. He didn't need to.

She'd kept that darkest, seediest part of herself from him. She realized now her whole relationship with him had been based on half-truth. She'd pretended to be someone she wasn't. She'd pretended to be normal.

He remained mute, and each second that ticked by seemed to widen the distance between them before Erin slowly eased off of him. Using up her last tiny scrap of dignity, she turned her back to him and began to get dressed.

* * *

Jay watched as Erin's hand reached for the doorknob, her petite figure once again dressed in a black pajama tank and pink boxers, her glossy brown hair trailing down her back. He didn't know what he felt anymore. He didn't want her to stay, but he didn't want to hurt her either.

"You don't have to go," he said out of obligation.

She waited a beat, and then, without turning to look at him, said, "I think I do."

His chest tightened at the quiet dejection in her voice. "It's okay," he lied. "I just need some time to think, to come to terms with . . . things."

She gave a small nod and, in the next instant, she was gone.

Jay released his elbows, letting his head fall back to the mattress, and stared at the old-fashioned white plaster ceiling. How could things have gone so wrong? His heart cried foul while his brain sought to distance itself. From what, he wasn't sure, but it was something that went deep, something that made his gut wrench.

Erin had touched his body in ways he hadn't been touched by a woman in a very long time. She'd touched him in places he'd never thought of as erotic before (like the inside of his elbow, for one) and had sent him to the brink of pure heaven; that is, until she'd kissed him on his hip, and he hadn't felt it. It was like she was kissing someone else, and the unfairness and wrongness of it had infuriated him.

Everything had been so incredible up to that point, until the kiss reminded him that a part of himself was missing. It was that useless part of his body that had cost him his marriage, among other things. He'd told Erin he wasn't hiding his body, but there was no doubt he wasn't ready for her to see him naked. He couldn't help but remember attempts at sex with other women he'd been intimate with since his accident—including his ex-wife—and he didn't want a repeat of the pity and revulsion he'd seen on their faces the first (and usually the only) time they saw him naked. He'd learned it was better to keep the woman distracted and pleased, to make her forget about his disability, not reveal the stark reality of it. It had been a good strategy until Erin.

Why wasn't he glad when she'd admitted his paralyzed body turned her on? Instead, he'd been horrified. He knew she was a dev, but he thought that he'd been wrong in the beginning, that he'd misunderstood what being a devotee meant.

He'd never actually talked to Erin about it, but what about all that stuff emanomaly had told Panhead? She'd said she wasn't attracted to a paralyzed body in and of itself. She'd made devoteeism sound noble, made it sound like it was the strong and classy way a wheeler adapted to his disability that attracted her, not his actual physical imperfections. She'd said she didn't perv on paralyzed legs, that it wasn't like she wanted to hump them. She'd made devoteeism make sense.

But when Erin had touched Jay's thigh, he'd seen a desire on her face that was unnatural, that was sick, and it had made his blood congeal. It was the thing that had so repulsed him about devs before he'd gotten to know her.

He raked his hands through his hair in frustration. Was he being an unfair bastard? He'd thought he could get past her devness after emanomaly had explained it better to him, but now that he knew the full extent of it, he wasn't so sure it was something he could overlook.

Then again, maybe it wasn't even Erin's fault. He was supposed to have come to terms with his injury a long time ago, accepted the way his body was now, but what if Luis had been right all those months ago when he'd said devs disgusted Jay because he wasn't comfortable in his own skin?

Like he'd told Erin, he needed time to think; he needed space. He knew avoiding her would hurt her, and he hated himself for it, but he didn't think he could be around her right now. How many times had she warned him, told him she was broken? But he hadn't listened. He'd begged her to give him a second chance to prove himself. Unfortunately, all he'd proven today was that he *was* a bastard. In his defense, though, she'd changed the rules on him. He hadn't known all the facts.

He thought of all the things he liked about her: She was hot and had those freakishly gorgeous hazel eyes; she had a great sense of humor; she was smart; she was kind. She was perfect for him in so many ways—so perfect he'd been falling in love with her.

Now he wasn't so sure.

Chapter 23

emanomaly: You there?

Erin waited, watching the hypnotic blink of the cursor on her screen, willing Panhead to answer. His status showed he wasn't online, but maybe he'd marked himself as inactive and forgotten to change it. He'd been unresponsive for days now, which sucked, because Erin was falling apart and needed someone to talk to.

It was four days since she'd creeped Jay out; four days since she'd revealed the true nature of her attraction to him; four days since she'd been kicked to the curb. It reminded her of when Trynt broke off their engagement, and her brain kept saying, *I told you so.*

Jay had been polite and cordial enough, saying "Hi" or "Bye" (but making only fleeting eye contact) as he dashed out the door to go to his office or disappeared into his room to work. He was suddenly the most dedicated IT guy on the planet. No one's computer was gonna die on his watch.

He was in his room now, still working (or hiding from Erin), even though it was almost ten in the evening.

If he was telling the truth, he'd been putting in fourteen-hour days, which couldn't be good for his back. The way he'd been shutting her out, she shouldn't be concerned about that, but she was.

Erin still held out the hope that Jay just needed time, that maybe it wasn't over between them, but each day he avoided her, her heart sickened a little more. She felt so alone and wished Zac was there, although it wasn't like she could tell him what had happened, even if he were. Besides, judging from the terse answers she got whenever she texted him, he was still pissed at her for not joining him on the tour.

She had friends, of course, but none of them knew she was a dev. The only person who knew, the only person she could really talk to, was Panhead.

It was her own fault, she supposed, that she'd lost contact with him. When things had been going great with Jay, she'd only chatted with Panhead once. Maybe ignoring her was payback, but Panhead didn't seem like the vindictive type. Maybe he was just busy. It wasn't like he'd tried to contact her in all that time either.

Maybe his radio silence was because he was on an awesome vacation somewhere exotic and didn't have reliable Internet access. Or maybe the dev he'd been pursuing had warmed toward him. Maybe they were so in love now that they were spending every waking moment together, and he just hadn't had a chance to chat. The longing and jealousy brought on by that visual cut deep, but Erin wouldn't begrudge Panhead his happiness, even if her own relationship with Jay had hit the skids.

Maybe, whispered the paranoid part of her brain, Panhead and Jay were one and the same. Was it a coincidence Panhead had gone missing at the same time Jay started treating Erin like the plague?

She propped her elbows on her desk and rested her head in her hands. God, please don't let it be that. Please don't let Jay turn out to be Panhead. She didn't want to angst over that again right now, not when she was already so raw and upset about everything else. Surely the universe wouldn't kick her while she was down.

She hoped something bad hadn't happened to Panhead. Her imagination, combined with a knowledge of what could go wrong when someone had paraplegia—urinary tract infections and pressure sores, to name a couple—had her worried.

Sighing, she lifted her head to look at her screen and decided to leave Panhead another message.

> *emanomaly:* Hope the reason you're MIA has something to do with that hot dev you wrote about, or else you're marooned on a tropical island with a bunch of virgin bikini models.

She paused, wondering if she should keep it light or say something that would let him know all was not right with her world. She settled on something in between.

> *emanomaly:* Seriously, hope you're okay. If you can

fit in a chat, I could really use a friend.

* * *

Jay stared at his laptop screen, at emanomaly's message.

"If you can fit in a chat, I could really use a friend."

Guilt gnawed at his belly, a nice addition to the chronic pain in his back and the annoying, jiggling spasticity in his legs. He'd been buried in work for days now, using that as an excuse for not talking to Erin, but burning the midnight oil had taken its toll on his body. He hardly ever had spasticity. Its appearance was a sign he'd been overdoing it. The back pain, however, was always present and had plateaued at "extremely painful ninety-five percent of the time."

He inhaled a deep breath and then exhaled, trying to breathe through a particularly vicious pang, and resisted the temptation to hold down his left leg, which was jiggling worse than the right. It kept working itself off the footplate of his chair. Holding on to it wouldn't make it stop, though. Lying down might help, but he didn't have time for that.

He'd seen the hurt in Erin's eyes every time he dodged her, but he wasn't lying to her when he told her he was swamped. Daniel, one of the other guys he worked with, was on vacation, so Jay had volunteered to cover Daniel's on-call shifts for help-desk. The extra work was a welcome distraction because none of Jay's confusion over his feelings for Erin had been resolved. He still needed time. One minute he missed her and thought he could get past the dev thing; the next, he didn't want to think about any of it because the whole situation made him want to punch a wall.

It all came back to one thing: How could she even want to touch his sticklike paralyzed legs, let alone be turned on by them? He just couldn't wrap his head around that. It had taken him years before he could touch his floppy, cold legs and feet without cringing. There was no getting around it: Erin was a freak.

And how could it not matter to her whether he could get a boner or not? He was insulted by that. It was just wrong. For the record, he could get an erection without taking Cialis, but it was unpredictable. With the pill, he could go for hours, but it took twenty minutes or so to kick in, which could seem like forever when things were hot and heavy. It was why he'd wanted to show Erin how good it could be in other ways, but no. She'd had to go and ruin everything.

He kept having this conversation with himself. It was on a continuous loop, going round and round in his head.

To make things more confusing, he kept remembering the things that were good about her, like the way she loved Chopper. Most people wanted to run when they encountered his diabolical-looking dog, but not Erin. She only saw the loveable, gentle dog beneath the scary exterior. She'd even called Chopper cute. Chopper was Jay's best bud, but he'd never in a million years describe the canine as cute.

Another case in point: the compassion she'd shown that shithead who'd tried to steal her wallet at HEB. She'd made up elaborate backstories to justify his actions because she didn't want to believe he was inherently bad.

Erin saw the beauty in things others couldn't see and always looked for the good in people—in everyone except herself. Jay had never known anyone with such a self-destructive streak. Now he fully understood what she'd been trying to destroy.

The cursor blinked on his screen, accusing and insistent. He should respond to her, if for no other reason than it might be suspicious that Panhead had disappeared at the same time he and Erin started having problems— and because he did still care about her.

He couldn't erase the past few weeks he'd spent with her. They had been good—really good—and no matter what his feelings for her were now, there was no reason for Panhead to reject her, too.

He started typing.

> *Panhead:* What's up?
>
> *emanomaly:* Oh. You're there.
>
> *Panhead:* Yep.
>
> *emanomaly:* You have no idea how glad I am to hear from you.
>
> *Panhead:* Sorry I didn't respond earlier. I've been busy with those virgins . . .
>
> *emanomaly:* Right.
>
> *Panhead:* I wish. Just been busy with work.

emanomaly: With the restaurant?

Panhead: Yeah.

It wasn't technically a lie, only he'd been busy with lots of restaurants, not just one.

He and Erin had talked about his work. She knew he supported restaurant computer systems, but she hadn't made the connection between Panhead's involvement with restaurants and Jay's. Yes. Panhead had mislead her by being intentionally vague, but it still wasn't exactly lying.

Ironically, her next sentence echoed what was in his head.

emanomaly: You never told me exactly what you do in the restaurant business.

Panhead: Not much to tell. It's boring. Just management.

Again, not quite a lie. He helped manage technology. Still, it was time to steer the conversation to something else, even if that meant jumping out of the frying pan into the fire.

Panhead: So why did you say you could use a friend?

emanomaly: Um, long story. Speaking of stories, did you have a chance to read the ones I sent you?

Panhead: Yes. I've been meaning to e-mail my comments but got sidetracked. I liked them. You should finish them. I even liked the romance.

emanomaly: Are you just being nice?

Panhead: No. I want to find out what happens. Especially in the romance.

emanomaly: I sense some sarcasm there.

Panhead: No, really. I want to know.

emanomaly: It's a romance. It's kind of a given what's going to happen.

Panhead: Let me guess: The dude believes his girl is dead so he drinks poison, then she wakes up, sees that he's dead, and stabs herself?

emanomaly: Ha. Uh, no. My novel is no *Romeo and Juliet*. It's a category romance, written for a certain type of readership. It's supposed to have a happy ending.

Panhead: Supposed to?

emanomaly: Not sure I know how to write one.

Panhead: Why do I get the feeling you're talking about something else besides your book?

emanomaly: Because, as usual, my love life is in the crapper.

Panhead: Does this have to do with your roommate?

emanomaly: Yes.

What was he doing? He shouldn't be encouraging her to confide in him, but he could ask her things as Panhead he couldn't as Jay and maybe get some answers without the awkwardness of having to look her in the eye.

Still, what he was doing didn't sit well with him,

and he felt agitated. He pressed his palms into his seat cushion, doing a quick pressure lift. It didn't help, so he rolled his head on his shoulders to release the tension in his neck and the pain in his back. That didn't help either.

He knew he was about to dig himself in deeper, but it didn't stop him from typing a response.

> *Panhead:* What happened?
>
> *emanomaly:* Things were going great until I freaked him out.
>
> *Panhead:* How?
>
> *emanomaly:* I'm afraid to tell you.
>
> *Panhead:* Why?
>
> *emanomaly:* Because I don't want to lose your friendship, too.
>
> *Panhead:* You won't. You can tell me anything, remember?

Yep. It was official: He was Satan.

> *emanomaly:* Like I said, it's a long story, but the gist of it is, I admitted I thought the paralyzed part of his body was hot, his legs and everything, and that I want to touch them and see them. He thinks I'm a perv now, and I guess he's right.
>
> *Panhead:* Wait a minute. Didn't you tell me you weren't into that, that you were attracted to a wheeler's inner strength or whatever and not the physical side of his disability?

> ***emanomaly:*** Yeah, I did. When I told you that, though, I believed it myself. I think it made what I am easier for me to accept. And it's true. I think the strength of character a guy with a disability exhibits is very attractive, the way he deals with it is cool, but I'm attracted to the physical aspects, too. I used to tell myself I wasn't necessarily attracted to the paralyzed parts but wasn't repulsed by them either. But with my roommate, it's more than that, more than just being able to overlook them. I can't lie to myself anymore. I am so physically drawn to him, to every molecule of him. My attraction to him is a compulsion. I can't get enough of him.

Jay could at least understand that. He'd felt the same way about her, but that was different. She was physically perfect. Her body was a work of art. His was far from it.

> ***Panhead:*** Are you sure your fascination with his paralysis isn't more of a morbid thing, like rubbernecking a bad car wreck?
> ***emanomaly:*** No. Absolutely not. When I look at him, I see nothing morbid or pitiful. All I see is perfection.

Jay was trying hard to let that sink in and not be biased, but he was having a hard time. How could she see perfection where all he saw was a reminder of loss, of weakness—that he would never again be what he once was?

Panhead: When did you realize you were attracted to the physical stuff?

emanomaly: When I saw my roommate out walking his dog one day. I know it's weird, but it just clicked for me. He looked so powerful, so full of life. His paralyzed legs, neatly contained by his chair, underscored his virility instead of detracting from it. They were beautiful because he was beautiful. He personified ability—not disability—and it was a huge turn-on for me. I couldn't deny any longer that I wanted to touch him, every single part of him. Later, I even fantasized about what it would be like to sit on his lap, to feel his legs beneath me.

Jay raised his brows. He didn't know what to think of that, let alone what to say. He noticed his legs had finally stopped jiggling, but he barely acknowledged it. He was more absorbed in what Erin had just told him. She'd fantasized about sitting on his lap? It was weird, yes; but, if he was honest with himself, it was kind of kinky, too.

emanomaly: You still there?

Panhead: Yeah.

emanomaly: It's disturbing, I know. I'm sorry. I probably shouldn't be telling you any of this, but I feel so isolated. I just need someone to talk to.

Panhead: No. It's okay. It's just a lot to take in.

emanomaly: I know. Thanks for at least hearing me out.

Panhead: Sure. It's just not what I expected.

emanomaly: I know. It obviously wasn't what my roommate expected either. I knew things wouldn't work out with him. It was too good to be true. I never should have let things go so far. I knew I was setting myself up for heartbreak, but, again, the physical attraction alone was too strong to deny. I think, judging by the way he used to kiss me, it was the same for him, too.

Panhead: Yeah, that's kind of hard to fake.

emanomaly: When I got to know him better, the physical attraction turned into something much deeper, something much more important. There's so much I like about him. He's so strong. I feel safe and protected when I'm with him. He's the perfect guy—thoughtful, affectionate, funny, smart, honest—and he even cooks. He deserves someone better than me, someone who's normal. It's probably best that he learned the truth now, before things went any further.

Jay sat there staring at the screen, rocked by all the things she'd said about him. She kept saying he was perfect, but he was far from it.

He was racking his brain for an appropriate response when another message popped up from her.

emanomaly: Losing him is so painful. I'm in love with

him, and I'm such an idiot for letting that happen. I feel
like I can't breathe, like my insides are being crushed.

Jay could identify with that. She was killing him.
Leaning his elbows on either side of his laptop, he
grabbed his hair with both fists and squeezed his eyes
shut. Jesus Christ. She'd just said she loved him. But if
she did, then why . . .

He opened his eyes and started typing.

> **Panhead:** Why did you admit that stuff to him about
> perving on his legs in the first place, especially if you
> knew it might end things?
> **emanomaly:** We were in an intimate moment, and he
> seemed so scornful of his body. I couldn't stand that. I
> wanted him to see himself the way I see him. I thought
> I could make him understand. And I think maybe I was
> tired of pretending. I wanted to be honest with him, so
> I gambled that I could trust him.
> **Panhead:** And you lost.
> **emanomaly:** Yes.

Neither of them typed anything for what seemed
like several minutes. Jay could sense her anguish, and
he hated himself for causing it. She loved him, even the
ugly parts. He should have seen that for the gift it was
instead of being such a jackass. His own deep-seated
hang-ups—things he'd thought he'd dealt with long
ago—had blinded him.

He was about to go to Erin, confess he was Panhead, and grovel for her forgiveness when she wrote something else.

> ***emanomaly:*** He hasn't talked to me in days, and it hurts. You'd think I would have learned my lesson. He's always provoked intense emotions in me, even in the beginning. I mean, my God, I almost offed myself because of him.

Jay's heart stopped and he went cold. What the hell was she talking about?

And then he knew.

Chapter 24

"Shit, shit, shit," Erin muttered to herself, wiping tears from her eyes with the Kleenex she'd grabbed from her nightstand. She hated crying, and she was glad Panhead couldn't see her. Talking with him about Jay had brought everything home, and the tears had started gushing. She hadn't cried this hard since Nana died.

And what the hell was she thinking, mentioning her pathetic suicide attempt to Panhead? She was distraught, and it had just come out.

She was dreading Panhead's inevitable response and trying to think how she'd explain when a knock on the door made her start.

"Erin," came Jay's deep, gravelly voice through the door, "we need to talk."

Tentative hope bubbled within her. Maybe he was going to give her another chance after all. Or—and this possibility squeezed her heart—maybe he was going to officially end things.

"Erin?" he called again.

Clearing her throat, she said, "Just a second," then hastily wiped her face and blew her nose with another tissue. She wished she had a bathroom connected to her room so she could wash her face, but only the master bedroom, which was Jay's room, had its own bath. She didn't want Jay to know she'd been crying, but there was no way her blotchy skin and swollen eyes wouldn't give her away.

Another knock. "Erin, please."

She closed out of the messenger program with Panhead and opened the window of the eMusic website. The last thing she needed was Jay inadvertently reading her chat with Panhead.

Smoothing an errant lock of hair that had escaped from her ponytail and tucking it behind her ear, she said, "Come in."

The doorknob clicked, and Jay pushed the door open and rolled through. Erin was still sitting in her blue secretary-style desk chair and hardly glanced at him, trying to look engrossed in the music site. She wanted it to appear she hadn't been pining away for him for four days, which was probably ridiculous. One look at her face and he'd know she'd been crying. She wondered if he could also tell that her heart was about to beat itself out of her chest.

Out of the corner of her eye, she saw him push himself up next to her. He was wearing one of his pale-blue oxford work shirts with Luis's company logo embroidered on it in dark blue and a pair of nicer jeans that weren't as faded as usual.

At some point, Luis must have relaxed the dress code

for his technicians because Erin hadn't seen Jay wear khakis since those first few weeks he'd lived with her. She tried not to admire how the pale blue of his shirt contrasted nicely with the tan coloring of his skin, and she refused to feel shabby in her well-worn Pixies T-shirt and black yoga pants. It was Wednesday, her night off, so she was in full-on lounge gear.

"Erin?"

There was such grief and urgency in the way Jay said her name that she forgot to be absorbed in her computer screen and turned her head sharply to look at him. When she did, she saw his face was tinged with red and his jaw was rigid, as if he was trying to control an intense emotion. Something that looked suspiciously like moisture made his eyes too bright, turning them a truer, more brilliant shade of blue.

His intensity disconcerted her. Another round of tears tried to surface, but she swallowed hard, willing them away. If he was about to permanently end things, she'd be damned before she would cry in front of him.

He held on to the edge of her desk with one hand for leverage. With his other hand, he grabbed the arm of her desk chair, which had casters, and swiveled her around so she was facing him, knee to knee. Then he leaned toward her, using one hand to brace himself on his thigh, and cupped her face with his other hand. "I'm sorry," he said, his tone grim.

He was like one of those giant magnets in a junkyard, and she was like a piece of scrap metal. Her body didn't have any choice but to gravitate toward him, bringing them close enough for him to kiss her forehead, then her eyes, then her lips. The pleasant tickle of his ever-present stubble against her skin made her stomach flutter.

"You've been crying," he said, outlining what were probably leftover tear streaks on her cheek with his fingertips. "Christ, Erin, I'm so sorry." His hand moved to the nape of her neck, and he pressed his forehead against hers.

Erin went stiff, not sure what to think. She'd been so sure he was going to break up with her, but his actions didn't reflect that. Why would he be kissing her? "What—what exactly are you sorry for?"

He reared back to look at her, his hand still on her nape, his forehead wrinkled in that soulful way he had. "For everything."

"You mean for blowing me off?"

"For starters, yes. I'm sorry for the last few days, for not talking to you. I was a jerk. I'm sorry for not understanding."

That hope she'd felt earlier started to bloom in earnest. "Are you saying—are you saying you still want to be with me?"

"Yes. The thought of losing you—" He had to stop, a muscle ticking in his jaw and that brightness in his eyes flaring again. He pulled her into a desperate, crushing hug. "Don't ever leave me," he rasped.

What the fuck?

Erin frowned as she hugged him back, her arms

much looser than his were around her, her chin resting on his shoulder. This wasn't what she'd expected at all. She was glad Jay was talking to her now, but this sudden desperation of his was freaking her out. What had gotten into him? Despite her confusion, the clean, masculine scent of his shampoo filled her nostrils, making her skin tingle with awareness of him. Her thoughts might be muddled, but her physical senses were operating just fine.

Reluctantly, she pulled away and rested her hands on his upper arms, feeling hard biceps just under the fabric of his shirt. "Why would I leave you? *You* wouldn't talk to *me*, remember?"

"You didn't deserve that." He swallowed. "I haven't been honest with you, Erin. There's something I need to tell you."

She got a sudden prickle on the back of her neck and a knot of trepidation in her stomach. "Okay," she said cautiously.

Jay sat back to where he could sit comfortably without having to brace himself and gently removed her hands from his arms, then laced her fingers with his. Erin relished the roughness of the calluses on his hands and the warmth of his skin, and that instant of trepidation she'd felt was gone—until he looked her in the eye.

"I'm . . . " He trailed off and closed his eyes, grimacing. Then he looked at her and began again. "The car wreck. It wasn't an accident, was it?" He'd said it like a statement, not a question.

She sat there in silence, her brain in denial and refusing to register all the implications of what he'd said, even as all the blood seemed to be draining from her body. The universe was kicking her while she was down after all.

He gave her hands a squeeze. "I never realized until now how hard what I said that day at Luis's hit you." He shook his head. "The thought that something I said drove you to . . . Jesus. I'm so sorry, Erin."

She couldn't move. Her body felt like cement, and she was utterly numb. Maybe if she didn't move, time would stand still and she wouldn't have to deal with what she knew was coming next. The tension in the room rose to an unbearable level.

Finally, staring at her hands intertwined with his as if they belonged to another couple, she cleared her throat and said, "How—how do you know this?"

There was a guilty pause and then, "I think you know."

A deluge of devastation, fury, overwhelming embarrassment, and a heart-wrenching sense of betrayal threatened to swamp her, but she held them all at bay. It was too painful to deal with and made her chest feel so tight she couldn't breathe. She fought to maintain the numbness, locking everything away in what was left of her heart.

In a voice that sounded far away to her own ears, she said, "You're Panhead."

Chapter 25

Jay was alarmed at how pale Erin was, and he tensed, afraid she was close to passing out. He didn't think what she'd said was a question, but when she lifted her eyes to his in inquiry, he felt compelled to answer. "Yes," he choked out. "I'm Panhead."

Erin just stared at him, still so pale, her face disturbingly blank.

"I'm sorry," he said again. He would say it a billion times over if it would do any good, but she showed no reaction.

In a flat tone, she said, "You've been lying to me for months."

"Yes."

"You know . . . everything."

She was referring to the suicide attempt, and a giant fist clutched his heart. He couldn't stand the thought of her almost dying, especially because of something he'd said. The fact that she'd been hurt in the accident because of him was bad enough. "Erin—"

"I let you read my work," she said, cutting him off.

Jay leaned toward her, ignoring the prick of back pain

the movement caused, and took hold of her shoulders to steady himself and to reestablish contact with her. "Listen to me. You're a talented writer, and I'm glad you let me read it. It was a privilege."

She looked at him, so calm it was eerie. Jay kept waiting for the anger to come, for her to throw something or rage at him. He wished she would. Anything would be better than this clinical indifference. It was like she'd shut down every single one of her emotions.

I didn't let you read it," she pointed out. "I let Panhead."

"I know, but it's good. Why didn't you want me to read it?"

"You know why. I explained it all to Panhead."

"Humor me."

"I wasn't ready," she said, oversimplifying it.

He gave her shoulders a little squeeze. "You are ready. You should be proud of what you've written, not hiding it from everyone."

She canted her head slightly and studied him. "How can I trust anything you say?"

"I swear to you," he said fervently, "the only thing I lied about was being Panhead. Everything else I told you was true."

"You said you were a restaurant manager," she accused.

"No. I said I was in the restaurant business, in management. It was true. I help manage the technology for restaurants."

"That's splitting hairs."

"Yes," he conceded. "But it wasn't an outright lie."

"And the dev you had the hots for?"

He moved a hand up to cradle her jaw. "You."

She jerked her head away from his touch. The abruptness of the movement threw Jay off kilter, and he had to grab his wheels to stabilize himself.

Resuming her interrogation, she said, "Why the name Panhead?"

"It's the type of engine in my bike. It's a 1951 Harley Panhead."

She watched him for a moment. "It's so obvious now, the similarities between you and Panhead. You must think I'm a complete moron."

"No," Jay said, shaking his head.

"I was so gullible, so pathetic. I made it so easy for you." She crossed her arms, putting up a barrier between them. "There were moments I suspected, you know, but I convinced myself you'd never do that to me."

Remorse burrowed into his gut like a thorn. Jay wanted to touch her again, to somehow make her feel how sorry he was, but her body language told him touching her was a bad idea. "Erin—"

"Luis must have given you my username."

"Yes. He didn't want to, but I talked him into it."

"Why?"

"You wouldn't talk to me, and I wanted to get to know you. I wanted to understand the whole dev thing."

"Why? Why didn't you just leave me alone?"

"Because I was attracted to you, and I didn't know any other way to get you to talk to me."

"You weren't attracted to me. You were repulsed by me."

"No."

She looked skeptical.

"Okay," said Jay. "Maybe at first. But Luis and I started talking about it, and he made me realize the whole dev thing might not be black and white. I wanted to find out more. And the longer I was around you, the more I wanted to know you."

She gave a short nod, as if something had been confirmed. "I was something new but taboo because of your own moral code. I was like the freak show at a carnival. You were disgusted but intrigued."

Jay felt his face heat with the force of his despair. "Dammit. No. That's not true. I was attracted to you, and I wanted to learn more, but the deepest conversation I could get out of you was about paying the fucking bills."

"And you learned something from what emanomaly told you. She—I—made the whole devotee thing palatable for you."

Jay didn't answer, but he knew his silence was damning enough.

Erin laughed, but the sound was dark and devoid of any humor. "But you didn't get the whole story, did you? Not until four days ago."

He leaned toward her again, one hand on a wheel and one hand daring to touch her knee. He felt a crucial need to break through to her before she finished this wall she was building around herself.

"Listen to me," he said. "Yes, what I did was wrong. I wanted to tell you I was Panhead months ago, but I was afraid of losing you. I was a chickenshit, and I know prolonging the lie made things worse."

No color had returned to her face. She was like a marble statue as she watched him, impervious to anything he said.

"But I've never lied to you about any of the important stuff, not about your writing or how I feel about you." Her stony gaze didn't let up, so Jay said the words that might be his only way of reaching her. "I love you, Erin."

She rolled her eyes.

It wasn't the reaction he wanted, but at least it was some sort of reaction, a crack in the armor. "I swear, it's true."

"I'm still a dev, Jay," she said woodenly. "I can't change that, no matter how much I want to." Her arms, still folded in front of her, tightened as if she were reinforcing the wall. "Declaring your love for me won't change it either."

"That's not why I said it, and I don't want you to change."

"Whatever." She tried to jerk her knee away from his hand.

He followed the movement, not letting her go. "I don't want you to change," he insisted. "I want you just the way you are."

"Oh, right," she said cynically. "Look, you're off the hook. Okay?"

He drew his brows together. "What?"

"You just found out I almost killed myself because of something you said, and you feel guilty about it. But you know what? It wasn't really because of you. It was exhaustion, pure and simple. I was tired of being alone, of being a freak and a perv, and I just wanted it to end."

Jay's heart split in two at that.

"But don't worry." She stood and placed her chair between them, hands resting on the back of it. "It won't happen again. I'm not suicidal, so you don't have to make meaningless declarations of love and pretend like the sight of me doesn't make your skin crawl."

"Goddammit, Erin! That's not how I feel at all!" Gripping his tires, Jay exhaled harshly, trying to rein in his temper. "I meant what I said. I'm in love with you."

Her tone was tart. "For some reason, I find that hard to believe."

"Give me another chance."

She turned her back on him and went to her closet, where she dragged out a large, black, soft-sided suitcase that was almost as big as she was.

His pulse spiked with fear. "What are you doing?"

"Leaving." She heaved the suitcase onto her rumpled bed and unzipped it. Turning to her dresser, she pulled some folded underwear and lacy bras from the top drawer and tossed them in the suitcase.

Jay wheeled over to her and clamped a hand on her

slim wrist, firmly enough to stop her but not enough to hurt her. She froze.

"Don't do this," he said. "I know you're pissed, but cool off first. Think about it."

"You have no idea how I feel. Let go of me."

"No. Give me another chance."

Her mouth tightened. "Sorry. Fresh out. You were already pushing it with two."

"Dammit. I know I don't deserve another one, but you told Panhead—me—that you love me. That has to be worth something."

She finally looked at him, her pale, green-gold eyes holding no mercy. "You're not who I thought you were."

Jay clenched his jaw. "No. You're right. I'm human, and I made a mistake. I'm not perfect. You put me on a pedestal that was too high, and I fell far. Real far. But doesn't the reason I did it count for something? I just wanted to get closer to you."

He'd loosened his grip on her wrist, and she broke free of him. She headed to her closet and began grabbing shirts and jeans. "Let's not forget you couldn't stand to be in the same room with me for the past four days," she said, yanking a flowing black top from the closet and adding it to the pile in her arms. "I'm not who you thought I was either. Face it. What we had was based on lies and half-truths." She stuffed the bundle of clothing in the suitcase, hangers and all, not bothering to fold any of it.

Jay angrily shoved at his wheels to get to her, then

placed his hands around her waist and pulled her onto his lap, enfolding her in his arms. Unfortunately, something shifted in his back in the process of grabbing her, and pain shot through him like sparks from a fire that had just been stoked, savage and pervasive. "Fuck," he gasped. He buried his fists in the back of Erin's T-shirt, and he had to force himself to loosen his grip.

At first Erin was stiff, not melding to him as she usually did, but when she realized he was hurting, she frowned and touched his face with her palm. Jay leaned into it, closing his eyes and riding the wave of pain. He was heartened by Erin's unexpected show of compassion until she said, "Go to California, Jay." The bite was gone from her voice, replaced by weariness. "Get your back fixed."

Eyes still clenched shut, Jay buried his face in the curve of her neck and shook his head. The last thing he wanted to talk about right now was his fucking back. "It's nighttime. Where will you go?"

"To my friend Angie's. Tomorrow, I'll figure out how to catch up with my brother on the tour."

Jay lifted his head. "Don't do this."

She hesitated, her expression uncertain for a split second, but she quickly squelched it, replacing it with that damned blank mask. She tried to get up, but he hugged her to him, their faces just inches apart.

"I'll cyberstalk you," he said fiercely, teeth clenched. "I'll text you every second of every day. I'll send so many e-mails your box will fill up. Same with the voice mail on your phone. You won't have a moment's peace. Do you hear me?"

Her eyes were filled with sadness, but her mouth quirked a little. "You don't do creepy very well, Jay. I'm not exactly quaking in my boots."

He knew she was slipping away, no matter what he did or said, and his heart thudded so hard he shook. Panic and desperation drove him to beg. "Please," he said, taking her face in his hands, "don't leave. I love you."

She shook her head and then touched her lips to Jay's in a light, bittersweet kiss that shredded his soul— because he knew she was saying good-bye.

Chapter 26

Jay: I miss you. I love you. I'm an asshole. I'm sorry.

* * *

Jay: Just give me one more chance. Just one more. I know you don't hate me. You're not capable of it. Let's work through this. Please.

* * *

Jay: Come on, darlin'. I'm sorry. We need to talk.

* * *

Jay: Just because you're not answering me doesn't mean I'll give up. You love me. I'll never forget you said that.

* * *

Jay: I'm sorry, darlin'. Talk to me.

* * *

Jay: Chopper is depressed. He says the house is lonely without you.

* * *

Jay: Actually, Chopper and I both are depressed. We need you.

* * *

Jay: I miss you. Maybe you're not even getting these messages, but I hope you are. Any response would be good, even if it's to tell me you're calling the stalker police. I'm not stopping until you talk to me again.

* * *

Jay: Erin, I'm going back to California. Luis wants me to open a branch of his company in Oakland. But if there's a chance you could forgive me or you have even an ounce of feeling left for me, please tell me. I won't go if there's a chance we could work things out when you get back to Texas.

* * *

Jay: I'm leaving San Antonio, Erin. Please tell me if you don't want me to go. I will renew my lease and wait for you if you just give me some kind of sign.

* * *

Jay: Last chance. I'm leaving for Cali tomorrow.

* * *

Jay: Back in Cali now. Still miss you. Still sorry. Still love you. Stay safe and don't eat too much junk food.

* * *

Jay: P.S. If you change your mind, I don't have to stay in Cali. I would come back to Texas for you in a heartbeat.

* * *

Jay: So, I found this website called sotruefacts.com. I'm discovering all kinds of things that are highly useful. For instance, did you know astronauts are not allowed to eat beans before they go into space because the gas damages their space suits?

Chopper's been pretty gassy lately. Good thing he's not an astronaut. On the upside, I haven't had to fumigate my place for vermin lately.

Hope all is well with you, darlin'. Take care.

* * *

Jay: So, ignoring me isn't going to make me go away. I need you to answer me. Just once. Please.

* * *

Jay: I saw that Silver made it to the Download 15 on that satellite college radio station. Congrats. Hope you're still finding time to write.

* * *

Jay: sotruefacts #959: In November 2013, a woman in Florida named Linda Duchame married a fairground Ferris Wheel named Bruce. Should I be worried that the Golden Gate Bridge is starting to look pretty sexy?

Have mercy on me, darlin'. I'm losing my mind without you.

* * *

Jay: Still missing you.

* * *

Jay: Watching the sunset here in Cali. It's almost as amazing as you are. Wish you were here. Love you more than my life. Hope you are okay.

* * *

Jay: sotruefacts #916: The founder of match.com, Gary Kremen, lost his girlfriend to a man she met on match.com.

How's that for irony? Poor bastard.

How are you? I can't stop thinking about you. Not that I want to.

* * *

Jay: sotruefacts #488: You can't hum while holding your

nose closed. It's true. I tried.

Still missing you.

* * *

Jay: sotruefacts #876: The North Face clothing company once sued The South Butt clothing company. Get it? South Butt? I hope North Face lost.

So, any chance you could let me know how you're doing? Just a clue would be good.

* * *

Jay: Two and a half months since you split. Talked to Zac yesterday. He said you're getting my messages. I know you think it won't work between us, but you're wrong. There's never been anyone more right for me. I know that now, darlin'. You're perfect. PLEASE forgive me.

P.S. Zac said you're sleeping with Norf. What the fuck's a Norf? He told me it's just out of necessity because the RV is cramped, that there's nothing going on between you. I want to believe him.

Christ, Erin. Don't hook up with someone else, especially not a dude named Norf.

* * *

Jay: "If you think nothing is impossible, try slamming a revolving door." —Anonymous

Thought you might think this quote was as funny as I did. I miss your sense of humor, darlin'. I also miss your smile, your voice, and the addictive scent of your skin. I want to touch you. I want to wrap my arms around you and feel the warmth of your body. I don't care if you're a dev. You have to believe me. Please.

* * *

Jay: Things are busy here, but I think about you constantly. I know you don't believe me, but I love you, Erin. Please talk to me. Please. I'll never give up on you. Never.

Chapter 27

Erin's phone bleeped in the silence of the '80s RV she shared with her brother and the rest of the band. She ignored the skip in her heartbeat and resisted the urge to snatch her phone up to see who the new text was from. She was the only one in the RV at the moment, so she didn't know who she was trying to impress with her show of self-restraint. Everyone else was in the bar where the band would be playing for the next two nights—a rare thing, to have two nights in the same place.

There was a ninety-five-percent chance the text was from Jay. Turns out, he'd meant what he said about the whole cyberstalking thing.

Erin could have easily blocked his number from her phone and relegated his e-mails (both from his regular e-mail account and the Panhead account) to her spam folder, but she couldn't bring herself to do it. She never answered any of them—the texts, the voice mails, or the e-mails—but she read every single one and never deleted them, no matter how inane. Even worse, she listened to the voice mails over and over, unable to stop herself from getting a fix of Jay's seductive dark-chocolate voice.

Feeling pathetically weak-willed, Erin picked up her phone off the RV's built-in, brown Formica table and read the screen.

> Did you know tacocat spelled backwards is still tacocat?

Erin laughed. It was small and rusty, but it was a laugh. She hadn't found much of anything to smile at in the last three months, but for some reason, this random text from Jay struck her as funny. Maybe he was finally wearing her down.

Except for a couple of odd days last month when she hadn't heard from him at all, he was persistent and managed to send her something or leave messages several times a day, no matter how meaningless or ridiculous, just to let her know she was in his thoughts.

She supposed the bombardment was serving its purpose. It was getting harder and harder to stay mad at him, especially when some of the stuff he said was really sweet. That didn't mean she wasn't still angry with him or that her self-respect wasn't in tatters.

She felt ill every time she thought of what a dupe she'd been and the depth of Jay's betrayal. She'd poured her heart out to "Panhead," had told him things she'd never told anyone else. If she'd known it was Jay, she never would have confessed the whole car wreck thing. She didn't know what had possessed her to even tell Panhead.

Jay'd had no right to pose as someone else, to trick her into confiding things she'd never wanted anyone else to know. It was the ultimate breach of privacy and trust. Of course, she was the dumbass who'd spilled her guts to an invisible stranger, but that was the point. She never thought she'd come face-to-face with him. He wasn't supposed to be real.

But he was real, and now he wouldn't leave her alone. Why? At first, she'd been certain Jay was acting out of a humongous case of guilt and the fear she might try to off herself again.

It seemed like his guilt and his sense of obligation should have started to fade by now, though, and if his messages and texts were any indication, he wasn't giving up anytime soon. Was it possible he really did love her? She didn't want to care, didn't want to get her hopes up, but it was getting more difficult to ignore him, to pretend indifference.

She let her head drop back against the ratty banquette she was sitting on, ignoring the jagged gash in the cream-colored vinyl seat that was poking her thigh and probably ripping a hole in her black tights. Not that it mattered. Her tights were full of holes already, and so was the black miniskirt she'd gotten from Goodwill. Ah, thrift stores: the clothier of choice for poor musicians.

Of course, some might argue that calling Erin a musician was a stretch. Since she'd joined the band on tour, she went through the motions onstage and managed to get most of the chords right on her guitar, but Zac was probably regretting making such a big deal out of her joining back up with them. She knew she had about as much charisma onstage as dryer lint, not to mention she was extra baggage in their already cramped RV (which wasn't much of a step up from Dale's RV in *The Walking Dead*).

Nate hadn't gone home to his baby mama after all. Erin suspected that had just been an excuse Zac made up, that Nate had never really intended to leave, so now she was a fifth wheel to the band's normal foursome.

Zac had welcomed her with open arms, literally, when she'd caught up with them in Nashville; it was as if their argument never happened. He was the leader of the band, so no one protested when she'd joined up. In fact, Norf had been happy to share his bed with her again.

As if conjured by her thoughts, Norf—past friend-with-benefits, current pothead and drummer extraordinaire—entered the RV and slammed the flimsy metal door behind him, breaking into Erin's reverie. "What's shakin', bacon?"

"Nothing."

He crowded in next to her on the banquette, and the smells of weed, cigarette smoke, and alcohol emanating from him were sweetly pungent in the cramped space. Norf had obviously been indulging in his usual debauchery in preparation for their upcoming show.

He smiled, his white teeth peeking through his auburn Grizzly Adams beard. The unstained state of his teeth was a miracle, considering he smoked like a chimney and had questionable dental hygiene.

He was cute in a grungy kind of way, with long hair the same auburn color as his beard and muscular arms from playing the drums. He always wore a slouchy beanie crocheted out of olive-green yarn. It was the kind of hat people with dreadlocks wore, although he didn't have any.

He inclined his head toward her phone. "You're gonna break that thing if you're not careful."

She looked down to see she was white-knuckling her phone. She tossed it onto the table.

"So what's up?" he asked. "I never see you these days."

That was ridiculous. "Norf, we live in a place the size of a space capsule and sleep in the same bed. You see me all the time."

They shared a bed out of necessity, not because of any sexual attraction, at least on her part. It was the same with her brother and Michelle. They also had to share a bed, but it was strictly platonic. Nate was the only one who got a bed of his own, but it was nothing to get excited over. The lumpy, thin berth that pulled down from the wall in the back of the RV was far from comfortable.

"Not true that I see you all the time," protested Norf. "You're always asleep by the time I get to bed."

"That's because you don't go to bed until seven in the morning."

Ignoring that logic, he continued as if she hadn't spoken. "And then you're always gone when I get up."

"You don't get up until three in the afternoon."

"Well, aren't we Miss High-and-Mighty." His tone was one of mock indignation, and the exaggerated look of disapproval on his face coaxed a small smile from Erin. "Nice," he said. "Haven't seen one of those from you in a while."

Feeling self-conscious, she looked down and started fidgeting with a fingernail.

"And when we are around each other," he went on, "you're usually typing away on that laptop of yours. We never really talk." He looked at the offending computer sitting on the table next to her phone. She'd bought a refurbished laptop when they were in Lincoln, Nebraska, with the meager paycheck she got for her part in the band.

She shrugged. "My writing is important to me."

She didn't try to keep it a secret anymore. When she wasn't sleeping, eating, rehearsing with the band or onstage, she was writing, and she didn't care who knew. She'd been stripped bare by Jay, and she'd survived it. Nothing else after that could be as painful.

She'd let Zac and Michelle read some of her stuff. To her surprise, Zac had liked the mystery novel with the wheeler hero, but—and this was not a surprise—he hadn't liked the romance. His criticism of it, though, wasn't nearly as hard to hear as she'd thought it would be. In fact, it had been constructive.

Michelle had supposedly liked everything. Erin found that harder to believe but tried to accept her friend's praise gracefully. Still, she appreciated Zac's blunt honesty. In the long run it would make her a better writer, and she was proud of herself for realizing that instead of freaking out and getting down on herself.

She'd sent a few query letters to agents regarding her mystery novel. So far, she'd gotten two rejections and hadn't heard from the others. The rejections, like Zac's criticism, didn't hurt as much as Erin had thought they would. If she couldn't find an agent or a publisher, maybe she would check into self-publishing. She might only make ten bucks from her novel that way, but who knew? Whatever happened, she would learn from it.

"It's cool you're so into your writing," Norf said, drawing her attention back to him. "I get that, but you know what Confucius said: 'All work and no play makes Erin a dull girl.'"

Amused, she said, "I think that's from *The Shining,* not Confucius."

Norf grinned. "Whatevs." He reached a long arm over to the mini fridge across from the table and grabbed a couple of Miller Lite longnecks.

Erin didn't want one, but Norf popped the cap off and handed it to her before she could decline. She curled her hand around it but didn't take a sip.

Norf eyed her. "That's called a 'beer.' You're supposed to drink it."

"I'm not really thirsty."

He snorted. "Since when is thirst a factor? It's *beer.*" He studied her face for a moment. "You're different these days. No more Party Erin."

She shrugged. "It always seems to get me in trouble."

His gaze grew thoughtful. "Was it the car wreck? I mean, that was some life-changing shit, wasn't it? You almost died."

She focused on the dark, amber-colored beer bottle in front of her, tracing the rim with her index finger. Where did that question come from? The car wreck was months ago, and Norf had been on the tour during her recovery. She wouldn't have expected him to think too much about it. "I wasn't wasted," she said, feeling like she needed to clarify. "That wasn't the cause of the wreck."

"I know. Probably just your usual crappy driving."

She shoved his shoulder playfully. "Hey, I'm a great driver."

"Right. That's why you totaled your car."

"Just bad luck," she said. She wasn't about to go into the real reason she'd crashed.

Norf sounded more serious, almost grave, when he said, "I was really worried about you, you know. Do you remember me visiting you in the hospital?"

She shook her head. "I don't remember much about that time."

"That's probably a good thing."

She gave a perfunctory nod.

"Hey," he said, gently cupping her cheek and bringing her face up to look at him. "I'm really—like, totally—so very incredibly fucking glad you're okay."

For Norf, that convoluted sentiment was pretty eloquent. Erin appreciated that he cared, even though he was looking into her eyes in *that* way, serious and intense—the universal look that said he wanted to kiss her.

For a second, she was tempted. It would be so easy to fall into her old pattern, to seek solace with a guy, especially with Norf. He was easy and familiar, but starting things up with him again wouldn't make her forget Jay. She'd learned that lesson with Duncan. It would just make her feel worse about herself and possibly hurt Norf in the process. Besides, she wasn't a slut. Not anymore.

Maybe there was a shred of her self-respect left after all.

Norf's lips were nearly to her mouth when she put a hand on his chest to stop him. "Don't."

He stared at her for a moment. "It's true, isn't it? Some dude broke your heart."

"No," Erin lied. "Why do you say that?"

"Zac. He said you hooked up with some guy, that you originally didn't want to come back to the band. I figure you only came back to us because things didn't work out. That's why you've been all mopey."

Erin didn't answer, just stared at her beer.

"Were you the dumper or the dumpee?"

"It was kind of mutual."

"You sure it's over?"

"Yes."

"Do you still have feelings for this guy?"

"No."

"Ah," Norf said with sympathy. "So you've still got it bad for him."

Erin shook her head and rolled her eyes.

After a faint beer-smelling burp, he said, "Well, if you need someone to help you forget, I'd like to offer myself up for your consideration. As you know from past experience, one night with The Norf Man will blow your mind."

Erin grinned. "Thanks. I'll keep that in mind."

He clinked his bottle with hers. "Cheers."

"Cheers."

"Seriously," he said as he got up to leave, picking up both her untouched beer and his, "call Dr. Norf if you need to talk or if you need some sex therapy."

She smiled dryly. "You'll be the first."

With that, he shut the door, leaving her alone again. Erin sighed and slid her laptop in front of her. It was about an hour and a half until the show. She had time to write before she had to go.

She tried to start where she'd left off, but she couldn't concentrate. The renewed silence of the RV was too loud, and her phone seemed to be staring at her, its little black screen beckoning and seductive.

No. She couldn't give in. She would never get over Jay if she opened up communication with him again. But her inner voice wouldn't be quiet. What if he meant everything he'd said, like the part about loving her? What if she was being too hard on him?

In the end, none of that mattered. She was still a

freak, and he still deserved someone normal.

She squared her shoulders and pressed her lips together. She was going to write. She was not going to think about Jay Bontrager or wonder what he was doing or if he was okay. She was not. And that was not her cell phone burning a hole in the table. As of this moment, it didn't exist.

Fingers poised over the keyboard, she sat there for a full five minutes and couldn't write a word. She glanced at her phone, which seemed to keep shouting at her, and blew out a breath that stirred the bangs on her forehead.

She should turn the phone off and hide the damn thing before Jay texted her again or before she did something dumb, like texted him back.

She picked it up, intending to get rid of it so she'd be able to concentrate. Out of sight, out of mind, right?

Right. And the road to hell was paved with good intentions.

Chapter 28

Yes. I know Tacocat is the same backwards and forwards. It's also a punk band from Seattle.

Erin didn't have to wait long for a response to her text. Her phone rang instantly. She let it ring a couple of times, her pulse pounding and her hands trembling with adrenaline. Finally, taking a deep breath, she got up the nerve to answer. "Hello?"

After a beat, Jay said, "Erin?"

She closed her eyes briefly, savoring the sound of him. "Hi."

"Hey." His voice was thick, the small word holding so much emotion and longing behind it that Erin felt a powerful tug on her heart.

Everything they both wanted to say clogged the line between them, so Erin cleared her throat and broke the ice. "So, um, Tacocat? Where did that come from?" It was trivial after everything that had gone down between them, but it seemed better to start with an anthill than a mountain.

"Just thought you needed a good palindrome to liven

things up."

She responded with a quiet snort, rolling her eyes a little. He sounded more like himself now, more sexy cockiness tinged with teasing.

"Thanks," she said. "I'm surprised you've even heard of Tacocat, though."

"Or a palindrome?"

Another little puff of amusement. "That, too," she teased. Although, for the record, he was one of the smartest guys she knew.

"I've been listening to some college radio."

"Oh. Really?" She was surprised. She didn't think he liked it that much, that he'd only listened to it when they were together to humor her.

"Yeah," he continued. "It's sort of grown on me. And I thought that was a cool name for a band."

"Yeah. It is."

"And it made me feel closer to you."

"Tacocat did?"

He gave a low chuckle that made her girlie bits get a little warm. "No. College radio did, especially when they played one of your band's songs."

"Oh." Cue the blush.

"You guys have been gaining momentum."

"Yeah. It seems unreal to me, though. I feel kind of like an interloper, more part of the audience than part of the show."

"I'm sure Zac doesn't feel that way."

"No. He seems glad I came back."

Neither said anything for a second or two, and then Jay said, "So . . . how have you been, darlin'?"

Darlin'. That buttery word slid through her, and now the warm girlie bits tingled. To think she'd once hated for him to call her that.

Crap. She needed to tread carefully here. Thirty seconds into their conversation, and Jay already had her melting for him. What was she doing?

She should never have responded to that text. She was weak. She would never be able to resist him. What had she been thinking, that maybe they could just be friends or something? Ridiculous.

She needed to dial back her need for him and be more wary.

"Erin? You still there?"

"Yeah."

"Don't do that."

"Do what?"

"Withdraw from me."

"I'm not."

"Yes, you are. You're starting to think you answered my text on impulse and that it was a mistake."

She huffed. "How can you tell all that from a half a second of silence?"

"I just can."

"Jay . . . ," she began, then trailed off. What did she want? Why was she even talking to him? She couldn't let it go anywhere. "I—"

"Erin, just listen. I'm sorry. I know I shouldn't have

lied to you."

"You made me feel like a complete dumbass."

A pained pause. "I know. Christ, darlin', if I could take it all back, I would. But you know what? I'm not sorry you opened up to me, and I'm that same guy you felt comfortable talking to online. I want you to feel like you can tell *me* anything, just like you could with Panhead."

"Oh, right. Like the fact that your gimpy legs make me all horny?"

To her surprise, he laughed. "Yes. Even that."

"I don't believe you."

He sighed. "I know you have every reason not to. I'm sorry for deceiving you. I wish I had better words than that, something more powerful, but I don't. Please, Erin, forgive me. Let me earn back your trust."

She let out a sigh of her own. "It's not that I don't forgive you, Jay. That's the easy part. I know you're sorry, and I know you didn't mean to hurt me. It's not even so much about the Panhead thing anymore. It goes a lot deeper."

"Erin—"

"And you know what? I saw it coming, and I still let it happen. It's in my DNA. God made me, and he proclaimed, 'Let it be written that Erin Marie Silver is destined to have her heart broken over and over and over forever.'"

"I don't think God does shit like that."

Anguish washed over her, making her eyes sting

and her throat constrict. She swallowed hard to keep the waterworks at bay. "Yes, he does, or he wouldn't have made me a dev."

In a quiet, intense tone, Jay said, "I think he made you for me."

And there he went, disarming her again. She wanted to believe that might be true, but she'd been beat down too many times to believe in destiny and soulmates. That only happened in fiction, not real life.

A couple of tears slipped free of her eyes, despite her best efforts, and she wiped them away. "I saw the revulsion on your face the moment you realized just how deep the creep goes in me, Jay."

"Dammit, Erin—"

"Let me finish. I don't know if I can get past that, any more than you can truly get past me being a dev. We can try all we want, but it will always be there. I think there's always going to be that doubt between us."

He was quiet for a moment before he spoke. "Okay. You've had your say, now let me have mine. I'm sorry I reacted the way I did. I was an ass. But I've had a lot of time to do some soul-searching since we've been apart, and I think the reason I had a hard time with the dev thing was because I still had some deep-seated issues with accepting my injury and what it did to me."

"But you've been injured a long time."

"I know. And I thought I'd come to terms with it, but apparently I hadn't. That's why I reacted the way I did." After a pause, he added, "I couldn't see how you could possibly find the paralyzed part of my body attractive because *I* was disgusted by it. Long story short: It wasn't you. It was me."

She gave a small laugh and rolled her eyes. "That's supposed to be an excuse for breaking up, not one for getting back together."

There was a smile in his voice. "Well, do you think it might work for getting back together?"

She wanted to say yes, wanted so badly to believe they still had a chance, but caution held her back. "I don't know. Maybe."

"I can work with 'maybe' as long as it means you'll keep talking to me."

She smiled, even as her brain kept shouting this was a big mistake. "I'll keep talking to you."

"That's all I ask, darlin'. That's all I ask."

Chapter 29

Erin read the e-mail again on the screen of her phone, and a grin split her face. She couldn't wait to tell Jay, but she would have to because she wanted to tell him the news in person.

Things had been going great with him in the last month. Although she was still cautious, she and Jay had been talking and texting every day. They were getting to know each other in a new way, without their hormones or other baggage interfering, and they were slowly but surely mending their relationship.

A gust of wind blew Erin's bangs away from her face, and she combed her fingers through to fix them. To gain some privacy, she was sitting at an abandoned picnic table a few camping pads over from the campsite where the band's RV was hooked up.

Switching to the favorites screen on her cell, she tapped Jay's name from the list. To her relief, he answered almost immediately. "What's up, darlin'?"

His voice sounded hoarse and kind of weak, and some of her excitement morphed into concern. "Nothing," she answered. "What's up with you? You sound kind of weird."

He cleared his throat, and his voice came out stronger. "Just tired. Things are busy here."

"But everything else is okay?" She meant his health, specifically his back, but it was a touchy subject. He got evasive whenever she asked him about it and usually steered the subject to something else.

"Everything's fine," he said, giving the same answer he always did, but that hoarseness had crept into his voice again.

Something was off with him. Erin could feel it, and she wanted to see with her own eyes that he was okay. Now she had the perfect excuse. "So, guess what. We're playing in San Francisco in three days, on Friday. I'll be just across the bay from you. I thought you might want to come see us." She added shyly, "Or, more specifically, me."

There was such a long pause that she pulled her phone away from her ear to see if the call had dropped. Putting it back to her ear, she said, "Jay? You still there?"

"Yeah. I'm here."

Okay. So, not exactly the response she was hoping for. She'd thought he would be more excited. She tried to be cool and not sound disappointed. "If you don't want to, that's okay. It's no big deal."

"No, no," he said hastily. "I want to."

"Is it—are you worried, you know, about accessibility? I think the venue is accessible. At least, they said it was when I called to check, but, if you want,

I could come see you instead. I'd have to get my brother or somebody to drive me to your place in the RV, but we could probably figure it out."

"No. I'm not—no. Don't come here. My place is a dump."

She snickered. "Trust me. It's probably way better than the RV."

"Trust me," Jay echoed dryly. "It's probably not. No," he said with conviction. "I'll come see you."

She smiled, relieved. Still, she gave him another chance at an out. "You sure? I don't want to twist your arm or anything. I just thought—"

"Erin," he said in that whiskey-tinged voice of his, "there's nothing I'd rather do."

* * *

Zac's glare was burning a hole in her, and Erin knew she'd hit another wrong chord. What key was she even in? Her fingers were stiff and clumsy as she tried to fit them on the strings of her guitar. She should just stop playing and pretend. It wasn't like the band really needed her. She was filler, a charity case. They only let her stay because Zac was her brother, and Michelle and Norf were still her friends.

She got the vibe from Nate that he couldn't care less whether she lived or died. After all, she'd stolen his thunder. Well, maybe not stolen it, but encroached on it. The feeling was mutual. Nate was barely a blip on her radar.

She tried to get her mind back on the song, tried to concentrate, but her thoughts kept going back to Jay. Where was he?

Communication with him had been sparse the last three days; she'd sent him the address of the bar and gotten a quick "OK" in return, but they hadn't talked on the phone since Wednesday. Still, she hadn't thought anything of it, just that he must be busy with work. He hadn't said anything that would make her think he wasn't coming to see her.

She squinted and strained to see if she could see him in the crowded venue where the band was performing, but the hot stage lights were too bright and blinded her. She'd expected him to come early and hang out a little before the show, but he hadn't. He hadn't sent her a text to tell her what time he would be there either, but maybe he'd shown up after the show started. Maybe he was there and she couldn't see him.

She faked her way through the rest of the show and then the encore, which she'd always thought was a stupid thing. Why didn't bands just play all their songs and tell everyone they weren't doing an encore? It was all so phony. It felt like they were fishing for adoration, making the fans beg for more.

The encore lasted forever, but finally it ended. Zac and the others started packing up instruments and breaking down equipment after the lights went up, but Erin dodged her way through the handful of groupies that always seemed to linger after a show and tried to make herself invisible. Unfortunately, a guy sitting at one of the few tables near the bar tapped her on the shoulder. "Hey. Great show."

She gave him a perfunctory smile. "Thanks."

"You're Erin, right?"

She stopped scanning the milling crowd long enough to answer. "Yeah." The guy was cute. He had short, dark hair and a nice smile, but she was more partial to blonds these days.

"I've been a fan of Silver pretty much since you guys first started," he said. "I'm from San Antonio originally."

"Hm," she replied absently, still searching the crowed. The place they were in was a warehouse that had been converted into a bar and live-show venue. She couldn't see Jay, but maybe he was hidden. He'd be sitting down, of course, while most of the people were standing.

"Small world, right? Been out here a couple of years now."

"Really?" she replied, barely registering what Cute Guy was saying.

Where was Jay? He wouldn't do this to her. He wouldn't stand her up. He wouldn't. Had something happened? What if he'd been in a wreck or something? The thought made her stomach lurch. She needed to check her phone, but it was in her bag behind the stage.

"So, how is your ankle?" Cute Guy asked.

That got her attention, and she frowned. "What?"

"Your ankle. I read you hurt it pretty bad last spring in a car accident."

It was weird, how complete strangers knew stuff like that. It had happened a few times since she'd been on the tour, but it always disconcerted her. Zac ate that kind of thing up, but Erin didn't like the invasion of privacy and had to force herself to be polite. Zac would freak if she was rude to a fan. "The ankle is a lot better." She patted his shoulder. "Thanks for coming out."

Before the guy could engage her again, she walked away, her search for Jay impeded several more times by fans of the band. She had to face reality, however, when the bar was nearly empty and Jay was still nowhere to be seen. Making her way back to the stage, she found her bag and checked her phone. There was a short text from him that had been sent shortly after their set started.

Sorry I couldn't make it, darlin'. Things got busy.

The excited buzz of anticipation she'd had at the prospect of seeing Jay again suddenly drained from her, and she sank down to the edge of the stage, feeling numb.

That was it? That was all he had to say? He didn't even seem bummed. She'd looked forward to this for days, but it hadn't even been important enough to him to warrant a voice mail. All she got was a lame text, as if he'd hardly given her a second thought.

What the fuck? Had she imagined the last few weeks they'd been talking? Had she imagined he'd practically stalked her for three months before that, begging her to talk to him? Why would he do this?

She closed her eyes and tried to shut out the disappointment crushing her lungs and stealing her breath, but it was no use. Once again, she'd let down her guard, and once again, her heart had been ground to dust.

Chapter 30

"So," said Zac, sitting down in the empty lawn chair opposite Erin, "you wanna tell me what planet you were on last night? Because it wasn't this one."

Erin took a sip of the coffee she'd gotten from a local coffeehouse across the street from the bar/warehouse where the band had played last night. They were still in San Francisco, and the autumn wind was blustery and cold. She was glad she was wearing a thick hoodie sweatshirt, even though it reminded her of the ones Jay always wore. Her battered heart twisted at the thought of him, while her brain shook its fist and yelled, "I told you so!"

The RV was parked in an alley behind the bar. Thank God the bar was located at the bottom of one of those crazy-steep hills San Francisco was known for. If it had been at the top, Erin had no doubt the RV, with its iffy, groaning emergency brake, would have careened to its death.

"You're up early," she said to Zac. It was early for him, anyway—almost noon. The rest of the band members, she assumed, were still asleep.

"Don't change the subject." He jerked his head in a maneuver to get his tousled mop of black, inky hair out of his eyes and hunched into his black leather jacket. "What's going on with you, Erin? You've been so moody since you came on the tour. First, for months, you were all mopey and quiet. Then, lately, you've been all happy, more like yourself. But last night you couldn't concentrate. It was like you'd never seen a guitar before."

"Gee, thanks," she said, pressing her lips together. "I wasn't that bad."

He looked dubious. "The truth hurts. You sucked."

She didn't say anything, just held her coffee with both hands and stared at the plastic lid.

"This has to do with Jay, doesn't it?" he said out of the blue.

She looked at him. "Why would you say that?"

"Because you lived with him."

She raised a brow. "So?"

"It's a law of nature. It's not possible for a guy and a girl to live together and not hook up, unless, of course, one of them is a troll."

"Or a freak," Erin murmured to herself.

"What?"

"Nothing."

"He's the one you were boinking, isn't he? He's the reason you didn't want to come back."

Even though Zac was right, she was indignant. "No."

His expression was calculating. "Yep. You guys hooked up."

"You and Michelle live together, and nothing is going on between the two of you," Erin pointed out. "And nothing is going on with Norf and me, even though we share a bed."

"Maybe not now," Zac said sagely, "but in the past, Michelle and I knew each other in the biblical sense—"

Erin rolled her eyes.

"—and let's not get started on your history with Norf."

"That was a long time ago."

"Yeah. Forever ago," he said dryly. "Like, last year."

"It's ancient history."

"Doesn't make it any less true."

She couldn't deny that. "Whatever."

"So, spiel," he said with a cheesy German accent. "Vat iss ze deal vith Bontrager?"

She took a sip of her cooling coffee. She usually liked her coffee black or drank tea, but, bummed about Jay and feeling sorry for herself, she'd splurged and gotten a mocha with raspberry. It was the epitome of "bittersweet," made with real dark chocolate and raspberry syrup, and was positively decadent. The smell alone was divine. "Your guess is as good as mine. I have no idea what's going on with Jay and me."

"Was the sex good?"

She felt her face heat a little. "God, Zac. That's none of your business."

"What? Don't go all prudish on me now."

She exhaled. "We never got that far."

"Uh-oh." He thought for a moment. "So, like, can he even have sex?"

"Yes," she said, not elaborating. Zac had an expectant look on his face, but she didn't want to go into the details of how sex worked with Jay's disability. Besides, that wasn't technically why they hadn't done the deed. "Jay wasn't the problem. It was me. I screwed it up, no pun intended."

"What do you mean? How did you screw it up?"

She couldn't meet his eye, so she focused on her coffee. "I freaked him out."

"How?"

"Because I'm a freak." She eased the lid off her coffee and took another lukewarm sip.

Zac threw his hands in the air. "Come on, Erin. Stop being so cryptic. Are you secretly into BDSM or something? Did you break out the whips and chains?"

Erin snorted. "I wish."

Okay," Zac said, his brows knitting together. "Now you're freaking *me* out."

Erin eyed her brother. Could she tell him? She was tired of hiding what she was from him. He was her best friend. She'd always told him everything—everything except that she was a dev. She hadn't had much luck in the past coming clean with people about her devoteeism, but she desperately needed him to understand, to accept her.

She looked down at the coffee in her hands again. "There's something wrong with me, Zac."

He rested his elbows on his thighs and loosely clasped his hands. "Tell me something I don't know."

She quirked her mouth to one side, annoyed. "I'm serious."

"Oh. Well, let's hear it, then."

She hesitated a full minute before she finally spoke. "I . . . have this attraction to guys with disabilities, especially guys like Jay—guys with paraplegia."

Zac sat back in his chair, his features scrunched into a *huh?* look.

Erin was too embarrassed to meet his eyes. Staring at the side of the dingy RV behind him instead, she said, "I know it's weird—perverse, even—but I can't help it." She had the urge to somehow hide and drew her knees up, hugging them to her chest, the soles of her beloved biker boots on the seat of her chair. She still held her coffee in her hand. "It's not something I choose. It's a strange attraction I can't help, no matter how much I try to fight it."

Zac watched her, not saying anything.

She soldiered on with her confession. "I've had this . . . fascination . . . ever since I can remember. Like I said, I'm especially partial to guys with paraplegia, but I'd also date someone with quadriplegia. In fact, I *have* dated someone with quadriplegia before."

The *huh?* look morphed into a *what the fuck?* look. "So, you'd date someone like, say, Stephen Hawking?"

"Uh, no. For God's sake, he's in his seventies. Way too old for me."

Zac smacked himself on the forehead. "Of course. If only he were younger." He was being sarcastic, but at least he no longer looked like he had a random piece of hair stuck to his tongue.

"If you're asking if I'd date any guy as long as he had a disability," she said, "the answer is no. There still has to be chemistry, and we have to have things in common. To me, the disability is just another trait, like eye or hair color."

She could see the gears turning in Zac's head. After what seemed like a year of silence, Erin couldn't stand it anymore. "What are you thinking?" She swallowed hard. "Are you disgusted?"

Zac took a deep breath and rubbed his hands on his thighs before answering, "I have to admit, it's pretty fuckin' weird."

Erin's heart plummeted. Had she just repulsed the last person left in her family, the only person in the world she knew for sure loved her? Would he want her to go now, to stay away from him?

To her surprise, he shrugged. "But, to each his own, right?"

She stayed absolutely still, afraid she was imagining it. "So . . . you don't hate me?"

"Hate you?" he asked, incredulous. He shook his head. "Of course not. You're my little sister, you dork. I could never hate you."

Warmth pooled behind her eyes, and Erin loved her brother more than ever in that moment. "I'm not your little sister."

He grinned. "One word, pygmy: size." He pointed to her, then to himself. "You little. Me big," he said, doing a bad imitation of a Native American from a John Wayne movie. He crossed his arms. "So what's the problem with Jay?"

She sighed. "It's complicated."

"Sounds like a match made in heaven to me. He's handicapped. You have a thing for handicapped dudes."

"Don't say 'handicapped,'" she corrected. "He shouldn't be defined that way. The only thing that handicaps him is an insensitive, able-bodied world that either forgets to—or won't—make things accessible for him."

It was Zac's turn to roll his eyes. "Let me start over. Jay has a disability. You have a thing for dudes with disabilities."

"It's not that simple."

"What are you not telling me?"

"I sort of misled him."

"Did he not know about your, uh, unconventional attraction?"

Erin gave a small smile at Zac's effort to sound politically correct and said, "It's called 'devoteeism.' We're called 'devs' for short."

"'We?'" Zac's brows went up.

"Yeah. There's a lot of us. There's this website where we meet other devs and wheelers."

"Wow. So you've had this whole secret life that I

never knew anything about?"

She grimaced. "It's not really something I wanted to broadcast."

"And Jay didn't know you were a—you know, a dev?"

Erin didn't want to get into everything that had happened or how she'd met Jay at Luis's, so she just said, "No. He knew."

"Then I'm really not seeing the problem."

"It's embarrassing, Zac. He knew I was a dev, but he didn't quite know the extent of it. When he found out, it drove him away." She would never forget the expression on Jay's face when she'd tried to explain the depth of her attraction. "He was disgusted."

"What do you mean, 'the extent of it'?" asked Zac.

She rested her forehead on her knees for a second and then faced him. "He thought my attraction had to do more with his strength in dealing with his disability, his character. I guess I wasn't totally honest with him, but, in my defense, I didn't understand it all myself. But it's not just about his strength of character and the way he adapts to his disability with such class. It's physical, too."

"Physical?"

"I think he's really hot, Zac, all of him, paralyzed legs and all."

"Okaaay." Zac's tone said he was a little weirded out but wasn't judging. "And that grossed him out?"

"Yeah."

"And that's why you left San Antonio?"

Erin groaned. "No. It's a long story, but I found out he'd been lying to me. He posed as a wheeler on the dev website I lurk on and started private-messaging me."

"Why?"

"He said it was the only way he could think of to get to know me better because I wouldn't talk to him in person. As you know, I didn't like him when he first moved in."

"Right. You thought he was a serial killer."

"Yeah," she said on a small, rueful laugh. "More like just an asshole. But anyway," she continued, "I was really angry with him for deceiving me on the website, for pretending to be someone else. I felt like such a fool, and I didn't think I could trust him ever again. That's why I left San Antonio. I thought it would never work with him, that we were never meant to be. I needed to get away from him to get over him, but he wouldn't leave me alone. He called and texted me every day, trying to get me to forgive him."

"And you eventually gave in and started talking to him again."

"Yeah. I thought things were going well between us."

"But?"

Her coffee was completely cold now, but she took a sip and let its bitterness and sweetness mix on her tongue. "You know he's in Oakland, now, right?"

"Yeah."

"I asked him to come to the show last night. He said he would."

"But he was a no-show?"

"Yep."

Zac frowned. "Did he call you? Did he give you a reason?"

She got up and threw her coffee cup in a smelly alley Dumpster that sat a few yards from the RV and then sat back down. "He sent me a lame text saying he was sorry, that things had gotten busy."

"And what? You think he was lying or something?"

God, Erin thought, why were guys so clueless sometimes? "Yes, I think he was lying."

"Why?"

"I don't know. Intuition."

Zac sat back in his chair, his manner doubtful. "Or maybe the dude was just busy."

"Zac, he practically cyberstalked me for months until I talked to him again. He even told me a million times that he loves me."

"Oh. Whoa."

"Yeah. Kind of a big deal. But now, after all these months, we have a rare opportunity to see each other, and he doesn't show?" She propped her chin on her hand, elbow resting on the arm of the plastic lawn chair. "It's weird. And he's had all morning to call me or text me, and he hasn't."

"Have you called or texted him?"

She gave him a dubious look. "No. I do have some pride, you know."

"Right. Pride," Zac said, in his I'll-never-understand-women voice.

She ignored that. "Know what I think? I think he changed his mind. I think he's not as over the dev thing as he insisted he was. Maybe the prospect of seeing me in person brought it all home again, and he balked."

"Or maybe he's just busy."

She shook her head. "I'm getting a different vibe."

Zac rolled his eyes again. "Look. Girls read shit into the things guys do and say, and most of the time they're wrong. Guys are pretty literal. If he couldn't come because he was too busy, he was probably too busy."

"Even if that's all it is, Zac, it still means Jay doesn't care about me as much as I care about him. I mean, if the situation were reversed, I would put everything aside"—she swept her arm in a dramatic arc—"no matter what it was, to go see him, especially if I knew he wouldn't be in town for long."

"Good point. Maybe he's just a scrote, then. You're better off without him."

Erin exhaled an exasperated breath. "You're not supposed to say that, Zac. You're supposed to say I should go see him for myself, try to get some closure and find out what's really going on."

"Now, see," he said, shaking his head, "that's what a girl would say."

She hadn't even entertained the thought of going to see Jay, but now that she'd said it, it was starting to take root. Her mind started racing, trying to figure out how she could find him and then get there.

She knew one thing: Time was running out. The band would probably be leaving in about an hour to head to Santa Barbara. If she was going to get up the nerve to go find Jay, she needed to act quickly.

Yet again, however, her heart was at odds with her brain. Her heart said that something else had to be going on, that Jay wouldn't have stood her up if he could help it, but her brain said she should let it go—let *him* go—before she made an idiot of herself . . . again. How many times was it going to take for her to learn?

Apparently, one more.

Chapter 31

Erin felt antsy as she waited for Luis to answer her call. Zac and the rest of the band would be leaving in fifteen minutes. She had to make the decision to stay and find Jay or go with them. Jay wasn't answering her calls or texts, which was another sign from the powers that be that she shouldn't try to see him.

What if Luis didn't answer? It was the second time she'd tried to call him. He hadn't responded to the voice mail she'd left him. What if he never answered her? What if he decided to ignore her as payback for all those messages he'd left after her wreck that she'd never returned?

But Luis answered on the third ring. "Hello?"

She moved farther down the alley from where the RV was parked so no one would overhear. "Luis? It's Erin. Erin Silver. You know, Jay's roommate?"

"Yes, Erin. Of course I know who you are." His tone was gentle, with that lyrical quality that came with his mild Hispanic accent. "Like I would forget you. You were my friend before you were Jay's. What can I do for you?"

She cleared her throat. "Um, do you know the address where Jay is staying while he's in Oakland?"

"Why do you want to know?" Luis didn't sound like he was being a jerk. He sounded genuinely curious.

"I'm in San Francisco, and I want to see him. I thought I would surprise him, since I'm so close." Erin thought it was better if Luis didn't know Jay had blown her off and wasn't returning her calls.

"As his employer, I can't give out private information like that. I'm sorry."

Erin gripped her phone tighter. "It's not like I'm a salesperson or somebody who wants to hassle him, Luis. I just want to surprise him. And I have some good news to tell him."

"What good news?"

"It's personal, and it's something I want Jay to know first, before I tell anyone else."

Luis let out a long sigh. "I would really like to help you, Erin, but Jay is a very good friend of mine. Aside from the fact that it really is against the law for me to give out his address, he asked me personally not to share his info. I have to respect that."

"Even with me?" Surely Luis knew about Jay's relationship with her.

Luis hesitated a beat. Then, with a hint of apology in his voice, he said, "Even with you."

"But you know we're kind of together, right? I mean, well, we were, and then we kind of broke up, but then—"

"I know, Erin. I know all of that. But I'm telling you,

Jay doesn't want to be found right now."

"But it's *me*, Luis."

"I know. But I think he especially doesn't want to be found by you."

Erin's stomach slid down to her toes. Jay had actually told Luis not to tell her how to find him? What the hell was going on? More than ever, she wanted to see Jay in person. Now that she was over the initial hurt and disappointment of him being a no-show, she was convinced something was fishy, and that feeling was underscored by Luis's dogged refusal to give her information.

"Luis, what is going on? Why wouldn't he want to be found?"

"Again, I'm not at liberty to say."

She made a guttural noise of frustration in her throat. "Is this really about Jay, or is it you?"

"What do you mean?"

"Well, you and I sort of had something going before that morning in your apartment. Is this some kind of revenge on your part? Are you trying to keep Jay and me apart out of spite?"

"Of course not," he said, sounding indignant.

"Then, for God's sake, what is going on? And don't give me all this crap about respecting Jay's privacy. You sure as hell didn't respect mine when you gave him my username on the dev website. You're no saint, so spill it. You owe me, Luis."

He didn't respond for a full minute.

"Luis, you still there?" If he'd been in front of her, she would have given him a good shake and yelled, "Come on!"

Finally, he muttered something that sounded like, "This is bullshit."

"What?"

His sigh was loud and long-suffering. "I'm going to tell you the truth, Erin, because, as you said, I owe you and also because you and Jay are two of the most stubborn, star-crossed people I've ever known. First you were mad at him and wouldn't talk to him, and now he's playing the martyr. If I don't intervene—"

"What do you mean he's playing the martyr?" she said, coming alert.

"—you two will never get together."

Erin was tense now, her pulse picking up speed. "What do you mean he's playing the martyr, Luis?"

"He's in a bad way, Erin. He didn't go to Oakland to open an office. He went there to have surgery on his back two months ago, and there's been complications. He's been staying in Stockton with his dad to recuperate."

As she processed that, a myriad of emotions swept through her—first shock, then anger Jay had lied to her again, and finally fear. It tangled her insides into knots, and her knees felt rubbery. She leaned a hand against the brick wall of the alley to steady herself. "But he was so stubborn about it. He wouldn't even talk about seeing a doctor. Believe me, I tried my best to get him to."

"The pain was affecting his work. I kind of gave him

an ultimatum."

She sniffed. "Right. Wouldn't want your bottom line to suffer."

"It wasn't really about that, Erin, but he wouldn't listen to me as a friend."

That, she could understand. "But why all the secrecy? It doesn't make sense."

"He's got his pride. He didn't want anyone to know. He didn't want to make a big deal of it, didn't want anyone worrying or fawning over him." Then, apparently feeling the need to defend his friend further, Luis added, "And it wasn't totally a lie. If all had gone like it was supposed to with the surgery and, depending on what did or didn't happen with you, he very well might have stayed and opened an office for me in Oakland. It would be a promotion for him. He'd be the boss."

"You said 'complications.'" A huge lump in her throat made it difficult to speak. "What complications, Luis? What's wrong with him?"

Another sigh. "The shit that often goes with SCI— bad urinary tract infection and a serious pressure sore on his ass. It's Stage III. He had skin-flap surgery on Wednesday to try to repair it."

Erin's hands were trembling, her heart racing. "Luis, you have to tell me what hospital he's in. I have to find him."

"I thought you'd never ask."

* * *

He was asleep when she got to St. Joseph's Medical Center in Stockton later that afternoon. He was lying on his side, pillows all around him and between his knees to help keep him in place, covered by a white sheet and lightweight, beige blanket. The bed was some kind of special hospital bed that redistributed his weight by pushing air into different sections of the mattress every five minutes or so, presumably to prevent any more pressure sores developing from lying in one position too long.

Erin had been watching the mattress subtly deflate and inflate for the last hour, the quiet hum of it hypnotically marking time. Judging by the other crisply made, empty bed in the room, Jay didn't have a roommate at the moment. She'd been alone with her thoughts, sitting in a standard-issue brown metal-and-vinyl chair by Jay's bed.

As he slept on, oblivious to the motion and noise of his bed, she studied him. He looked pale, and she wondered when he'd last been able to work on his bike in the sun.

Luis said Jay'd had the back surgery two months ago—a month after Erin had left San Antonio. He'd been living with his asshole dad in Stockton while he recuperated. Jay had been vague about exactly what had happened to cause the pressure sore and the UTI, but since, after his accident, he'd always been very diligent in trying to prevent both, Luis suspected Jay's dad had something to do with it. Erin suspected the same.

Jay would have needed help with a lot of things—transfers to and from his chair, for instance—if his mobility had been limited by a back brace after his surgery. Relying on his dad, especially for help with the more personal issues, would have rankled.

And from what Erin knew of Jay's father, she doubted the jerk would have been very vigilant in doing what was required to care for his son—like making sure Jay was out of his chair enough that he wasn't sitting on the same spot on his ass all day. Jay's pride and his father's general dickweedery would have been a bad combination.

Jay was facing her, his arm resting on a pillow that had been placed in front of his chest. Although his tan had faded, his skin still contrasted sharply with the white pillow. An IV was taped to the back of his hand and snaked up to the IV pole by his bed, and a hospital ID bracelet around his wrist somehow emphasized the sinew and masculinity of his arm and hand, the latent strength there, instead of taking away from it.

His golden surfer-boy hair was flat and looked a bit darker—it probably hadn't been washed for a few days—and he had a blond beard that was way beyond the stubble stage, passing into Ragnar the Viking territory. Despite his rather unkempt look, his lips looked even more kissable outlined by the beard.

Although he was still the hottest fallen angel she'd ever seen, it was hard to see him so vulnerable. Her heart broke to think he'd been going through all this alone, but, at the same time, she could have easily wrung his neck for not telling her the truth. She blew out a loud, angry sigh.

It must have penetrated his sleep, because his lashes fluttered open, revealing the deep grayish blue of his eyes. The waning afternoon light from the window behind her made them appear the color of a lake at midnight, reflecting the moon. "Erin?" he whispered, almost like he thought he might be imagining her.

"Hi," she said, trying to sound neutral. She wasn't ready to put her cards on the table yet. She wanted to see what he would say for himself.

"Hi," he rasped. Even hoarse, his voice still sent pleasant little shivers down her spine. That was all he said, though. He watched her, clearly waiting for the other shoe to drop, for her to lay into him.

"Nice place you got here," she said with false cheer, pointedly looking around the stark, sterile-looking hospital room.

"Thanks," he said, going along with the game, but wary and still waiting.

"I was in the neighborhood, thought I'd come say hi, see how the work was coming."

"It's . . . been busy."

She nodded like she wasn't about to have steam coming out of her ears. "Yeah. That's what you said in your text—you know, the one where you explained why you were a no-show last night?"

He held her gaze, still going along with the fake banter, but she thought she saw guilt flicker in his features.

"Too bad you couldn't make it," she said. "I have some news I wanted to tell you. I got an agent. She's going to shop my mystery novel around, see if she can sell it to a publisher."

His wariness faded for the moment, and he smiled. "I knew you could do it."

"I know you did. So thanks for believing in me."

"You're welcome."

Their eyes locked, and he seemed to be facing her as if she were a firing squad, as if he knew he was a condemned man. Unable to hold back any longer, Erin said, "What the fuck, Jay?"

His jaw went rigid.

She folded her arms over her chest and tried to make her voice sound less bitter than the betrayal and hurt simmering inside her. "So, you know how you begged me to forgive you for lying to me? How you said you wanted to earn back my trust? Well, here's a tip: Lying to me and telling me you were in Oakland instead of in a hospital in Stockton and then standing me up is *not* a good way to go about it!"

He closed his eyes, and his forehead creased in that ardent, sincere way he had that always made her want to believe anything he said. "I'm sorry."

"Okay. Good start." This time Erin was the one who waited, but he apparently wasn't going to say any more. "Is that it?"

He opened his eyes and met hers, but he still wasn't

talking.

"Tell me why you would do that, Jay. Tell me why you would lie. Again!"

"How did you find me?" he deflected.

Erin's eyes stung, but she was not going to let him see her cry. "Luis."

"He wasn't supposed to tell anyone."

She drew in a hard breath and looked up to the ceiling before training her gaze back on him. "I don't understand you. After everything that's happened, after you bugged the shit out of me to talk to you for months, I thought I meant more to you. For fuck's sake, you said you loved me. More than once! Was that a lie, too?"

He didn't answer.

She was outraged that he was being so closed up. "You know," she said, picking up her purse and throwing the strap over her head, "I wanted to see you in person, to find out what's going on with you and between us. Looks like I got my answer. Nothing." She stood up. "Thanks for the closure, shithead."

She stalked over and grabbed her big black suitcase on rollers that was against the wall near the door. She'd lugged the thing on three different buses to get to Jay's hospital. And what the hell was she going to do now? Zac and the band were at least three hours away, over halfway to Santa Barbara. She'd have to find another bus.

She shouldn't have come (understatement of the century). She was now the undisputed queen of idiots.

Her brain gloated, saying, "I told you so," while her heart cracked in two.

She had her hand on the handle of the door when Jay spoke, his deep, anguished voice slicing through the quiet of the room. "I didn't want you to see me like this, Erin."

She froze. If he'd said just about anything else, she probably would have kept going, but that, she couldn't ignore. She let go of her suitcase and walked back over to sit down in the chair by his bed. "Why?"

Again the muscle in his jaw went taut. "I didn't want your pity. I thought I'd have the back surgery and be better by the time I saw you again—if you ever forgave me. That's why I didn't tell you. But then there were complications."

"I heard. You give new meaning to the term 'bad ass.'"

He gave her the ghost of a playful Jay smirk, but his eyes were bleak.

She wanted to reach out and touch his cheek but refrained. She was in no way sure of what was happening here, although hope was trying to drag the two pieces of her cracked heart back together. "Does it look like I'm pitying you?"

He didn't comment.

Sighing, she took her purse back off and set it down, then leaned forward and idly ran her finger along the inside edge of his ID bracelet. It was as close as she dared get to touching him, at least for the moment. She didn't trust herself to do more, not until she knew where she stood with him. "I would have been here for you, Jay. All these months you've been dealing with this, and I wouldn't even talk to you." She looked him in the eye. "I was such a bitch. I'm so sorry."

His nostrils flared. "Now see, darlin'? That's what I'm talking about. You had good reason to be pissed at me, and I didn't want you to forgive me just because you felt sorry for me. I wanted you to forgive me because you were ready, because you wanted to."

She stopped the motion of her finger. "So why did you keep lying after I forgave you? I thought we were getting close again. And why let me think you were coming to see me and then not show?"

"I'm sorry. I didn't know how to tell you."

"Try words. I would have understood."

He squeezed his eyes shut for a second as if pained and then said, "What was I supposed to say? 'Sorry, darlin', but I've got this nasty extra hole in my ass that I have to get fixed, so I can't make your show. But once I'm over that in a couple of months and not pissing my pants anymore because of this urinary tract infection I keep getting, how about we get together for dinner?'"

"Yes, Jay," she said fervently. "That's exactly what you should have told me." She was deliberate when she spoke, trying to make him hear her. "I would have understood."

"Take a good look at me, Erin!" he growled, his features reddening.

Startled, she couldn't help but obey the furious command. Her gaze traveled over him. She was a little embarrassed to see a catheter winding its way from beneath his covers to a bag collecting urine that was hanging on a hook on the side of his bed. She quickly bounced her eyes back to his face, but it was too late. He knew what she'd seen.

"That's what I'm talking about," he said.

She sat back in her chair. "What? It's just a catheter, Jay. It's not a big deal. I don't care."

"You don't get it." He fisted the pillow his arm was lying on. "I'm a fucking mess!" he raged. "This isn't some dev fairytale where the wheeler overcomes adversity, then gets healed, and everyone lives happily ever after. I've been bedridden for weeks. I keep getting UTIs, and then there's this goddamn pressure sore that will take me months to get over—and that's if everything goes the way it's supposed to. Welcome to the land of SCI, Erin! Is this what you want, a man who can't even sit up in a fucking chair anymore?"

"I don't know what you want from me, Jay! Are you trying to scare me away? You want me to leave?"

His fury seemed to have run its course, and he slowly closed his eyes. "You're a writer," he said wearily. "You know how it goes. This is the part of the story where the author kills me off. The future for me isn't glamorous or romantic. I'm facing a lifetime of health problems, and there's no miracle cure. The cripple's not supposed to get the girl."

"Where does that leave me, then, the freak who still wants you, who still loves you? By your reasoning, I should be written off, too."

He frowned. "What?"

"You know"—she pointed at herself with both of her index fingers—"pervy dev here. I'll never be normal. I'm not fit for polite society. I'm subhuman, a bottom-feeder. Remember?"

His nostrils flared again. "You're never going to forget that, are you?"

"No," she said, giving him a rueful smile. "But I can forgive it." She leaned toward him, elbows on the edge of his bed and chin resting on her interlaced fingers. "Let's face it, though. I'm certainly not your typical heroine. I should definitely be killed off. In fact, too bad I didn't succeed in killing myself. That would have been a profound and just ending. Don't you think?"

"No," he said. "That's bullshit. And stop saying you're a perv. I think . . . " He trailed off and his eyes darted away, as if looking for words.

"You think what?"

He focused on her again, intense and penetrating. "I think you have this . . . I don't know . . . this tremendous capacity to see the beauty in everything—even in things that sometimes inspire pity or repulse others. That's a gift, not a perversion."

The sweetness of his words bloomed within her, and this time Erin's eyes welled up with love for him.

He took one of her hands in a gentle arm-wrestler's

hold, palm to palm, then laid their hands together back onto the pillow. The warmth of his hand spread through her whole body. "So don't ever fucking say that shit again about dying," he said in a husky grumble. "Don't ever even think it."

"Same goes for you, hot shot," she said softly.

He brought the back of her hand to his lips, and a joyful energy hummed through her. She couldn't take her eyes off his mouth. "Does this mean you don't want me to leave?"

"I should be all noble and tell you to go."

She rolled her eyes. "Good thing you're not noble."

He grinned, flashing his pearly whites, and it stopped her heart. "Good thing."

She tugged on his beard with her free hand. "So, I think we need to promise each other full disclosure and honesty from now on. Slate of bad stuff is erased. We start clean."

His grin faded. "Okay. Then I'm going to be honest here. You sure you want to get pulled into my shit?"

"Would you shut up? I know this sucks and you're in a funk right now, but it's not forever. You're going to get better, Jay."

He hesitated, his gaze brimming with strong emotion. "What if I don't?" he said on a ragged breath.

That was the crux of all this: He was scared. Erin reached forward and combed her fingers through his hair, needing to touch him, to allay his fear. "You will," she said gently. "You're one of the strongest people I know."

"I've been lucky since my injury, Erin. I haven't had a lot of the issues others with SCI have, until now. It's like it all converged on me at once."

"And that's why you're so freaked out. Plus, you've been going through all this alone. I'm guessing your dad wasn't much help?"

His expression hardened, and the disdain for his father came off him in a wave that was almost palpable. "No."

She squeezed his hand. "See? There's your problem. You'll be fine now that I'm here."

He let go of her hand and reached for the nape of her neck, pulling her to him so they were almost nose to nose. "I think this is the part where you convince me life is still worth living."

She smiled, happy to oblige. She brushed her lips over his, light at first but quickly getting swept up in the euphoria of sharing his air, of finally being with him again, of feeling his beard tickle her mouth and her chin, of having him open up to her and their tongues mingling in a hot, wet dance. Toes were curling. Heart rate was soaring. And he smelled like heaven: eau de hospital disinfectant mixed with the musky scent of Jay.

When they broke apart, she said a little breathlessly, "How was that?"

His mouth curved into the sexy Jay grin. "I suddenly have a new lease on life, darlin'." And he pulled her to him again.

Chapter 32

"**G**od*dammit,*" Jay groaned, putting his arm over his forehead and closing his eyes, mortified. He'd just farted—there was no mistaking the sound—at the worst possible time imaginable, right when he and Erin were planning to have sex.

It was another fun side effect of paraplegia, the fact that he couldn't control when he passed gas. He was past the point of being embarrassed about it and usually ignored it or, if the moment called for it, uttered a polite "excuse me." But this was different. Stinking up the bed wasn't exactly the method he had in mind for seducing his girlfriend.

"Hey, Bontrager, you got a squirrel under the covers, or are you just happy to see me?"

Then again, this was Erin he was talking about.

He opened his eyes to see her standing by the bed. She'd been in their bathroom doing whatever girls did to get ready for sex. She was buck naked, her tight, petite body curving in all the right places. She looked magnificent, and Jay couldn't wait to get his hands on her.

If possible, she'd grown more beautiful in the six months they'd been together. She was more confident and no longer so hard on herself, and there was something really sexy about that. It also hadn't hurt her self-esteem that her agent had finally sold her mystery novel to a small publisher.

She'd stuck by Jay through his long recovery from the pressure sore and all the other shit he'd dealt with, including his old man. They'd stayed with him in Stockton until recently, when Jay had been well enough to go back to work. He and Erin had rented an apartment together in Oakland, where he was finally heading the effort to open a branch of Luis's office. Erin was waiting tables part time at a nearby sports bar and working on her next writing project.

His dad had been his usual asshole self around Erin, but she'd given as good as she got. Jay had been afraid for her, since his old man wasn't above hitting a woman (his mom being a perfect example), but Butch had never laid a hand on Erin. Instead—maybe because she was one of the few people who'd ever stood up to him—he seemed to have developed a grudging respect for her toward the end of their stay with him. That had been a good thing because Jay would have happily killed him if he'd touched a single hair on Erin's head.

The pressure sore had finally healed, the back surgery hadn't completely gotten rid of his back pain but had reduced it to a level he could manage, and so far Jay had gone a month without a UTI. He drank cranberry juice by the gallons, even though he hated it, and it seemed to be helping stave off infection—that, and the simple fact that he was active again and better able to take care of himself. He knew better than to think he was home free, but he was taking things day by day and enjoying the good ones while they lasted.

He followed Erin's amused gaze down to where the bedsheet was tented just below his waist and laughed. Apparently the Cialis he'd taken earlier had kicked in. "A squirrel?"

Erin's light-hazel eyes were dancing. "Hmm. You don't like 'squirrel'?"

"Dudes don't want their dicks compared to squirrels. How about 'rod' or 'staff'?"

"Nope. Too biblical," she said, shaking her head.

She grasped the top of the covers as if to pull them back, but Jay put his hand over hers to stop her. "In the interest of full disclosure, I wouldn't do that if I were you," he said.

"Why?"

He sighed, hating that he had to tell her. "Because I farted while you were getting ready for bed. Trust me. You don't want it to escape."

"Nice," she said on a laugh, and something uncoiled inside Jay. She didn't care. To her, it wasn't a big deal, and he loved that she could joke about it. It took the weight from it, made it ordinary.

She yanked back the covers, and he grinned, suddenly not feeling even a hint of embarrassment that she'd so abruptly exposed his naked body and set the fart free.

"Peeugh!" she exclaimed, making a comical face, not blinking an eye at his state of undress or his very erect penis. "You're right. That one was something to be proud of." She waved her hand back and forth and flapped the sheet, shooing away the odor. "I'll be right back."

Disappearing into their bathroom, she reappeared with his deodorant and sprayed it under the covers, filling the room with the smell of Degree Sport antiperspirant for men.

"At least my dick won't get B.O.," he said wryly.

She crawled under the covers and pulled them to her shoulders. "That's better. I love your deodorant. Your armpits always smell nice."

Jay smiled and put his arm around her, snuggling her close as she laid her head on his shoulder. "You're weird."

"Yep," she said matter-of-factly. "And you love it."

He kissed the top of her head to let her know she was right and got a tantalizing breath of her apple-scented hair.

She traced his nipple with her fingertips, and a current ran through him. Jay had never paid much attention to his nipples, but lately, with Erin, he'd discovered they were much more sensitive than he'd ever realized and could be a source of incredible sensation.

With other women, he'd been so focused on proving to himself and to them that he could still give a woman pleasure, he'd ignored his own needs. He couldn't feel anything where it counted, so he'd thought it was futile to try.

He'd been wrong. The parts of his body where he still had feeling were extra sensitive, like his nerves had rerouted themselves to make up for the places where he couldn't feel. He'd read about this when he'd first been injured, but he'd thought it was all bullshit.

Erin said with a smile, "I think you're taking this full disclosure thing a little too far." She grazed her fingers around his nipple and then along his chest muscles.

It felt so good he had to make an effort to concentrate on what she was saying. "Nope. I made you a promise. I will always be straight with you, no matter what. I'll never lie to you or keep anything from you ever again."

She trailed her fingertips between his pecs, then down to his ribs. Jay closed his eyes, letting the exquisiteness of it wash over him.

"Well," she said, "I guess I should appreciate the red alert."

"Yep. And there's nothing like a good backdoor breeze to set the ambiance. Do I know romance or what?"

She snickered and kissed his jaw. "Oh, yeah. You're a regular Nicholas Sparks."

He grinned. They were so comfortable with one another. There were no secrets between them anymore, and they could completely be themselves. Jay had never been as close to anyone as he was to Erin, not even his ex-wife. He felt like he could tell Erin anything, and he hoped she felt the same.

She rose up to straddle him, the covers slipping down to her waist and exposing the pale softness of her skin and the round globes of her breasts. She leaned forward to kiss his lips. "I love you, Jay," she said against his mouth.

He burrowed his fingers in her hair and caressed her cheekbones with his thumbs, kissing her more deeply. "I love you, too," he said. He'd never said anything he meant more, and his heart felt too full, like it might explode.

She began to kiss him again, light, open-mouthed nips accompanied by a little swirl of her tongue that was sheer ecstasy over his tingling, hypersensitive skin. She started with his mouth, then his chin, then down his throat to his collarbone, then over his chest and stopping at his nipple. She traced her tongue around the brown circle surrounding the peak, and then the peak itself. His nipples were so hard now they could chisel stone.

Jay gave an unsteady laugh. "You're stealing my thunder, darlin'. I'm supposed to be doing that to you."

"Don't worry. You'll get your chance," she said, then gently bit his nipple.

"Jesus!" The sweet prick of pain made him wild with desire, and he had the sudden, fierce need to pull her to him, to feel all of her against him, skin to skin. His palms pressed into her back, desperate to meld her to him, but he tried to control himself enough not to hurt her.

Her hands were on his shoulders, her forearms

framing his chest, and her breasts rubbed against his ribs and the part of his stomach where he could feel. She responded to the pressure of his hands and began to rub her body over him, slow and seductive. "I can feel you, Jay. Your cock is pressing against my lower abdomen. It feels so good, lets my body know what's about to come." She licked the other side of his chest, making her way to his other nipple. "The anticipation is driving me crazy," she said against his skin. "It's making me so hot for you."

He loved it when she described the things he couldn't feel. It was more than just dirty talk. It was essential and enhanced the sexual experience for him. He closed his eyes and wished to God he could feel her belly rubbing against his cock, but just the thought of it, knowing it was happening, filled him with need and excitement.

Yes, the sensations were in his head and other places that weren't his dick, but if he let himself get into it and really think about what he and Erin were doing, it was still something special and wonderful. She had made it her mission in life to discover how to make him feel pleasure. She'd researched it—both by reading about it and by hands-on experimenting (Jay's personal favorite)—and preached to him all the time that the brain was the biggest sex organ in the body.

His dick, he had to throw out there, was a close second.

Again, Erin's teeth bit his nipple, and he couldn't take it anymore. "Come here," he growled, and she obeyed, writhing up until her face hovered over his, her long hair tickling his overly stimulated nipples before her breasts came down against his chest. Her lips found his neck, just under his jawline, and then she kissed her way to his earlobe and began to suck on it.

"What am I doing to you, Jay?" she whispered, darting her tongue into his ear. It was on that list of erogenous zones where the pleasure was magnified more than it might have been before his injury.

He was panting now, his heart beating a thousand beats a minute. If he'd been able, he would have arched off the bed. As it was, he clenched his fists into the sheet underneath him, trying not to spontaneously combust.

"Tell me what I'm doing to you," she said between suckles of his earlobe and tonguing his ear.

He'd intended for it to be her turn, to take her breast in his mouth and give her pleasure as good as he'd gotten, but she'd distracted him with the ear thing, and his brain was rapidly disintegrating. She liked to get inside his head, knew that sex for him was as psychological as it was physical, and making him give commentary was another way she drew him in.

"Tell me, Jay," she said. "What is my tongue doing to you?"

"It's . . . " He closed his eyes to better focus on what he wanted to say, but she was still driving him insane tonguing his ear. At the same time, her fingertips were drifting over his eyelids, down his cheek, onto his neck, and caressing the outer shell of his other ear. She was all hands, fingers, and tongue, a wealth of sensory delights,

making sure no parts of his body where he had feeling—
and, knowing her, probably the parts where he didn't—
were neglected.

He felt her fingers run along his arms, to the area
inside his elbows, where, even there, her touch caused
a kaleidoscope of light and color behind his eyelids. His
upper body was greedy, soaking in and amplifying her
every stroke, and what he was feeling was incredible.

It wasn't the same as how sex had been before
his injury—no build-up to a climax, just a steady
bombardment of bliss that was no less enjoyable because
it was different. And it was all the more amazing because
it was Erin—the girl he loved so much he would gladly
die for—who was doing it to him.

She switched to his other ear. "You haven't answered
me," she said, her warm breath tickling him. Her smoky
doll voice was sin itself. "What am I doing to you?"

He couldn't stifle a moan as her tongue thoroughly
traced his ear, then plunged in deeper, as if she was trying
to lick his eardrum. "You're . . . " He swallowed hard,
letting the sensation consume him. "You're fucking my
ear with your tongue."

She gave a husky chuckle. "Do you like me fucking
your ear with my tongue, Jay?"

A particularly deep thrust stole his breath. "Yes," he
managed to hiss.

"Good. Because I like fucking you with my tongue."

Christ almighty. She was going to kill him. He was
sweating and panting, even though she was doing all the

work. It was time he stopped neglecting her. He reached down to her pussy and inserted his middle finger. She was already drenched, her lips swollen and so ready for him. Not for the first time, he was amazed at how turned on by him she was, how just touching him seemed to get her off. He was the luckiest man alive to have someone who accepted him so completely.

When he began to rub his finger inside her, along her G-spot, she said, "That feels so good, but I want you inside me."

Jay removed his finger, and she whimpered in protest. "Not so fast, darlin'. I believe I still owe you some breast action."

She gave a raspy little laugh. "I'll take a rain check."

He took one of her nipples between his thumb and index finger and gave it a little twist, then kneaded her breast.

"Oh, God," she said, closing her eyes. "On second thought . . . "

Jay smiled and, with his hands on her hips, coaxed her to move close enough that he could take her breast in his mouth. He ran his tongue along her areola and then sucked on her pebbled nipple, all the while kneading her other breast with his hand.

She groaned, and Jay loved that he could do this to her, could worship her body the way she deserved.

"I'm going to come," she said with a hitched breath. Her arms were braced on either side of his head, and he could feel the warm moisture of her pussy sliding on his belly as she gyrated against him. She rose up and sat back for a second to look at him, her delectable little nipple popping out of his mouth as she did so.

Jay met her eyes as if to say, *Go ahead*, then pulled her back down, bringing her other breast to his mouth, licking and sucking on that nipple while rubbing the nub of her clit with his free hand.

She moaned an "Oh, yes" under her breath, then tensed for a few seconds, and finally shuddered. She was such a sexual being, so sensual. And, by some miracle he knew he didn't deserve, she was his.

She scooted down and rested her forehead against his, panting.

"Good?" Jay asked, arching a brow.

Erin raised her head and smiled. "It was a nice appetizer, but I'm ready for the main course. I want you inside me. Now."

He kissed her mouth first, and then she shifted over him and eased herself down on top of his erection, taking her time, the enraptured look on her face telling him she was savoring it. "Oh, my God." She closed her eyes, then arched her back, her fingertips on his ribcage for stability.

Jay had never seen anything more beautiful or more provocative.

"You're huge," she said, eyes hooded, throat bared to him. "You fill me up. We fit together"—she gasped as she adjusted herself—"so perfectly."

He couldn't feel any of it, and it was surreal, like he was watching the hottest porn he'd ever seen in his life. He had to remind himself this was real, and it was happening to him.

As if reading his mind, Erin said, "Don't zone out on me, big guy. Stay with me." She grabbed his hand in both of hers and brought it to her mouth, then took each of his fingers, starting with the smallest, and methodically sucked on each one of them, ending with his index finger.

Oh, yeah. He loved it when she did this. It kept him in the game, and the heat of desire pumped through him again, his heartbeat picking up speed. When she touched her tongue to his palm and licked it in tiny circles, her breath coming out in steamy little puffs, his eyes rolled back into his head. His hand was one big erogenous zone, and what she was doing was mind-blowing.

She took his thumb next, licking around it and sucking on it, then pulling it in and out of her hot, wet mouth in a way that was incredibly erotic. The symbolism wasn't lost on him, especially when she started moving on top of him in a rhythm that matched the in-and-out of his thumb.

Both of her hands had slipped down to his wrist, and she let go of it to place her palms on his chest. Her eyes locked with his, and he knew she wanted him to keep his thumb in her mouth. He did, his other fingers of the same hand splayed out across her cheek. It made a picture that was wickedly carnal.

He watched her hips move up and down on his cock and, at the same time, felt her suck on his thumb. He closed his eyes and concentrated, letting his thumb act as a surrogate, letting each stroke drive into her mouth the way he wanted to drive his dick into her body.

She began to moan, her sucking became frenzied, and the way the bed squeaked told him she was fucking him faster and faster down below. Jay got caught up in it, felt his excitement grow until pinpoints of light pricked his body all over. His breathing was labored; his heart was beating out of his rib cage. Then a starburst exploded in his mind, euphoria rushing through him like a freight train.

He opened his eyes to meet Erin's, and he couldn't help the big, incredulous grin that spread across his face. He was still panting as his body came down from the high.

Had he just had an orgasm? He hadn't experienced one since he'd been injured, hadn't thought it possible, but this was . . . awful damn close. Again, it was different, not like before his injury, but still pretty fucking awesome.

Erin smiled around his thumb. He took it out of her mouth, then slid his hands down to her hips, feeling their rocking motion. She leaned into her palms, which were still on his chest, and he eased his thumb over to the nub of her clit again. "Does this help?" he asked.

"Oh, God. Oh, yes," she gasped, her body pumping up and down on his cock.

Jay kept up with her, never letting his thumb leave her, until she came.

"Oh, God!" she yelled, closing her eyes, a hurts-so-good expression on her face. "Oh, God. Oh, yes. Yes!"

Jay watched her come down, loving the way her breasts heaved and the dewy sheen on her skin, until she was finally breathing normally again.

"You are the most beautiful woman in the world."

She sank down on top of him, heated skin to heated skin, chest to chest, and kissed his neck before laying her head on his shoulder. "You're the hottest guy in the world."

Jay kissed the top of her head and wrapped his arms around her. "I think I loved you the first moment I saw you."

"Oh, please," she said, skeptical. "We all know that's BS." She kissed his collarbone to take the sting out of her words. "You're saying that because we just had really great sex. It's clouding your memory."

"That's not true. I would have done anything to get to know you. Maybe, subconsciously, that's why I blackmailed you."

"Whatever."

He smiled. "In the interest of our honesty pact, I have another confession to make."

"What?"

"You know how your TV was broken?"

"Yeah?"

"I probably could have fixed it. I'm good at that kind of thing, but I liked that you had to come to the living room every time you wanted to watch TV. It meant I got to be near you, so I didn't tell you."

She was quiet for a long time, then she said, "I should

confess something too."

"What?"

She idly ran her finger along his bicep. "My TV was never really broken."

He was stunned for a moment as the meaning of that sank in, and then he burst out laughing.

"Guess I 'subconsciously' wanted to be with you too," she said, a smile in her voice.

He hugged her to him as his laughter faded to a grin.

She tilted her head back to look at him, her mouth curved into a coy smile. "So, you know what?"

"What?"

"I think I finally got my happy ending."

Jay gave her a gentle, languorous kiss. "Nah, darlin'. This is just the beginning."

So, what did you think? Reviews are an author's lifeblood, so please consider leaving a review at Goodreads or your favorite book retailer.

If you would like to leave the author a personal message, she can be reached at mollymirrenauthor@gmail.com.

ACKNOWLEDGMENTS

Thank you to H. This book is better for your input and encouragement. Actually, it probably wouldn't have been published without you. Thank you for reading it so many times!

Thanks to my mom, who didn't disown me after she read it. Sorry for all the profanity, Mom. My next book will be family friendly. I promise.

Thanks to my editor, Christi Stanforth. You know I think you're a genius.

Thank you to Robin Harper at Wicked by Design for creating my cover.

Lastly, I owe a big apology to all the indie authors (and even some traditionally published authors) whom I've scorned for not having perfect copy. I tried to weed out all the mistakes in this book, but now I understand. It's easier said than done.

About the Author

Molly Mirren loves being a writer. She also loves good company, good food (too much, if you ask her bathroom scale), good wine, and good music. When not writing, she is doing laundry. She is also a firm believer in the Oxford comma and defends it fiercely. Long live the Oxford!

www.ingramcontent.com/pod-product-compliance
Lightning Source LLC
Chambersburg PA
CBHW050905250626
47155CB00001B/112